A SENIOR CITIZEN'S GUIDE TO LIFE ON THE RUN

Also by Gwen Florio

The Nora Best mysteries

BEST LAID PLANS *
BEST KEPT SECRETS *
BEST PRACTICES *
BEST BE PREPARED *

The Lola Wicks series

MONTANA
DAKOTA
DISGRACED
RESERVATIONS
UNDER THE SHADOWS

Julia Geary legal thrillers

THE TRUTH OF IT ALL
THE LEAST AMONG US

Novels

SILENT HEARTS

* *available from Severn House*

A SENIOR CITIZEN'S GUIDE TO LIFE ON THE RUN

Gwen Florio

SEVERN HOUSE

First world edition published in Great Britain and the USA in 2025
by Severn House, an imprint of Canongate Books Ltd,
14 High Street, Edinburgh EH1 1TE.

Paperback edition first published in Great Britain and the USA in 2025
by Severn House, an imprint of Canongate Books Ltd.

severnhouse.com

Cover and jacket design by Panagiotis Lampridis

British Library Cataloguing-in-Publication Data
A CIP catalogue record for this title is available from the British Library.

ISBN-13: 978-1-4483-1358-7 (cased)
ISBN;13: 978-1-4483-1810-0 (paper)
ISBN-13: 978-1-4483-1359-4 (e-book)

All Severn House titles are printed on acid-free paper.

FSC www.fsc.org MIX Paper | Supporting responsible forestry FSC® C013604

Typeset by Palimpsest Book Production Ltd., Falkirk,
Stirlingshire, Scotland.
Printed and bound in Great Britain by
CPI Group (UK) Ltd, Croydon CR0 4YY

The manufacturer's authorised representative in the EU for product safety is
Authorised Rep Compliance Ltd, 71 Lower Baggot Street, Dublin D02 P593
Ireland (arccompliance.com)

Praise for Gwen Florio

"Florio continues to put a contemporary spin on the old-fashioned whodunit"
Kirkus Reviews on *Best Be Prepared*

"A satisfying cozy"
Booklist on *Best Be Prepared*

"Enthralling . . . Florio never stretches credibility with Nora's talents, making it a treat to sleuth alongside her"
Publishers Weekly on *Best Be Prepared*

"A breathtaking page-turner"
Kirkus Reviews Starred Review of *Best Laid Plans*

"Florio's suspenseful mystery will have readers rooting for amateur sleuth Nora"
Library Journal Starred Review of *Best Laid Plans*

"Engrossing series launch. Fans of strong female leads will look forward to seeing more of plucky Nora"
Publishers Weekly on *Best Laid Plans*

About the author

Gwen Florio grew up in a farmhouse filled with books and a ban on television. After studying English at the University of Delaware, she began a decades-long career in journalism that has taken her around the country and to more than a dozen other countries, including several conflict zones.

Her first novel in the Lola Wicks mystery series, *Montana*, won the Pinckley Prize for Crime Fiction and the High Plains Book Award, and was a finalist for the Shamus Award, an International Thriller Award and a Silver Falchion Award. She has since released four other books in the Lola Wicks series, two legal thrillers and a stand-alone novel. *Best Laid Plans* was her first book in the four-book Nora Best series, and her first with Severn House.

gwenflorio.net

For Kate,
always

ONE

Frail, they called them. *Elderly*.

Those were the polite terms, the ones used by the newspapers and television networks. Social media bypassed courtesy and went straight to the 'Over the Hill Gang' or 'The Fossilized Four.' The friends couldn't figure out which were worse – those or 'The Sexy Seniors.'

The latter made them sound like one of those polyamorous entanglements that seem to be all the rage these days, even though only two of them – Sasha and George – were romantically involved. Good thing the press never found out Alice had slept with him first. Given that she was approaching her eighties, they'd have had a field day with it.

The nicknames offended Alice most of all.

'Look at the Chicago Seven. The Minnesota Eight. The Beaver Fifty-Five.' Trust Alice to harken back to the Sixties, an era whose outlook she'd carried into her own sixties and beyond, with a hardened suspicion of all forms of authority and corporate control that had proven prophetic when it came to their community of Timeless Pastures. 'Nobody called them the *Young* Chicago Seven.'

Sasha peered into the burner phones they were all carrying by then. 'Of course they're calling Timeless Pastures "Out to Pasture." Hah. Like we didn't call it that first. And here it is again. "The four elderly neighbors . . ." We're none of us elderly.'

'Ahem,' said Alice.

The few people remaining at Timeless Pastures had celebrated Alice's seventy-sixth birthday six months earlier, joking at the time that she'd have to start thinking about leaving their planned community designed for so-called active adults. (Translation: one step below the sort of going-going-gone facilities that ushered you through your dotage to the lip of the grave.) Given Timeless Pastures' distance from major hospitals, most residents tended to move out when eighty and its escalating frailties loomed.

George raised his hand. 'The Beaver who? I've never heard of them.'

Alice pulled her waist-length silver curls over one shoulder and began weaving them into a fat braid. ‘This was in Saint Paul, 1970, I think. They destroyed draft records.’

‘No wonder I’d never heard of them. I was in Vietnam then.’

Sasha patted his arm. ‘We know. You might have mentioned it once or twice.’

Alice and Mia exchanged eye-rolls. In private, they called it the used-to-be syndrome, the way the residents of Timeless Pastures invariably identified themselves. Used-to-be a teacher’s aide. A township clerk. A car salesman. Whatever they’d all been before ending up in a collection of prefab pastel duplexes on the edge of New Jersey’s Pine Barrens, far enough from anywhere desirable to be affordable for the likes of them.

In addition to his permanent status as a Vietnam vet, George was a used-to-be high school principal; Sasha was a used-to-be realtor and Mia, a used-to-be personal trainer. As for Alice, she was vague about her own used-to-be when they introduced themselves at one of the Getting to Know You sessions everyone was forced to endure upon moving to Timeless Pastures.

‘Waitressing mostly,’ she’d shrugged. ‘A little retail. That was the worst. Give me twelve hours on my feet in a diner any day.’

Innocents that they were back then, they’d all just smiled and nodded and turned their attention to the next person.

Turns out Alice’s actual used-to-be was more interesting than all of theirs put together.

Way more.

Lavina Township Police Department
Transcript of interview with Mia Sullivan
Present: Detective Travis Meacham, Officer Sherilee Townsend

Townsend: Could you please state your full name and age?
Sullivan: Mia Elizabeth Sullivan, sixty-six.
Townsend: Occupation?
Sullivan: Retired. Not by choice.
Townsend: Oh?
Sullivan: Seems nobody wants an over-the-hill personal trainer, even though I could probably kick half their butts.

I can prove it. Look at these guns. (Rolls up sleeve, flexes.) Want to arm-wrestle?

Townsend: Um, maybe later. Residence?

Sullivan: It's going to be my van, as soon as you guys release it.

Townsend: Technically, it's evidence in . . . well, this is an investigation into about five different things. Including, possibly, homicide. You all have been busy.

Sullivan: Homicide? You mean murder? Are you kidding? Do I need a lawyer?

Townsend: This is just an informal interview. No one's been charged with anything yet.

Sullivan: Good. Because I didn't kill anybody.

Townsend: I didn't say you had. We're just trying to sort things out, compile a narrative that we can provide the FBI when their agents get here. Let's start at the beginning, shall we?

Sullivan: I guess that would be the party.

Townsend: What party?

TWO

Of course, Sasha planned the weekend.

Every organization, every office, every family has its de facto cruise director, and Sasha took on that role the minute she moved into Timeless Pastures.

She didn't just plan the usual holiday parties – Christmas/Hanukah/Kwanzaa, Easter/Passover and the like. She made sure Timeless Pastures had an event to celebrate every month – St Patrick's Day in March, Cinco de Mayo in May and, of course, International Talk Like a Pirate Day in September. You get the idea. *Arrrrrrr.*

She always went above and beyond. Take Christmas. Don't even think about tinny carols from a phone plugged into a speaker and a few sad trays of store-bought cookies, along with some poor guy roped into donning a bedraggled Santa suit.

This year, she'd installed so many Christmas trees in the community manager's office that Johnny Natale could barely get through to his desk, and staged a decorating contest, along with a bake-off to ensure enough treats. She held the party early, right after Thanksgiving, with individually wrapped presents for everyone – little things like Christmas ornaments, because most of their duplexes were already overstuffed with the things from their larger, used-to-be lives. As for the eggnog, you'd better believe it was spiked.

And now, because she and her three best friends would all be moving out on New Year's Day thanks to months of punishing fee increases from Timeless Pastures' new owner, there was only one thing to do: have another party, just for them.

'Should we invite Babs?' she asked after announcing she'd found the perfect lakefront rental at the perfect off-season rate for what she'd dubbed The Great Timeless Pastures Farewell Weekend. 'We know she wouldn't come, so we're safe. But it would be a nice gesture. She's about the only other one left in our section of Timeless Pastures.'

Keep in mind that Sasha had spent decades in real estate. She liked to say no situation was so dire it couldn't be improved, although in private she'd acknowledge that as wishful thinking, given her lifetime of experience as a Black woman in America.

They all held their breath when Sasha asked about Babs. Except Alice. Those blue eyes of hers went hard as Arctic ice.

Lately, there'd been the slightest bit of quaver in her voice, along with the tremor in her hands – age is full of indignities – but there was none in her answer.

'No way in hell.'

Lavina Township Police Department
Transcript of interview with Sasha Coverdale
Present: Detective Travis Meacham, Officer Sherilee Townsend

Townsend: Could you please state your full name and age?
Coverdale: Sasha Larae Coverdale, seventy.
Townsend: Occupation?
Coverdale: Realtor, retired. But my license is up to date.
Townsend: Residence?
Coverdale: I was in the process of moving out of my home in Timeless Pastures when this happened.
Townsend: Moving where?
Coverdale: Maybe Atlanta. My son is there.
Townsend: Maybe?
Coverdale: We hadn't worked out the details. I might stay with his family for a bit, get some time with my grandchildren. Look, speaking of my son, he's really worried about me – understandably, under the circumstances. How long is this going to take? What happens next?
Townsend: You'll be here as long as it takes us to figure out what happened. As to what's next, it depends on the information you provide. To that end, you were the one who told the others about Barbara Stevenson, right?
Coverdale: Who? Oh, you mean Babs.

THREE

Just like every group has a cruise director, every planned community has a Babs. Sometimes it's the community manager, sometimes the chairperson of the homeowners' association.

Babs bypassed both those roles and had fake-charmed her way straight to the position that held real power: chairperson of the Standards and Appearances Committee.

The committee was responsible for an endless list of regulations, punctuated by italics – *no off-leash pets outdoors* – and capital letters. SERIOUSLY.

Pets (limit of two and only dogs, cats, birds and fish; NO ferrets or rodents or anything that might be considered livestock) were the least of it. Plants, barbecue grills, types of vehicles and where they might park – the list filled a book so fat and detailed that residents' voices took on italics of their own when referring to *the book*.

Say you fell in love with that silver maple you saw at the local garden center and had the audacity to plant one behind your house despite its listing in *the book* as forbidden because its roots might infiltrate the sewer system. Expect the grounds crew to show up outside your bedroom window at six in the morning and fire up a chainsaw to remove your pride and joy. Oh, and there'd be a fine, too.

An excess of lawn ornaments, jangling wind chimes, newly painted shutters a shade off from the approved hues listed in *the book*? All of those could bring a stern email from Babs, followed by a written warning, followed if necessary by the appearance of Babs herself on your doorstep, and you did not want that, by God, you did not.

So the friends went to the lake house without her, with Mia and Alice arriving Friday afternoon, and Sasha and George a couple of hours later, just as a snowstorm hit. They shed their coats and headed for the welcoming warmth of the fireplace.

Alice sat before it in a deep chair, swaddled in one of her characteristic shapeless sweaters, her feet pulled up under her long skirt. A bottle of wine and two half-full glasses stood on a low table. A pack of cigarettes sat next to one of the glasses. For all her granola-crunching vibe, Alice remained a committed smoker.

Sasha stepped around Mia who was pretzeled into a yoga pose in front of the fireplace.

'You won't believe what we have to tell you.' Sasha blinked snowflakes from her eyelashes and rubbed at her cheeks, scarlet with a combination of cold and excitement.

George followed her, blotting frost from his clipped white beard. 'Show them your phone, Sasha.'

'In a minute.' Sasha went into the kitchen and came back with two more glasses. 'Have you already finished all the wine? There's some left? Good, then pour another round. You're going to need it. Look what's on the community Facebook page – oh, heck.'

She tapped the screen. 'It's gone. Don't we have Wi-Fi out here?'

Mia grabbed her ankle and stretched one leg high behind her. 'It comes and goes, probably because of the storm. Anyway, the whole idea was to get away from things. What's the big news, Sasha?'

Sasha gulped her wine.

'It's about Babs.'

'Oooh.' Mia unkinked herself.

Sasha held up her glass in acknowledgment of the flexibility she'd long ago lost. 'Show-off. Just because you're younger than the rest of us.'

Mia stood and shook out her arms and legs. 'Never mind that. What's your news? Is it about Babs' big fight with Alice?'

'What big fight?'

'Glenda said she saw—'

Alice broke in. 'Glenda? Are you serious? She'd turn a simple "hello" – which is about the longest exchange I ever had with Babs, if I could help it – into World War Three. There was no fight.'

Sasha waved her phone. 'Both of you, hush. It's not about any fight. She's gone.'

'What do you mean, gone? Where?'

'No idea. Somebody posted a story from the *Community Caller*'s website – "Local woman missing," something like that. Seems a delivery guy called the police when he saw her front door standing open and she didn't answer when he rang the bell. Anyway, the police went by the house and saw the back door was open, too. Her car was there; nothing seemed to have been disturbed, but you know what people think about us old folks. They're sure we have Alzheimer's and are wandering off somewhere. They put out an alert.'

Alice punched the air. 'Good riddance. Hope she never comes back.'

She wouldn't.

Lavina Township Police Department
Transcript of interview with J.R. 'Johnny' Natale
Present: Detective Travis Meacham, Officer Sherilee Townsend

Meacham: Could you please state your full name and age?
Natale: John Robert Natale Jr. I'm fifty-five.
Meacham: Occupation?
Natale: I'm the community manager for Timeless Pastures.
Meacham: What does that entail?
Natale: I supervise the grounds crews, show prospective buyers the model unit, handle the sales and all the paperwork when they arrive and when they leave.
Meacham: Isn't that unusual? Why wouldn't a realtor do it?
Natale: The model for communities like ours is a little different than a traditional sale. The residents finance their homes with loans, not mortgages. They own their homes – duplexes, in this case – but not the ground beneath them. They pay a monthly 'lot fee' for the land.
Meacham: What are your responsibilities to the residents?
Natale: Not much more than what I've already said. They're pretty self-directed. They've got a committee and a club for everything you can imagine.
Meacham: What about disputes? Who handles them?
Natale: There's a Judicial Committee. But a lot of the time, they come to me, wanting me to settle some difference or another. I try to steer them back to the committee. Sometimes I think they just want someone to listen to their concerns. Most of which, frankly, aren't a big deal.
Meacham: What counts as a big deal?
Natale: Birds. They're a very big deal.
Meacham: Birds?
Natale: Not just any birds.

FOUR

Pigeons.

Along with smallpox, measles and Norway rats, pigeons hitched a ride on European ships and were even more effective North American colonizers than their unwitting transporters. A female pigeon can begin laying eggs at seven months, depositing them in pairs as often as six times a year. Even factoring in losses due to disease, weather and predation, a single breeding pair and their offspring can be responsible for nearly fifty pigeons a year – a number limited by the fact that pigeons are monogamous. Imagine if they were as promiscuous as humans!

As fecund as they are in terms of chicks, their poop production is truly astounding. It's estimated that a single pigeon produces twenty-five pounds of droppings a year. Another estimate: the United States and Canada are home to more than eight million pigeons, nearly a million in New York City alone. That's a lot of crap crusting park benches, sliding down the faces of stone monuments and all too often turning a Park Avenue ingénue's fresh blowout into a sticky disaster.

More to the point, the ever-increasing flock that descended daily upon the patio behind the Timeless Pastures duplex that housed Babs on one side and Alice on the other turned it into an unholy mess.

Which is the most charitable way Alice described it to Johnny.

'I can't take it anymore. She won't stop feeding those damn birds. She's out there every day, sitting in her chair, scattering birdseed by the bushel. Those birds are nothing but flying rats. My patio looks like a Jackson Pollack painting. It's disgusting.'

He agreed.

'It's not fair, Johnny.'

Right again.

'You've got to do something about it. Or I will.'

FIVE

Johnny Natale took the job at Timeless Pastures with the idea that it would ease him into his own retirement years.

He'd spent the previous decades in the family contracting business, a stressful job under any circumstances, one increasingly at odds with his essentially amiable nature. While his father, Big John Natale, relished his ongoing wrangles with recalcitrant subcontractors, Johnny – somehow he'd never shed the childhood diminutive – just wanted everybody to get along. Delays on the projects he supervised were legendary. A psychiatrist would have had a field day with the fact that he'd married a woman who was the distaff version of his father, one who radiated disappointment in his lack of ambition.

When Big John succumbed to a heart attack in mid-screaming fit over a sloppy tuck-pointing job, Johnny rushed to Confession to cleanse his soul for the depth of gratitude he'd felt, then turned his part of the business over to his relieved brothers, upon which his wife promptly divorced him. Johnny settled into the Timeless Pastures job with the air of a condemned man granted a full pardon.

He rented a ramshackle cabin tucked away in the pines, ate take-out washed down with PBR in front of a sixty-five-inch television and – except for what Alice called the damn birds – had never been happier.

Compared to Johnny's former job, managing Timeless Pastures was a walk in the pre-retirement park. At least, it had been. Johnny's pleasurable stroll toward Social Security had ended a year earlier when Hawk Boneham III strolled into his office and introduced himself.

Johnny, whose ex-wife's relentless strivings had given him an acquaintance with such things, looked the elegant older man up and down and clocked the swirled silver haircut at two hundred bucks, with another sixty for the manicure. He didn't even want to think about the suit, the kind with those pipestem pants that stopped at the ankle.

But who wore a three-piece suit to a two-bit development in the far reaches of South Jersey?

Timeless Pastures' new overseer, Hawk informed him.

'I'm a vice president for expansion for Weller Holdings. They own this place now.'

A vice president. Not *the*. Johnny's previous life in the midst of endless power struggles had left him with an ear finely tuned to such nuance. If he'd learned anything, it was that the likes of Hawk Boneham, the Third if you please, would have his sights trained on becoming *the*.

'We're a holding company,' a term that meant nothing to Johnny. 'Timeless Pastures is our most recent acquisition.'

Johnny half stood and offered a shake. 'Johnny Natale. I'm the community manager.'

Hawk withdrew his hand as quickly as possible and discreetly touched it to the hem of his jacket, not obviously wiping it off, but still. He slapped a thick folder on to the desk.

'Our business model follows a standard funding formula, one that creates impressive efficiencies. You'll find all the details, including your new budget, in here. My card is attached. Feel free to contact me with any questions. But you won't have any. As I said, there's a formula, one we've found successful.'

He nodded toward the Solitaire game on Johnny's computer screen. 'Trust me, you'll have a lot more time for that.'

Johnny waited a moment to be sure he was really gone. He reached for the folder, unclipped the business card and pushed it to the lone uncluttered corner of his desk. He leafed through the contents, quickly at first, then more slowly. He closed the folder and pushed it away from him, knocking Hawk's business card unnoticed to the floor. He raised his head and stared at nothing at all.

He should have known as soon as Hawk said 'trust me' that the man was a lying sack of shit.

Lavina Township Police Department
Transcript of interview with George Sterling
Present: Detective Travis Meacham, Officer Sherilee Townsend

Meacham: Could you please state your full name and age.
Sterling: George Frederick Sterling, seventy-one.
Meacham: Residence?

Sterling: A bit unsettled at the moment. Those robber barons who took over Timeless Pastures last year keep raising the lot fees. Everybody's leaving. The four of us are some of the last ones left in our section of the community.

Meacham: As I've explained to everyone, we're trying to get a timeline here. When did you make your acquaintance with Alice Sanders? For the record, to reduce confusion, that's the name we'll be using in these interviews.

Sterling: I got to know Alice when I joined the Timeless Reads book group shortly after I moved in.

Meacham: When did your involvement become, ah, more intimate?

Sterling: How did you . . . That's none of your business. And it has nothing to do with any of this. It ended quite some time ago. Amicably, I might add. I feel as though it's time to call a lawyer.

Meacham: It may become our business. But for now, we'll proceed with the timeline – and while you're of course free to contact an attorney, this is strictly an informational interview. You're not under arrest. When did you become aware of any dispute between Alice Sanders and Barbara Stevenson?

Sterling: I've known about it as long as I've known Alice. Poor thing. She had no idea when she moved in that she'd be sharing a wall with a crazy lady who fed hundreds of pigeons every day.

SIX

Babs knew the residents hated her.

She read the message boards, saw how people described her: *mean as a snake*, *the proverbial turd in a punchbowl*, *sad, lonely, friendless soul*.

She'd long ago learned how to deal with such characterizations. *Hit back harder*. She'd applied her father's counsel on dealing with high school mean girls ever since to anyone who crossed her. She knew exactly how unwelcome her appearance was at any community gathering. Half the residents were dealing with outstanding Standards and Appearances complaints she'd filed against them.

But friendless? Untrue. Because she had her birds.

She knew the names people lobbed at pigeons were on par with what they called her. Especially that witch-that-starts-with-a-B who lived next door: *dirty*, *disease-ridden*, *vermin*.

Sure, there were plenty of other birds. Robins, happy harbingers of spring. Cute little finches, flashes of gold around feeders black with thistle seed. And cardinals, strutting their showy scarlet stuff among the dull sparrows and wrens. All of them easy to love.

Babs had never known easy. She was naturally drawn to outcasts. She'd never forgotten the first time a pigeon landed briefly on her patio one morning, its lovely lavender chest feathers glorious in the morning light. It cocked its head, staring at her through the patio door.

She tore a hunk from a piece of perfectly good sourdough and tossed it on to the patio. Then she closed the sliding glass door and waited. Nothing.

The bread sat there all day. A couple of sparrows fluttered out of the pine forest that began only a few yards from her patio and pecked at the soft part before the famously crackly crust defeated them. But the next morning, the crust was gone.

It could have been anything. A whole host of determined sparrows. A raccoon. Or even one of the feral cats that plagued the community, the main reason Babs had Animal Control on speed dial.

The next time she slid open her patio door, a pigeon paced the flagstones.

By then she'd read up on them, about their high level of intelligence, the experiments that showed their ability to count, to discriminate among various images, to recognize words. She wasn't surprised by her lone visitor, nor by the fact that others soon appeared.

She procured an old canvas coat and brimmed hat from a thrift store and found that if she pulled a chair into the center of the patio and scattered birdseed around it, then sat very still, the pigeons used her arms and sometimes her head as perches, bobbing and cooing and looking her directly in the eye as though to say good morning and thank you.

For the first time in more or less forever, Babs started her mornings with a smile, at least until the day when Alice banged on her door, *the book* in hand.

'Babs. You of all people. There's bird crap all over my patio.'

'Call Johnny. He's got the number for the power-wash guy.' She started to close the door.

Alice jammed her foot between the door and its frame. For someone her age, she was surprisingly quick.

'I don't want to have to pay someone to fix a problem I didn't create. If anyone should pay, it's you. Feeding all those birds. It's against the rules. It says right here' – she held open *the book*, a passage highlighted in screaming neon.

Babs pushed it away. 'It says no such thing. It says we're only allowed two bird feeders. I don't have any feeders.'

She brought her own foot down hard atop Alice's, grinned at the resulting squawk and slammed the door.

It didn't end there, of course.

A few days later, when she was on the patio with her lovies, she spied Alice walking Glenda Ferguson's little Scottie, Sugar Plum, a chore the remaining Timeless Pastures residents shared on rotation after Glenda had sprained her ankle on a patch of ice.

Sugar Plum went wild at the sight of the birds, yapping and straining at the leash. Somehow, it slipped from Alice's hand.

Oops.

The birds arose en masse and en mess, raining chalky splats.

Sugar Plum tore up to Babs, stood on his hind legs, balanced his forepaws on her knees and barked a frenzy in her face.

Alice reached the patio just as Sugar Plum homed in on a wet white splotch on Babs' coat and turned his attention to licking the coat clean. When Babs bent to shoo him away, he swiped his tongue across her mouth.

Hit back harder.

It took a few days, using the skills she'd acquired during her job as a forensic accountant, to assemble the perfect weapon. Once Babs had it in hand, she set up a fake online identity and crafted an email. It wouldn't contain everything she'd learned. Just enough to get things started. She could always drop more hints later, prolonging the satisfaction.

For a moment, she considered sending it to the police. But no, it would be better for the police to receive the news from a third party, one with a direct interest. A person providentially placed in her path. She paused to savor her imminent triumph before hitting 'send.'

She lurked by her front door until she heard Alice leaving her side of the duplex. She stepped out on to her stoop, beaming a smile so startling it stopped Alice in her tracks.

'Well, if it isn't Carol. Carol Ann Kaminski.'

And now, not a week later, Babs was gone.

Lavina Township Police Department
Transcript of interview with Mia Sullivan
Present: Detective Travis Meacham, Officer Sherilee Townsend

Townsend: We understand there was bad blood between Alice Sanders and Barbara Stevenson.

Sullivan: That's an understatement. Can you blame Alice? Living next to that?

Townsend: Did it ever get physical?

Sullivan: No, not really. No.

Townsend: Not really?

Sullivan: I didn't see this myself. So, it's – what do you call it? Circumstantial evidence.

Townsend: Ms Sullivan, we're not in court. What did you hear?

Sullivan: Alice has a neighbor, Glenda Ferguson. She's

about the only one left on the street besides Alice and Babs. We've all been taking turns walking her dog ever since Glenda sprained her ankle, but Alice probably takes him more than anyone. Sugar Plum's just the cutest little thing you ever saw . . .

Townsend: The dispute?

Sullivan: Right. This was about a week or so before we left for the lake house. Glenda said she saw them toe to toe in the driveway that they share. Alice was always going after Babs about the birds. Glenda said Babs just smirked and said something real low. Glenda couldn't catch it. But she said Alice went white as a sheet.

Townsend: That's it? That's not exactly physical.

Sullivan: She scared Alice. I can't imagine what she said to do that. Alice is the most unflappable person I know. So, like a threat. Isn't that almost the same as physical?

SEVEN

Babs was missing. Babs was missing. Babs was missing.

Somehow, Alice made it through dinner despite the drumbeat in her brain, responding appropriately – at least, she hoped she had – as her friends chatted over Sasha's lasagna. *Babs was missing.*

At the end of the interminable meal, she volunteered to do the dishes, waving away offers of help.

'I've got a whole system. You'll just get in the way.'

She shooed them out of the kitchen, practically collapsing in relief as the door closed behind them. She cracked a window, standing next to it and indulging in a quick smoke before turning to the dishes, scrubbing in a fury, berating herself. She'd gotten far too comfortable at Timeless Pastures. No. More than comfortable. Sloppy.

She'd spent years perfecting the blank stare at the sound of Kaminski. It came up every so often, mostly in anniversary stories on the evening news, invariably with the headline: 'Still At Large.'

But those stories grew farther and farther apart as time passed, first yearly, then every five years, then each decade until finally they vanished altogether. Alice, fatally, relaxed.

And then, after all those years, there was Babs just a few days ago, hissing – what did the kids call it these days? – her dead name, resurrected by the worst person possible.

It was all her fault. That stone face she'd perfected so long ago? It dissolved at the sound of the name she foolishly assumed she'd successfully escaped.

At her stammering reaction – 'W–w–what did you call me?' – Babs had been only too happy to tell her how she'd figured it out.

'Your real name. It's all over the internet.'

'I'm not on the internet.' True, mostly. She eschewed social media, and her friends made fun of her antiquated flip phone. She'd spent decades working under-the-table jobs, paying her bills with cash orders and hiding a smile whenever someone joked about people who kept their money in the mattress. Her own mattress was cash-free, but the bankers' boxes stacked neatly in her closet were worthy of their name, each one home to neat rectangles of twenty-dollar bills beneath a layer of old *National Geographics* that she'd gleaned from garage sales.

She'd surprised even herself with how much money you could accumulate from a series of minimum-wage jobs when you needed next to nothing. It was even more gratifying to realize how many landlords were happy to take deposits and rent in cash. Even the loan payment on the Timeless Pastures duplex was low enough that Johnny barely raised an eyebrow at her cash offering.

She knew how to use the internet, of course. Once she'd realized it had become essential to 99.9 percent of the population, she sat in on one of those senior citizens' classes at a local library and occasionally availed herself of their public computers. But never once had she typed the name she'd worked so hard to lose into a search engine.

She'd spent all those years not being stupid. Until she had been – as Babs was happy to tell her.

'You want to know how I uncovered it? Those Getting to Know You meetings. All I needed to do was figure out where you'd gone to college.'

'I didn't go to college.' Alice was shocked to discover that she could actually form words. Her mouth, her face, her entire body felt frozen.

'No, you said you dropped out. From Smith. Right after you said you'd worked mostly as a waitress. I thought, how'd a Seven Sisters type end up as a waitress? So I looked up everything I could find about Smith during the time you might have been there.'

But she hadn't gone to Smith. Which Babs had also figured out.

'Do you play poker, Alice?'

Where was Babs going with this? Alice shook her head.

'I didn't think so. Do you know what a "tell" is? No, of course not. I remembered that just before you said "Smith," you hesitated. So all I had to do was look through the rest of the Seven Sisters. Turns out you're a Holyoke girl. And that's not all you are, is it, Carol Kaminski? Don't you think it's time everybody knew? Because soon enough, everyone will.'

Remembering, Alice bent over the sink, gasping. A soapy plate slipped from her hands and shattered against the tile floor.

The door swung open.

'Everything OK in here?'

Mia looked from the shards on the floor to Alice's face. 'Oh, sweetie. It's no big deal. It's just a plate. Here, let me help you clean it up. Why in the world are you washing those by hand? Just put them in the dishwasher.'

Alice complied, glad for an excuse to turn her back on Mia, lest her damnably undisciplined face betray her yet again.

Who knew where Babs might have taken her secret? Or to whom?

EIGHT

The pigeons had already begun to gather, perching in the pines behind the duplex, occasionally fluttering to the patio. Babs donned her old coat and hat in preparation for their daily feeding, savoring the feeling of being wanted, needed.

She glanced at the clock. She was expecting a delivery of birdseed but didn't want to interrupt her time with her sweethearts. She went to the front door, opened it a bit so the delivery man would know she was home and then walked through the house and slid open the patio doors.

Clouds hung low and heavy, underscoring the weather service's warning of a pending snowstorm. The patio, with its high wall dividing her portion from Alice's, was sheltered from the wind, giving it the illusion of warmth. One by one, birds started landing on it, bobbing and cooing at her feet.

She rubbed her hands together, thinking of the dirt she'd dug up on Alice. The email she'd sent should get results soon. She couldn't wait to watch Alice squirm. The woman had been a thorn in her side for far too long with her incessant complaints about the birds.

Babs knew that Alice was gone on her getaway weekend. She walked around the dividing wall and boldly explored Alice's patio, seeking an infraction worthy of a write-up. The birds fluttered along behind her, eager for their daily treat.

There, along the base of the dividing wall. A line of moss and mold, creeping upward. Babs fished her phone from her pocket and bent to take a photo.

A split second later, the birds lifted in a silvery cloud as she crumpled into the corner of Alice's patio.

Lavina Township Police Department
Transcript of interview with Bert Miller
Present: Detective Travis Meacham, Officer Sherilee Townsend

Meacham: Can you please state your name and age?
Miller: Albert Scott Miller, sixty-three.
Meacham: Residence?
Miller: Lavina Township.
Meacham: Occupation?
Miller: Until they find a better way to get rid of me, I've been sentenced to serve as the Our Towns columnist for the Community Caller.
Meacham: Huh. We'll parse that later. How did you become involved in this story?
Miller: My editor somehow forgot I'm not supposed to be allowed anywhere near real news and assigned it to me. Look, I can save you a lot of time. Am I under arrest?
Meacham: Of course not. We're just trying to flesh out the narrative—
Miller: Then read my stories. That's where you'll find anything that might be relevant to whatever you're looking for. Beyond that, we're done here.

NINE

Bert Miller's exile to the Our Towns column of the *Community Caller* had been swift, merciless and permanent.

As the oldest reporter on the *Community Caller* by at least a couple of decades, he was too expensive compared to the staff that barely populated what had been a bustling newsroom back when he'd started, oh, never mind when. As far as he could tell, management's rule was to replace each two reporters who'd left with a single new hire, younger by at least ten years, preferably twenty.

Management wasn't stupid. Wary of an age-discrimination suit, instead of firing him they'd simply moved him off the police beat that he'd owned for decades, routinely putting reporters from the bigger city papers to shame when they came sniffing around the crimes that happened with surprising regularity and creativity in the vast, largely uninhabited section of central and southern New Jersey known as the Pine Barrens.

Now Bert was limited to combing the region's small towns for the sort of human-interest stories that he knew better than to publicly deride as fluff/filler/absolute reeking crap. He wrote a column about a woman who turned her entire yard into a rose garden. A town's contest to name its fire trucks, which yielded such imaginative monikers as Big Red.

At his lowest point, God help him, his editor prodded him during a prolonged heatwave into trying to fry an egg on a sidewalk. (It didn't go well.) More recently, he held his nose and typed a column about a man who walked his pet rat on a leash.

But given the fourteen months left before he could qualify for Medicare and two and a half years until he could collect a reasonable amount from Social Security – he had calendars marking countdowns to both dates – he'd be damned if he'd quit, which is what management clearly hoped he'd do. And he'd perfectly calibrated the least amount of effort he could put into his job without giving management a legal reason to fire him.

So when his editor's number popped up on his phone on a

Saturday morning, he didn't answer on the first ring. In fact, he didn't answer until the third call within fifteen minutes.

Madison Baker didn't bother with hello.

'Today's your lucky day, Bert. Two weeks before Christmas and half of what passes for a staff is on vacation, and now Don calls in sick. He says he's got Covid.'

Don was the reporter who'd been assigned Bert's old police beat, in addition to covering schools and some of the area town council meetings. Madison clearly didn't believe Don's Covid story, meaning that, for perhaps the first and only time, she and Bert agreed about something.

'Remember the woman who went missing from that old folks' place over in the Pine Barrens? We put up a brief about it yesterday on the website.'

Bert didn't. But he knew better than to say so. 'What about her?'

He braced himself to remind Madison that it was Saturday and, given all the other insults the paper had heaped upon him, he was not about to give up a day off; no, he was not. He opened his mouth to say just that when Madison spoke again.

'They found her.'

Lavina Township Police Department
Transcript of interview with Glenda Ferguson
Present: Detective Travis Meacham, Officer Sherilee Townsend

Townsend: Could you please state your name and age?

Ferguson: Glenda Jean Barrington Smythe Hopkins Ferguson. Those last three are my married names. Seems like every time one dies, another one pops up. Gerry's been gone six months now. It's about time for another one to come knocking.

Townsend: Goodness. Age?

Ferguson: A lady never tells.

Townsend: Nonetheless . . .

Ferguson: Old enough to know better. But I keep getting married anyway.

Townsend: Ma'am, this is potentially a homicide investigation. But if you're thinking about calling an attorney, I need to let you know that this is just an informal interview at this point.

Ferguson: An attorney? Why in the world? I'm happy to help. What do you need to know?

Townsend: Your age, please.

Ferguson: Oh, all right. My driver's license says I'm seventy-three. But if you looked at the photo, you'd say sixty-three. And if you look at me in person, just like you're doing now, you'd say sixty. Right?

Townsend: Right now, I'm looking at this timeline and the people involved. Can you please describe your relationship with these four people – Mr Sterling, Ms Coverdale, Ms Sullivan and Ms Sanders? Five, including Ms Stevenson. Were you close friends?

Ferguson: Oh, heavens, no. Just neighbors.

Townsend: Yet you seem to have been the source of quite a bit of information about them.

Ferguson: I like to pay attention. That's the thing missing in society these days. If more people looked out for one another, we wouldn't have so many terrible things happening. Like this. It doesn't get much more terrible than this.

TEN

If Alice thought the news of Babs' disappearance had vanquished her friends' curiosity about the fight, she'd thought wrong.

They'd spent Saturday at a small-town Christmas festival, drinking mulled wine, being serenaded by adorable young carolers and indulging in a sleigh ride pulled by two amiable Percherons, their harnesses decorated with jingling brass bells. Babs' name hadn't come up at all.

So she was relaxed on Sunday morning as they clustered around the fireplace, balancing plates on their knees, enjoying a casual breakfast before packing to leave.

Mia held up the bakery box of chocolate- and cream-filled croissants. 'Another, anyone?'

Sasha waved it away. 'Not for me.'

Mia waggled the box at her. 'Don't you know calories don't count when you're on vacation?'

Sasha shook her head so hard her chin-length locs swung. 'Speak for yourself. You're the one out there running marathons. You can eat whatever you want.'

'Half marathons. Slow ones.' Mia bit into a croissant and spoke around a mouthful of cream. 'Alice, it's about time. We've managed to get all the way through this weekend without asking, but have mercy. You said there was no fight, but Glenda said it was a real knock-down, drag-out.'

'Really? We're back to this? Glenda needs to get a life. I might have said something to Babs about the birds again, but that's all.'

'Glenda said things got so intense that she was ready to call nine-one-one in case it got physical.'

Sasha reached into the bakery box and pulled an end off one of the croissants. 'To be fair, Glenda is a gossip.'

'I'll take the rest of that.' Alice reached for the croissant Sasha had mutilated. 'That's exactly what Glenda is. More than a gossip, she's a drama queen. Every time we get so much as a flake of snow, she's all over the message board yammering about a blizzard. I can only imagine what she's saying about this weekend's storm. I just told Babs that I was moving out along with everyone else and that I hoped she and the birds enjoyed having the place to themselves. End of story.'

Mia pouted. 'It was a lot more fun the way Glenda told it.'

A faint ding sounded. 'Sounds like we've got a signal again.' Sasha bent over her phone. 'Speaking of the message board.'

'If there are any chocolate ones left, send the box down this way,' George said. 'Please.'

'Alice?' Mia wasn't going to let her off the hook. 'We're waiting.'

Alice rolled her eyes. 'Maybe if I see Babs again before I leave for good, I can liven things up, punch her in the nose. That should keep Glenda going until she moves out.'

'I heard Glenda's stepdaughter is taking her in. Glenda never liked her . . .' Mia began.

'Oh my God,' Sasha breathed. She held the phone closer to her face. 'Alice, you're not going to be punching Babs.'

'Well, of course I'm not. Not any more than I was getting up in her face the other day.'

'No. That's not it.' Sasha held out her phone, showing the shaded rectangles of the message board, as though any of them could read it from more than a few inches away.

'For heaven's sake, Sasha. What does it say?'

'Wait, I'm reading. It links to a story on the newspaper's site.' The others clustered close.

'Alice isn't going to get a chance to punch anybody. Babs is dead.'

MISSING LOCAL WOMAN FOUND SHOT DEAD
By Bert Miller
Community Caller Our Towns Columnist

An elderly woman reported missing on Friday was found dead late Saturday afternoon. Barbara 'Babs' Stevenson, 70, was shot once in the head, according to Police Chief Oscar Martinez.

Stevenson's body was found behind the Timeless Pastures duplex at 120 Yorktown Way, he said.

Stevenson was reported missing after a delivery person noticed her front door open when he arrived. When no one answered after he rang the bell and called a greeting, he alerted the community manager, J.R. Natale, who in turn called the police, Martinez said.

Nothing was discovered during an initial check, but Natale later returned to the property in order to deal with a report of a vermin problem and discovered the body partially concealed between lawn furniture and a wall, police said.

Stevenson lived in a neat, light-blue duplex at the end of a cul-de-sac in Timeless Pastures, a retirement community within Lavina Township on the edge of the Pine Barrens. A wooded area, thick with underbrush, lies behind the home. The resident in the other half of the duplex was not at home and several of the other houses on the street are unoccupied. Stevenson's house sat forlorn, tended only by a row of pigeons perched on the rooftop.

Lavina Township Police ask that anyone with information contact their confidential tip line or fill out the anonymous form online.

Lavina Township Police Department
Transcript of interview with Sasha Coverdale
Present: Detective Travis Meacham, Officer Sherilee Townsend

Townsend: Tell us about the cellphones.

Coverdale: The phones? That's when – excuse my French – shit got real.

ELEVEN

Sasha's hand went to her mouth.

George turned. 'What's the matter?'

Sasha handed him the phone. 'Look. It's not just that Babs is dead. This says she was murdered.'

The four friends simultaneously moved closer to the fireplace, as though the fresh snow squall had found its way through the lake house's leaky window frames, accounting for the sudden collective chill.

Alice wielded a poker, jabbing at the logs in the fireplace until they collapsed, sending flames shooting high and showering the hearth with sparks. She set it aside and held out her hands.

'Everybody. Phones.'

'Why?'

'Never mind. Just get them.'

Mia and George commenced a general fumbling through purse and pockets – the usual places phones tended to disappear whenever anyone most wanted them.

'What the heck?' Sasha, who was always the first to adopt the newest technology, tossed her sleek titanium iPhone on to the coffee table. 'They hardly work out here anyway.'

Alice's flip phone joined the rest. She lifted the hem of her long skirt and scooped the phones into it. The other three trailed her to the foyer, where she stuck her feet into boots and shrugged one-armed into a coat as she gathered her skirt tight around its cargo.

'Are you actually taking a smoke break in this weather? Why do you need our phones?'

The door closed in Mia's face.

She rushed to the bay window. Sasha and George crowded behind her. The gusting wind calmed for a moment, and the snowfall changed from a weatherman's dire warning to a Currier and Ives print, drifting gently down around Alice as she walked the few yards to the lake and out on to the dock.

'I'm going to get her.' Sasha's tremulous voice belied her words. George wrapped a protective arm around her.

'Don't even think about it. What if you were to fall?'

'Shhh!' A collective hiss. No one, ever, wanted to think about what they all called the F-word, the thing that would boot them right out of their 'active' lifestyle and into a dreaded care facility, from which – according to the accepted wisdom – the only way out was in the proverbial pine box.

With a final great whoosh, the wind carried away the last of the clouds and the sun shimmered through.

'Oh,' Mia breathed. 'It's so beautiful.'

Sasha elbowed her. 'What's she doing?'

They all figured it out at the same time, screaming into the double-paned glass as Alice drew her arm back, whipping it forward, sending the first phone sailing.

The ice petered out beyond the dock, an inky stretch of open water beyond, its surface marred by a series of concentric circles as one after another the phones splashed into it.

Lavina Township Police Department
Transcript of interview with J.R. 'Johnny' Natale
Present: Detective Travis Meacham, Officer Sherilee Townsend

Meacham: You're the one who found Ms Stevenson, correct?

Natale: Yeah. When you guys didn't.

Meacham: Ahem. Our officers went through her house, as would be standard procedure when someone calls for a welfare check and the doors are standing open.

Natale: All they had to do was look over the patio's divider wall.

Meacham: How did you happen to look over the wall?

Natale: The next day, when Babs still hadn't turned up, I went over there.

Meacham: Because?

Natale: I was dealing with an ongoing complaint about pigeons.

Meacham: It's a shame no one thought to inform us immediately about the interpersonal dynamic involving Ms Stevenson. But moving on, what led you to the patio?

Natale: I just walked around the outside of the duplex, looking to see if anything was out of order. I saw a bunch of birds over on Alice's patio, which was weird, because Babs was the one who fed them. They were all clustered around something up against the patio wall. It turned out to be Babs.

Meacham: Mr Natale, do you own a firearm?

TWELVE

Johnny Natale issued a forceful 'no comment' and clicked out of the call, permitting himself a moment of nostalgia for the old-fashioned Bakelite phones in his father's office that gave the satisfaction of banging down a receiver.

Bad enough that there'd been a murder on his watch, necessitating his working on a Sunday. Within a couple of hours of the story appearing on the *Community Caller*'s website, it seemed that every newspaper, radio and TV station in the area had seen it and was determined to match it. He could only imagine social media's spin. He couldn't really blame any of them – who could resist a story about someone's granny killed just before Christmas? – but their interference meant he was missing the Sunday-afternoon football lineup.

The meatball parm he'd picked up on a quick Wawa stop on his way into the office was getting cold. He was halfway through it when he glanced out the office window and realized there were worse things than being besieged by the press. Hawk Boneham strode toward the building.

He cursed. If he'd looked up just a minute or two sooner, he'd have seen Boneham's brawny black Range Rover pulling into the lot and could have made his escape through the back door. Now, there wouldn't be enough time to duck into the pines behind the office without Hawk spotting him. If Hawk had driven all the way down from corporate headquarters on a Sunday, it probably meant he'd found a way to blame Johnny for the bad publicity spurred by Babs' killing.

Johnny gave the sandwich a longing look before pasting a smile on his face, clinging to the faintest hope that things wouldn't be as bad as he feared.

Hawk didn't even give him a chance to say hello.

'The woman at one twenty Yorktown Way, the one who was killed. What was her name again? Betty, Beatrice, something like that?'

So much for hope. If Johnny had to bet, he'd put money on Hawk knowing exactly what the name was. Maybe this was some sort of a test, part of a new way to make his life miserable. For sure, he wasn't going to tell Hawk that Babs actually lived next door, at one twenty-one.

'Babs. I mean, Barbara. Barbara Stevenson.'

'Corporate would like to update its initial statement of concern with our offer to help with funeral expenses, that sort of thing.'

Johnny blinked. Not once in his interactions with Hawk had discussions of money involved spending the stuff.

'What a . . .' He stopped himself from saying 'surprise.' 'What a generous gesture. But you could have just emailed me. You didn't have to drive all the way down here on a weekend.'

'And you didn't have to come into the office on a Sunday. Yet here we both are,' Hawk countered.

Except that Johnny lived five minutes away, while Hawk had subjected himself to an hour on the New Jersey Turnpike. The man was, as usual, dressed to impress. Maybe he'd stopped by on the way to the Atlantic City casinos, where he no doubt installed himself at one of the tables for high rollers.

Hawk tapped on the desk, snagging Johnny's attention. 'I don't suppose you have a photo of her. It would help personalize things.'

'Maybe on the community Facebook page.' Something Hawk could have checked on his own – unless he was one of those older people who'd never embraced social media. It only took Johnny a few clicks. 'Here's one.'

He swiveled his computer screen to show a group photo from one of the parties Sasha organized. 'It's not the greatest quality, though.'

Hawk bent toward the screen. His lips tightened. He shook his head. Clearly, he'd found Johnny wanting once again. 'You're right. That won't work. I'll send you that statement from corporate about Mrs Severson.'

'Stevenson.'

'What?'

'Her name. Stevenson.'

'That's what I said.'

Johnny's eyes narrowed as he watched Hawk leave. The name mix-ups nagged at him. Still. For all the unwelcome intrusion, the offer to help Babs' family made him – almost – reevaluate his opinion of the man. Was it possible that somewhere beneath the designer threads lay a beating heart?

Lavina Township Police Department
Transcript of interview with Sasha Coverdale
Present: Detective Travis Meacham, Officer Sherilee Townsend

Townsend: You weren't kidding that, as you put it, shit got real.

Coverdale: No. We were all pretty much in shock.

Townsend: And then – at least the way you've described it – things got even crazier.

Coverdale: So much crazier.

Townsend: Yet you all just went along with her.

Coverdale: Speaking solely for myself, I was curious. Wouldn't you be?

Townsend: Believe me, everything about this case has provoked the utmost curiosity.

THIRTEEN

They set upon her as soon as the door opened.

'What the hell, Alice?' Sasha grabbed her shoulders and shook her so hard her head snapped back and forth. 'I just got that phone!'

George tugged Sasha away.

Mia took her place. 'What the hell?'

Alice pulled free and kicked out of her boots, stepping aside to avoid the puddles of melting snow. She hung up her coat and headed for the stairs.

'You'd better pack. We're leaving.'

Mia jumped in front of her and held out her arms. Alice tried to dodge around her. No dice.

'Point guard, Eagle High School's 1973 state championship girls' basketball team. We can do this all day. You're not getting past me. Why are we leaving?'

'Because we have to. They'll be able to track us this far because of our phones.'

'Track *us*?' Mia quick-stepped to one side, blocking another feint by Alice. 'Why would anyone want to track us?'

Alice dodged to the other side, Mia a half-step ahead of her. 'If we leave now, we've got a fighting chance of getting away without them knowing where we're going. But we have to get rid of the cars.'

Sasha took up Mia's refrain. 'What do you mean, *we*? Getting away from whom? And why the cars? Are they going into the lake, too?'

'Not funny.' Alice shoved Mia, moving her barely at all. Her eyes were wild, her voice near breaking. 'Mia, get out of my way.'

George leaned close to Sasha and spoke sotto voce. 'This is really concerning. Shouldn't we call someone? A doctor? What about family? Maybe Johnny would have an emergency contact.'

Alice turned on George so fast he stepped back.

'I'm not crazy, George. This isn't some sort of psychic break or descent into dementia, or whatever it is you're thinking. This is the most rational thing I could possibly do, not just for my own sake but for all of yours.'

'Then we're going to need an explanation,' George said, even as Sasha shook her head at him. 'Enough,' she whispered. 'She's too upset.'

Alice drew a shuddering breath. 'Stop patronizing me, all of you. Explanations can wait. Now is the time for action. We'll need another vehicle. Mia, where's that RV you bought?'

'In a storage lot.' She named a township bordering Lavina.

'Guarded?'

'Do I look like I have the money for a guarded lot?'

'Terrific. We'll leave our cars in the lot and use the RV.'

'We'll do no such thing,' George said as Sasha sighed and turned away. 'No one is going anywhere, and we're certainly not getting rid of our cars. This started off as crazy talk and is getting crazier by the minute. You've said nothing to persuade us otherwise.'

Alice gulped more oxygen.

'You want a reason? Here it is. It's like the story said. Babs isn't just dead. She was killed. I'll be the main suspect. And all of you are with me.'

Lavina Township Police Department
Transcript of interview with Mia Sullivan
Present: Detective Travis Meacham, Officer Sherilee Townsend

Townsend: If I'm understanding things correctly, you left your cars and transferred to the RV. Can you tell us about that?

Sullivan: It's so cool. I got it cheap because it's really old and pretty beat-up. But I could afford it, which is more than I could say about my place at Timeless Pastures after they raised the lot fee for the fifth time. I'm going to travel around the country in it. You know, like in that movie?

Townsend: The thing I remember about that movie was how small it was, even for one person. I can't even imagine what it would be like with four people.

Sullivan: Are you thinking we stayed in it? Because we didn't.

Townsend: Actually, I'd like to know what happened after the, ah, phone incident. Why'd you switch to the RV?'

Sullivan: Oh. But I should probably tell you that it's not exactly an RV.

FOURTEEN

The friends parked their cars in the storage lot and stared in disbelief when Mia pointed. Leave it to George to state the obvious.

'You said it was an RV,' George said.

'But it's just a camper van. An old one,' Sasha resorted to a realtor's ultimate skill: turning the proverbial sow's ear into a . . . 'Retrofitted, I presume?'

'Of course.' Mia beamed with pride. 'Check it out.' She wrestled with the side door until it slid back with a screech, revealing a sink barely larger than a mixing bowl and a mini-fridge beneath a countertop that held a hot plate. A platform bed with storage cabinets beneath it took up the rest of the space. Curtains screened what Mia euphemistically called the 'living area' from the driver's and passenger's seats.

'Where do you eat?'

Mia pointed to a tray table tucked behind the passenger seat. 'And I've got a couple of folding chairs, so that I can sit outside when the weather's nice.'

Sasha continued running through her mental checklist.

'Bathroom?'

Mia shook her head.

'Let me guess,' said George. 'The woods.'

'For you, maybe. Not as easy for us women,' Sasha reminded him. Then, 'Lord save me,' as Mia lifted a five-gallon bucket topped with a plastic toilet seat. 'Even I can't put lipstick on this pig' – confirming with every word Mia's worst fears about her impulsive decision to buy the van.

Sure, she'd made it sound interesting – the open road! No loan payments, no possessions! Freedom! Adventure! At least, that's how she talked it up.

But she'd seen the movie, knew what she was really in for. Crouching over the bucket in the middle of the night when the dash to a campground toilet seemed entirely too far. Taking a crappy job to pay for a van breakdown – because vehicles always broke down.

And worst of all, no matter how warmly that movie portrayed the weird tribe of voluntary nomads, no real friends to speak of, certainly none to compare to the bonds she'd forged at Timeless Pastures.

But now, in the proverbial blink of an eye, she found herself on a real adventure, far more thrilling than anything she'd imagined when she bought the van.

Alice was getting more interesting by the moment.

In addition to hustling them out of the lake house and into the van, Alice had insisted that they pay cash for whatever motel they ended up in that night – where, she'd promised, they'd get an explanation. And it *would* be a motel.

'All of us in this thing – I'm getting claustrophobic just thinking about it,' Sasha said. 'I'll spring for a room for me and George, and another for you two.' She waved a credit card.

'No!' Alice snatched it away as deftly as she'd pocketed their phones. 'No credit cards. They leave a trail. In fact, don't leave yet, Mia. Purses and wallets in the cars, everyone.'

Mia piped up. 'Then how are we supposed to get a motel? Food? Gas? Because I need to fill the tank before we go anywhere.'

'Seriously? We'll use cash,' Alice said.

'I never carry it anymore,' Sasha protested.

'None?'

Sasha rifled through her wallet and waved a five. 'I stand corrected.'

'I brought some for the weekend. Maybe fifty,' George said.

'Thirty for me,' Mia said.

Alice waited while they stowed things in the cars. 'I've got plenty,' she said when they returned. 'But it's at my house. And I don't dare go back there. None of us do.'

'But they don't know the van,' Mia pointed out.

'Still, a van pulling up in front of my house. Probably not the best idea.'

'I still don't see how the rest of us are involved in this . . .' George began before Sasha shushed him.

They sat in silence.

Alice took out her cigarettes, shook one from the pack and rolled it longingly between her fingers. She never smoked in front of her friends.

Sasha clasped her hands together and stretched her arms forward, flexing her wrists.

George opened his mouth. Snapped it shut at a warning look from Sasha.

'I know!' Mia's smile lit up the van. 'I'll run. Alice, give me your house key.'

She took in their bafflement. 'I'll park the van a mile or so away. Maybe at the supermarket. I'll jog on over to Timeless Pastures. I'll look like any runner. Just tell me where to find the cash.'

Alice held out her key but refused to relinquish it. 'Bedroom closet. Banker's box. But a jogger running up to my front door and letting herself in? What if police are still at Babs' place?'

'No, silly. Those pines come almost up to your back door. I'll cut through the trees. If cops are around, I'll use my own best judgment. I need to get in a run today anyway.'

'What if someone recognizes you?'

'I never run in the community – all those cul-de-sacs, it's too boring – so no one ever sees me in my running gear. Anyway, there's hardly anyone left in Timeless Pastures to see me. Besides, I'll be in the pines most of the way, but just in case, I've got a gaiter I'll pull up over the lower part of my face. Makes sense, with the snow and all. People think it's colder out than it really is.'

'I don't know,' Alice began as Mia ushered them into the van, Alice in the passenger seat beside her, George and Sasha on the folding chairs in the rear.

The van jolted to life.

'We're off,' Mia cried. She turned out of the storage lot and on to the road. Gave it some gas.

George and Sasha clutched the arms of their flimsy folding chairs. 'Is this safe? We don't even have seatbelts.'

'Probably not,' Mia called over her shoulder, entirely too cheerfully. 'Alice, how much money would you like me to get?'

'Um, maybe a thousand?'

The van lurched. 'Sorry,' Mia said. 'You have a thousand dollars? In cash?'

'Emergency fund.' Alice turned toward the window and stared at the passing landscape, signaling an end to the conversation. Or so Mia thought.

Alice poked her shoulder.

'On second thought,' she said, 'get three.'

Lavina Township Police Department
Transcript of interview with J.R. 'Johnny' Natale
Present: Detective Travis Meacham, Officer Sherilee Townsend

Meacham: Good news, Mr Natale. Ballistics tests cleared your gun.

Natale: Of course they did. Am I free to go?

Meacham: We're still working on the narrative. Just a few more questions. Believe me, no one wants this cleared up more than I. When did you become aware that you might have a bigger problem on your hands than the death of Barbara Stevenson?

Natale: Glenda Ferguson brought it to my attention. To be perfectly honest, at first I didn't think of it as a problem. Glenda can be, let's say, excitable.

Meacham: We're aware of Ms Ferguson.

Townsend: Very aware. Hardly a week goes by without a call . . .

Meacham: I was in the midst of a question, Sherilee. What exactly did Ms Ferguson say? And why did you decide to take it seriously?

Natale: I'm a little embarrassed to say this, but it had more to do with Sugar Plum than what Glenda said. Alice loved that little dog. When Glenda told me Alice hadn't shown up to walk Sugar Plum, it got my attention. Alice is just about the most reliable person in Timeless Pastures. Walks in at nine a.m. on the dot of the fifteenth of every month to pay her home loan and lot fee in cash. I wish all our residents were like her. Not that we have that many of them these days.

FIFTEEN

Johnny was at his office window, watching Hawk's Range Rover wheel out of the parking lot, when Glenda pushed through the door with Sugar Plum, ignoring as she always did the sign specifying 'Service Animals Only.'

'I hope you got that guy's license plate,' she huffed. 'The way he drives, he could have killed Sugar Plum.'

The Range Rover hadn't come within fifty feet of Sugar Plum, but Johnny knew Glenda liked her drama, which no doubt explained her presence in his office. Just as Babs monitored perceived wrongdoing within the community, Glenda was hyper-alert to anything that might pose a threat from beyond its gates.

He wondered what it would be this time. Kids riding bikes through the community? Timeless Pastures made a handy and mostly traffic-free short-cut between a middle school and a nearby development of considerably larger and more expensive homes. Despite their bookbags and school logo gear, Glenda persisted in labeling them juvenile delinquents.

Suspicious vans? According to Glenda, vans reliably sheltered serial killers, even though most of the ones navigating Timeless Pastures' cul-de-sacs bore the logos of worldwide delivery companies. 'Fake logos. That's how they lure you into a false sense of security,' Glenda maintained with a knowing sniff.

Reports on the police scanner – because the scanner app was the one bit of technology Glenda mastered quickly – of a break-in two towns over? In her world, it stood to reason the burglars would move on to Timeless Pastures.

Johnny sighed and waited.

'Well? Did you?'

'Did I what?'

'Get the license plate. Because if you don't report him, I will. But it would really help the police to have a tag number.'

Johnny heaved a deeper sigh. Glenda's near-daily calls were the reason he and Police Chief Oscar Martinez were on a first-name basis, occasionally bumping longneck beers in sympathy whenever both fetched up at the same time in the Dew Drop Inn.

'He's my boss, Glenda. Yours, too, I suppose. Or, at least, your landlord. He's a vice president of Weller Holdings.'

'Doesn't give him the right to swan around like he owns it . . . Oh.'

She wore the same involuntary grimace he saw on all the residents' faces whenever they heard the name behind their ever-increasing lot fees.

'Right. What brings you here today, Glenda?'

'Alice.'

'Alice? What about her?'

'She's missing. I'm afraid someone took her.' She bent and scooped Sugar Plum into her arms and hugged him so tight he yelped.

'What do you mean, *missing*?'

'She was supposed to walk Sugar Plum for me today. She walks him twice a day, at eight in the morning and four in the afternoon. She didn't show up this afternoon, and they were supposed to be back from their weekend by then. Her house is dark and she's not picking up her phone.'

Johnny looked at the clock. 'It's only four fifteen.'

Sugar Plum yelped again at a fresh squeeze.

'But we're talking about Alice.'

'Why don't you put Sugar Plum down? Nobody's going to get him in here.' Johnny played for time. For once, Glenda had a point. Alice was punctual nearly to a fault.

'I just want to keep him close. I held my breath and paid one of those dog-walking services while they were gone. I was scared I'd never see Sugar Plum again. According to the internet, dognapping's a big business these days.'

Johnny reached for Sugar Plum, but Glenda clutched him tighter still.

'You were saying about Alice?'

'They should have been back by now. Don't you usually have to check out of places like that by noon? It was only about an hour away from here. But we had that awful snowstorm a couple of days ago. What if they got in some kind of a wreck? What if their car ran off the road and they're all lying down at the bottom of a ravine somewhere where no one can see them? You read about things like that – people dying just out of sight even as cars zoomed right past them.'

'This is South Jersey, Glenda. We don't have ravines.'

Sugar Plum managed a whimper. Johnny thought that if the dog had been human, his little face would be purple from lack of oxygen.

'Tell you what, Glenda. I'll give you and Sugar Plum a ride home, then I'll go around to all their houses and check things out,' he said, more for the sake of the dog than anything else.

And told himself the spasm in his gut was solely the result of the wolfed-down meatball parm, and not the unthinkable.

What if, for the first time, Glenda was right about something?

Lavina Township Police Department
Transcript of interview with Mia Sullivan
Present: Detective Travis Meacham, Officer Sherilee Townsend

Townsend: About the cash.
Sullivan: What about it?
Townsend: How much are we talking about?
Sullivan: About three to start with.
Townsend: Three hundred?
Sullivan: Thousand.
Townsend: Three thousand *dollars? Where'd all that money come from?*
Sullivan: It was Alice's.
Townsend: Where'd she get it?
Sullivan: You'll have to ask her.
Townsend: You see the problem with that.
Sullivan: For you, maybe. It's not a problem for me.

SIXTEEN

Mia parked in the shopping center about a mile from Timeless Pastures and set out at a decorous jog until she could no longer see the van behind her.

Then she leapt – more of a hop; she was, after all, sixty-six – and let out a whoop.

Not twenty-four hours earlier, she'd bemoaned the future that would see her leave her newly unaffordable duplex, sell or donate most of her possessions and move with just a few essentials into the van.

Now, a life she'd long fantasized had become reality. Over the years, their Timeless Reads book group had revealed its members' preferences – true crime for George, a blushing acknowledgment of romance for Sasha, and poetry for Alice, meaning that her suggestions for the next month's read were routinely rejected.

For Mia, it was spy novels. Not the silly stuff – no James Bond and his babes and lethal gadgets. Only the real deal: the likes of le Carré, Furst, Gerritsen. Threads tucked into closed doors each and every time upon leaving. Tailing by car or on foot. Being the gray man; woman in her case. She'd always thought she'd be good at those things; the hours of boredom – her marriage had certainly taught her about that – and the split seconds of terror.

On her runs, she sometimes amused herself by memorizing details of passing cars, their make and color, license plates, distinguishing features. You never know, she'd tell herself, when you might see something – an accident, maybe – and be the only person able to supply crucial details.

She loped along the development's main street to a short stretch where the pines lined each side. She did a quick check over her shoulder. Not a soul in sight. At least in this case, the relentless emptying out of Timeless Pastures proved an advantage.

The Pine Barrens were an added benefit – a million acres of trees backing right up to Timeless Pastures. People liked to talk about the Pineys, descendants of early White settlers who lived deep within the pines and kept to themselves, their wariness of outsiders often downright hostile. Of the ne'er-do-wells who took refuge within its remoteness, from escaped slaves and moonshiners in the early days, to more recent drug runners. Of its occasional location as a dumping ground for the victims of mob hits. Of the Jersey Devil, a two-legged creature whose characteristics confusingly included horse hooves and maybe a horse head – or was it a goat head? – bat wings and claws, and a blood-curdling scream.

But the Jersey Devil was a nighttime denizen, and hers was a midday mission. She ducked into the trees and began working her way back to the duplex uneasily shared by Babs and Alice – a murder victim and a maybe-murderer! She'd stopped running, thankful that she was merely making her way through a short stretch of the trees, one that gave glimpses of the houses ahead. The pines were a featureless tangle, each skinny twisted trunk looking so much like the other that it gave credence to the stories of hikers who went missing each summer. Most were found. Not all.

Despite her slow pace, her pulse picked up as she reached the edge of the trees, and the houses – Babs' and Alice's duplex a bit apart from the rest – came fully into view.

She stopped. Stared hard.

No movement. No sound. Nothing.

She gathered herself to sprint toward the duplex. Checked the impulse.

If cops were in Babs' house, a woman charging their way would raise suspicion.

Heart jackhammering, knees wobbling, Mia sauntered across the narrow open space, trying to convince herself that a woman walking out of the trees was perfectly normal, in the process gaining a whole new appreciation for the spies in her novels.

Her hands shook so that it took her three tries to fit the key into the lock. She pulled the back door closed behind her and slumped against it. Still shaking, although now from relief, she hurried to the bedroom and flung open the closet door.

A banker's box, Alice had said. As in, one. But an entire side of the closet was stacked with bankers' boxes from floor nearly to ceiling. She stood on tiptoe and reached for the top box. It was surprisingly heavy. She gave it a hard shove, stumbling backward as it fell into her arms. The box was taped shut. She sat it on the floor, slit the tape with her thumbnail and lifted the lid.

Only a bunch of *National Geographics*. Similar troves populated garage sales all over Timeless Pastures as people moved out. She edged the box aside with her foot and reached for the next one. Same thing. She sat it atop the first, and reached for the third, fighting a sense of rising panic.

Alice was pretty old. What if she'd gotten confused? Told Mia to look in a banker's box when she'd stashed the cash in the mattress instead? What if three thousand dollars in cash was only the figment of fading memory?

What if, what if, what if? She slammed the third box down atop the other two, so hard it tilted and slid from its perch. The brittle, yellowed tape securing the lid tore and a gold-and-black wave of *National Geographics* broke across the floor, followed by a veritable tsunami of green.

Mia sank to the floor and raked stacks and stacks of cash toward her.

She lifted one of the bundles – all twenties – and riffled through it, holding it close to her face to feel the breeze, until she realized she had no idea how much was in each bundle, and that time was passing. She did a quick count – five hundred dollars per bundle. She set six bundles aside, then put the rest back in the box and covered it with the magazines.

She lifted the covers from the other two boxes. Same layer of *National Geographics*, covering unimaginable amounts of cash. She pulled another down from the stack. Same. She counted the boxes and started to tally the stacks of cash in one, but the math made her head swim. Who had that kind of money lying around in cash? Drug dealers. Mob bosses. Crooked politicians – they lived, after all, in New Jersey.

But a seventy-six-year-old woman who lived in a budget retirement community and whose personal style could most charitably be described as thrift-shop bargain bin?

Which took Mia right back to the drug dealer/mob boss/crooked pol category. Nobody amassed that sort of cash legally, did they? Alice's self-professed status as a murder suspect suddenly seemed a lot more likely – which made Mia's own situation feel a lot more fraught.

One of the things she admired most about her fictional spies was their ability to perform split-second adaptations to changes in circumstances, kicking into survival mode when a casual bystander might notice nothing amiss. As of just a couple of hours ago, Mia was no longer a casual bystander.

She opened one of the boxes again, slid her hand beneath the magazines and, with only the slightest twinge of guilt, removed two more bundles. If this situation turned out to be much ado about nothing, she'd hand them over to Alice. If Alice was the sort of person Mia was starting to suspect she was, she'd understand.

She stacked the boxes back as best she could, only to realize that despite her every-other-day free weights routine, she couldn't possibly hoist the last two atop the rest. Who knew money was so heavy? She finally shoved them into a corner of the closet and stashed two of the bundles in the pockets in her running tights that usually held her late, lamented phone. She stuffed two more in her sports bra and tucked the final four into the waistband of her tights, snugged hard against the small of her back, reminding herself to hide two somewhere safe as soon as possible after handing the rest to Alice.

And wondered, as she jogged back toward the van, her breath coming fast and hard all out of proportion to her leisurely pace, if what she'd just done made her a criminal, too.

Lavina Township Police Department
Transcript of interview with J.R. 'Johnny' Natale
Present: Detective Travis Meacham, Officer Sherilee Townsend

Meacham: Would you call yourself a cautious man, Mr Natale?

Natale: The last time we spoke, you said just a few more questions.

Meacham: I had hoped it wouldn't take this long. Perhaps your response will help move things along. This should be an easy one. Cautious? Yes or no?

Natale: It depends on the situation. Safe to say I don't enjoy taking unnecessary risks.

Meacham: Checking on residents after they'd been reported missing – you'd consider that risk avoidance, then?

Natale: I wouldn't call it an official report. Just speculation by our resident gossip.

Meacham: My question stands.

Natale: Sure. I didn't want to jump to conclusions.

Meacham: Let's look at the situation from another angle. Failing to pass along a report of four missing people – that could be considered quite a risk, couldn't it?

Natale: I guess I didn't see it that way.

Meacham: Four people, four vulnerable *people, missing. You didn't see that as a risk? Something that should have been called to the attention of the authorities?*

Natale: I wouldn't describe any of those four as vulnerable.

SEVENTEEN

Johnny dropped off Glenda and Sugar Plum and then looped back toward Alice's house.

As usual, Timeless Pastures' streets were deserted, save for a solitary jogger, face wrapped against the cold.

He turned on to Yorktown Way and parked in front of the duplex anchoring the cul-de-sac. The police had removed the yellow crime-scene tape, but a stray bit still fluttered atop a crust of snow. At some point, he'd have to deal with Babs' side of the duplex. So far, he'd been unable to locate any relatives who might have had an interest in her belongings.

He shrugged, reminding himself that it wasn't as though Timeless Pastures was losing money by letting the duplex sit unoccupied. For some reason, Weller Holdings wasn't advertising any of the vacant properties for sale.

Alice's side of the duplex, like Babs', gave every appearance of being unoccupied, although, unlike Babs, Alice had drawn her curtains. He walked around the duplex, shuddering at the dark stain on Alice's patio where Babs had fallen. The pigeons that had so bedeviled Alice fluttered disconsolately about, wheeling away at his approach, then swooping back toward the home.

He waved his arms. 'Shoo!' A few more days without Babs' regular feedings and they'd probably disappear for good. If nothing else, Babs' death had solved one of his most persistent problems.

He nearly decided against checking the homes of the other three – he hated driving past all those abandoned duplexes – but the thought of another visit from Glenda propelled him into the next cul-de-sac. George's home stood dark and quiet. A flagpole jutted empty from the porch. Johnny frowned. George flew the American flag every day when he was home, attaching it in the morning and taking it back inside, properly folded into a triangle, at sunset. Which was still a half-hour away. George wasn't home.

Same story at Sasha's freshly painted beige house with the burgundy shutters, and Mia's with its array of race trophies displayed on a shelf across the picture window.

Johnny went back to the office, fired up his computer and looked up their cell numbers, calling each in turn, only to have the calls go straight to voicemail.

He put the phone down. Picked it up again. Stared at the private number he'd been given as a courtesy after Glenda Ferguson had called the police one too many times.

The logical move would be to call Chief Martinez. Wouldn't it?

But if he did, Martinez would be duty-bound to do something. Maybe put out another alert, the way he had with Babs – something that might bring Hawk Boneham breathing down his neck anew.

He reminded himself that Babs had gone missing under very different circumstances – house standing open, nobody home when the delivery guy showed up as expected. Exactly the sort of thing to cause concern.

But four fully functioning adults just a hair past their scheduled return from a planned weekend getaway? They were probably fine. Anyway, didn't the police usually require twenty-four hours before investigating a missing-person report?

He'd be well within his rights to wait until the following morning. He'd check again then, and if they were still gone, he'd call Martinez. And if, in that time, they returned?

He wouldn't have to worry about another visit from Hawk Boneham.

Lavina Township Police Department
Transcript of interview with George Sterling
Present: Detective Travis Meacham, Officer Sherilee Townsend

Meacham: You were the first one to connect Alice Sanders with the original crime, yes?

Sterling: Correct.

Meacham: How did that come about?

Sterling: I'm something of a history buff.

Meacham: Hey, me too. I've heard there's something like fifteen thousand books written on Lincoln alone. I aim to read every last one.

Townsend: Nerd.

Meacham: Ignore her. What about you? Civil War? World War Two?

Sterling: Neither. For whatever reason, I homed in on the Sixties.

Meacham: Seems an odd choice for a military man such as yourself.

Sterling: Maybe that's why I'm fascinated by it. So much norm-busting and rule-breaking. I couldn't imagine dodging the draft or doing all of that protesting. Or worse.

Meacham: Worse, of course, is what brings us here today. This is the Wanted poster for the woman you know as Alice Sanders. It lists some extremely serious charges. Is it true she admitted to them?

Sterling: Not in so many words.

EIGHTEEN

After the van, the no-tell motel on a two-lane road lined with pawnshops, liquor stores and used-car lots felt almost luxurious.

They lounged on the beds covered by slick patterned spreads – George and Sasha on one, Mia and Alice propped up on pillows stacked against the headboard of the other – and passed containers from a Chinese take-out place back and forth.

'May I have the dumplings, Sasha?' Alice held out her hand.

George cleared his throat. 'I think this is the part where you tell us what's going on, Alice.'

Alice popped an entire dumpling in her mouth and chewed for a very long time.

'This was back in the Sixties, early Seventies,' she said finally. 'Everybody was on edge.'

'Let me guess. You were one of those hippie kids.'

Sasha shot him some side-eye. 'You say it like it's a bad thing. Weren't we all? I had a 'fro out to here.' She held her hands six inches from her head.

'I so wanted to be one of them,' Mia chimed in. 'But I was stuck in Catholic school. The nuns made us kneel to check that our skirt hems touched the floor. The minute we got out of school for the day, we'd roll up the waistbands to those little pleated skirts until we'd hiked the hems up to our butts, throw our sweaters over our shoulders and untuck our blouses and tie the tails up under our boobs. Not that I had much in the way of boobs, then or now.'

George tried to rein things back in. 'I'm just guessing Alice's hippie years involved more than a fashion statement.'

Alice's lips tightened. 'Fighting that obscene war – it was my everything.'

'Really?' Sasha's eyebrows arched high. 'Why? The Army wasn't coming after your college-boy buddies. They were too busy filling their ranks with Black and brown boys.'

'Which is one more reason that war was so awful,' Alice shot back.

George pushed the food aside.

'Alice, where did you say you went to school again?'

'Holyoke. Babs figured it out.'

Mia leaned forward. 'Is that what you two were fighting about?'

'Glenda was the one who called it a fight. I think Babs could tell I wasn't happy my privacy had been invaded.'

'Wait,' George said. 'Holyoke? What year?'

'1968. That's when I started. I left in 1970.'

Of course.

'Remind me, Alice. Where's Holyoke?'

'South Hadley.'

It drew a blank.

'Southern Massachusetts.'

George sifted through his memory – bombings at the University of Wisconsin, the U.S. State Department, the Pentagon. And one at a military materiel manufacturer in Connecticut. A small state. He'd been stationed there briefly, and while he couldn't place South Hadley, he knew you could drive all the way through Connecticut and be in Massachusetts in an hour and a half.

He squinted at Alice, trying to erase the wrinkles, darken the hair.

Damn her for throwing away his phone. There was a time when all the names were safely filed away in his head, a sort of mental card catalogue. Poke the crease in his brain that stored radicals on the run, and the names and images used to pop right up. Some still did.

Bernadine Dohrn, her straight dark hair parted in the middle and flowing over her shoulders, staring square-jawed and clear-eyed into the camera.

Mustachioed Bill Ayers, cocking his head at a quizzical angle.

And a woman with long, wavy hair, dark in the black-and-white Wanted poster photos, but described in newspapers as a striking redhead. Her name was . . . it was . . .

'Are you . . .? Is it possible? I mean, you look as though you could be Carol . . . Carol . . . oh, shoot. I can't pull up the last name. Something Eastern European.'

'Carol who?' Mia and Sasha chorused.

George talked fast, lest his memory fail him again.

'A munitions plant was bombed. Some sort of anti-war message. And people—' He stopped.

Mia's and Sasha's faces mirrored shock.

'A bomb? George, that's crazy. Isn't it, Alice?' Mia's voice was small. 'Alice?'

Alice looked George in the eye. 'Yes. People died.'

Lavina Township Police Department
Transcript of interview with Sasha Coverdale
Present: Detective Travis Meacham, Officer Sherilee Townsend

Townsend: The night in the motel was the first time Alice Sanders told you about the people she kil— about the people she's alleged to have killed, correct?

Coverdale: Your words, not mine.

Townsend: And yet she acknowledged people died.

Coverdale: She did.

Townsend: Complete strangers? Or did she have some relationship to these people?

Coverdale: How should I know?

Townsend: It was a yes-or-no question.

*Coverdale: *silence**

Townsend: Yes? Or no?

Coverdale: I got the feeling she was invested in them.

NINETEEN

George was on his feet, his voice rising. 'People killed. Families destroyed. Did you even know who they were?'

Alice lifted her chin.

'Victoria Carpenter, chemist, daughter of the company president, married, mother of twins. Roosevelt Jones, custodian, widower, father of four and grandfather of seven. And Larry Raynolds, assembly-line worker, married with a baby daughter. If we were at home, I'd show you their photos. I keep them on my nightstand.'

'What a touching gesture. I'm sure their families would appreciate it.'

Alice flinched but held his gaze.

'Alice, I think the three of us are going to need a minute to discuss a few things. Would you mind waiting in the van?' George looked to Mia and Sasha for agreement.

Alice turned to Mia. 'The van's locked, right? What if I just wait in the other room?'

'These walls are like paper,' George said. 'When Sasha and I were getting settled, we could hear every word you two said.'

Mia tossed Alice the keys with an apologetic shrug.

'The locks are sticky. You have to wiggle the key. And if the heater doesn't come on, just bang the console.'

They sat in silence until she left the room and they heard the van's door open and close.

George stabbed at the contents of his carton with his chopsticks, as if somewhere beneath the oyster sauce and cloud ear mushrooms lay the careful words he'd need.

'This has already gone too far. We need to get ourselves out of this situation. Maybe even go to the police.'

Wrong words.

Mia and Sasha shook their heads in unison.

'We don't even know the whole story of what happened back then,' Mia said.

George folded his arms. 'I'm not talking about what happened back then.'

'Go on,' Mia said finally.

Sasha merely glowered, sitting on the same bed with him, just inches away, although her body language telegraphed a different emotional solar system.

'I'm talking about now,' he said.

'I'm talking about the possibility that Alice might have killed Babs.'

Lavina Township Police Department
Transcript of interview with George Sterling
Present: Detective Travis Meacham, Officer Sherilee Townsend

Meacham: Let me get this straight. Alice Sanders tells you she's, let's say, involved *in a fatal bombing that happened several decades ago, and you recognize her as a woman who's been in hiding or living underground or whatever you call it, all these years. And the three of you just go along with her without a moment's hesitation?*

Sterling: Oh, there was hesitation. More than a moment.

Meacham: Glad to hear it. I was starting to wonder about your mental faculties.

Sterling: If you're suggesting any of us are suffering from dementia, you can take that suggestion and . . .

Townsend: I'm sure he didn't mean it that way. Did you, Detective Meacham?

Meacham: I chose an unfortunate turn of phrase. For sure I was starting to worry about your sanity.

Townsend: Is that better, Mr Sterling?

Sterling: If I thought he really meant it. Not certain I do.

Townsend: Then I'll pose the question instead.

Sterling: So now we're playing bad cop/good cop?

Townsend: We're just giving Detective Meacham a time-out. Here's my question: Didn't anyone have second thoughts?

Sterling: I did.

TWENTY

George squared his shoulders against the inevitable outburst after his suggestion about the police.

It didn't come.

Sasha slowly rose from the bed and moved toward the door.

'Where are you going?'

'To get my things from the other room. I'm going to sleep in here tonight.'

Even as she spoke, Mia shifted on the other bed and patted the spread. 'You can sleep with me. Let's let Alice have the other bed. She must be exhausted.'

Resignation tugged at George. He'd always feared Sasha would walk away someday. What was it his students said? TGTBT – too good to be true? He'd never imagined it would end over something like this.

The relationship with Sasha had taken him by surprise, immersing him in a gratitude so profound he'd never dared look beyond any given day, for fear the future would only involve the same sort of stabbing, swirling sense of loss into which he'd plunged after his wife's death.

Alice had pulled him out of it, at least partially, arriving empty-handed at his door one day, as opposed to the 'widow brigade' he'd been warned about – lovely, well-meaning women bearing casseroles and oblique offers of more. They scared the bejesus out of him.

Alice set him straight. 'They want relationships, George. It's not time for that yet. It will be, and sooner than you think. But now, you need to learn how to find joy in life again.'

He'd snorted. 'Impossible.'

She'd shown him it wasn't.

And she'd been right about something else. To his shock, he found himself wanting deeper involvement, just as she'd predicted. Alice smiling at him across the breakfast table, sharing coffee and trading sections of the newspaper – because he preferred his current events old-school – rather than sneaking out in the middle of the night. Strolling hand-in-hand on Timeless Pastures' walking trails along the edge of the pines, heedless of who might see them. Accepting his flowers with delight rather than consternation.

She'd been firm. 'Yes, you're ready. But I'm not the one.' She'd had to say it more than once before she mentioned Sasha. He knew who she was, of course. She was in their Timeless Reads book group and, beyond that, one of the community's few Black residents.

Alice noted his hesitation, harsh judgment at the ready. 'Is there a problem, George?'

He wasn't that guy. Was he? He and his son were estranged, so he'd never told him about Sasha, and he gathered she hadn't told her son's family, either. So they both had misgivings; would be foolish not to, given sadly regular reminders that racial animosity was alive and thriving. But the longer they were together, the more he let himself wonder, *Could there be more?*

He'd thought about having *that* talk; had hoped, in fact, that the weekend getaway might be the opportunity.

Sasha reached for the door handle.

George found his backbone. He couldn't stop the cancer that had stolen his late wife. But this – maybe he had a fighting chance.

'Sasha, wait.'

She didn't turn, but at least she stopped.

'Hear me out. Both of you, please. You're right. We don't have the facts of what happened all those years ago. But we know a little about what happened to Babs.'

He dropped the chopsticks into the carton, set it aside and held up his hand, counting on his fingers.

'First, just a few days ago, Babs and Alice have a big fight.'

'About the pigeons,' Mia countered. 'Which they've been fighting about forever.'

'Right. But this one was so bad that Glenda was ready to call nine-one-one.'

'Glenda would call nine-one-one over a hangnail.'

'I wasn't finished. Then we plan this trip out of town. Sasha, didn't you tell me Alice was the one who suggested we go immediately?'

'Yes – but she said it was because the rates would only go up the closer we got to Christmas.'

'Noted. But then we get to the lake house and find out that Babs is missing.'

'So?' Sasha's chin still jutted defiance. But at least she left the doorway and joined Mia on the other bed.

'And it turns out that Babs has been shot dead and that Alice, if not an actual killer, at least has a passing acquaintance with murder.'

He held up his hands to forestall another outburst.

'I'm not saying she did it. I'm just saying it looks bad. Really bad. Any cop will tell you there's no such thing as coincidence. A cop would also say something else. Because Alice told us she's wanted for murder, we could all be accessories to harboring a fugitive.'

He'd expected to see shock as reality sank in. Some hesitation.

But Sasha shot back without a second's pause.

'Any real cop? Or just the ones on those shows you watch?'

His heart lurched at Sasha's tone. He lobbed a Hail Mary.

'You know what else a cop would say? That we need more facts – both about that earlier business, whatever it was, and about her beef with Babs. The only thing to do is to ask her ourselves. Let's get her back in here.'

He strode to the door with far more confidence than he actually felt.

Sasha's words were like a knife in his back. 'You could've led with that, George. Instead of threatening to go to the police.'

'I'll get her. We'll talk. I never meant to threaten—'

He opened the door. Looked out.

'But maybe I should have.'

He held the door wide, heedless of the frigid air gusting into the room.

'Come see for yourself. Alice is gone. Along with the van.'

Lavina Township Police Department
Transcript of interview with Mia Sullivan
Present: Detective Travis Meacham, Officer Sherilee Townsend

Townsend: Just like that, you handed Alice the keys.
Sullivan: I had no idea she could drive. None of us did.
Townsend: If she couldn't drive, how'd she get around? Timeless Pastures is miles from any public transportation.

Sullivan: She had a bike. Nothing fancy, just an old cruiser, the kind you backpedal to brake. You know, like ones we probably all had as kids. She had a milk crate on the front for her groceries from the supermarket just down the road. We just thought it was part of her old-hippie shtick. Anyone who asked her about it got the whole climate change lecture – everybody had to do their part, blah blah blah.

Townsend: What about in winter?

Sullivan: Even then. If there was snow on the ground, she'd walk to the store. It's only a mile or so away. For an old lady, Alice is a lot tougher than she looks.

Townsend: We're starting to figure that out.

TWENTY-ONE

Alice gave thanks for the slope in the motel parking lot. It took her a few moments to locate the emergency brake, disengage it and put the van in neutral. She couldn't remember the last time she'd driven. For sure, she'd used a stick shift, and the van was automatic, along with being larger than anything she'd ever driven. But it couldn't be helped.

She only had a little while for what she needed to do – if she could even achieve it – and get back to the motel before the others rightfully panicked and went to the police. To her relief, the van rolled smoothly in reverse, stopping at the far side of the lot.

She turned the key in the ignition and kept an eye on the motel-room door, fearing her friends would hear the van sputtering to life.

But the room's door stayed closed, at least as long as she could see it in the rear-view mirror, and she turned out on to the main road and headed for the shining oasis she'd seen on their way to the motel.

It beckoned ahead, its blaze of light a signal that it was still open. Of course it was. That's why they called them convenience stores.

She parked the van out of the light's glare and spent a couple of minutes searching through it for a hat, or even a rag she could twist around her hair. Nothing. Finally, she wove her hair into a braid and tucked it into her collar. The clerk probably saw hundreds of people a day. She knew that old women in particular were said to be nearly invisible. Some apparently resented that. Alice relished it.

She smoked a calming cigarette, then went into the store, wincing at the light, and paced its aisles, looking for something she didn't see.

'Can I help you?'

She turned her back on the clerk and pretended to inspect a wall of snacks. 'Just looking for a newspaper,' she called over her shoulder.

'Good luck. We only get a few a day and we end up throwing most of them out.'

She gritted her teeth. 'Where would I find those few?'

'You wouldn't.'

'Sold out?' She headed for the door. Where there was one convenience store, there were bound to be more.

'Nah. I already took out the trash. I think we still had a couple, but they're in the Dumpster now.'

She left, angling her face away from the security cameras. She maneuvered the van out of its parking space and steered around the back of the building where – huzzah! – the Dumpster stood at the far end of the lot. She pulled up alongside it so that the van shielded it from the cameras and heaved open the lid.

'Ugghh.' She reeled away from the stench. Forced herself back. The darkness for which she'd given thanks a minute earlier now proved her enemy. She finally resorted to sticking her hand into the Dumpster and feeling around until her fingers touched a plastic sack. She pulled it up and over the lip of the bin. It fell to the ground, splitting open and spilling its reeking contents.

Paper and Styrofoam cups, crumpled chip bags, receipts, wads of tissues and paper napkins, empty snack boxes, all of it coated in a slurry of coffee and soft-drink dregs, decomposing hot dogs and blobs of something that might have been yogurt. At least, she hoped it was.

She clawed through it, barely daring to hope. But at the bottom – of course it was at the bottom – barely recognizable, was a sodden mass of newsprint. She lifted it carefully with both hands, fearing it would disintegrate, and laid it like something precious across the passenger seat.

Then she drove the van a couple of blocks and pulled into an office supply store's parking lot, not wanting to wait until she got back to the motel. She had to know exactly what the story about Babs' death had said.

She flicked on the overhead light and checked the date – Saturday – and shrugged. A day-old story would be better than nothing. She began to pull the pages apart one by one, trying her best not to tear the wet paper.

When she found the story, it was so small she nearly missed it, tucked as it was between an ad for hearing aids and a notice of an upcoming car wash by a local high school. She held it close to her face, squinting at the tiny print, ignoring the smell.

It seemed to be a fleshed-out version of the initial story Sasha had seen on the paper's website, with a plea from the police for anyone with possible information to come forward, along with a pro forma statement of sympathy from the corporation that had bought Timeless Pastures.

Her gaze stopped at a detail.

'Oh, no,' she breathed. 'No, no, no.'

Someone pounded on the window. She screamed.

A man stood beside the van, wearing a uniform and a hat bearing a security company's name.

'Sorry, ma'am. Didn't mean to scare you. There's no overnight parking in this lot. You have to—'

Whatever else he said was lost as Alice jammed her foot to the gas pedal and sent the van roaring back on to the road.

Lavina Township Police Department
Transcript of interview with Sasha Coverdale
Present: Detective Travis Meacham, Officer Sherilee Townsend

Townsend: I'm curious as to why you so readily went along with the other three.

Coverdale: You mean because they're White and I'm Black?

Townsend: Not necessarily.

Coverdale: I've noticed that even though you two are about the same age, he's a detective and you're an officer. Why is that?

Meacham: I don't like what you're insinuating.

Coverdale: I wasn't talking to you. But I'll move on. Officer Townsend, do you typically investigate murders?

Townsend: I'm supposed to be the one asking the questions.

Coverdale: Humor me.

Townsend: We don't have many homicides here.

Coverdale: Detective Meacham, how many murders have you investigated?

Meacham: Let me think. I've been with the department a good while. Several.

Coverdale: Officer Townsend, how about you?

Townsend: This is my first. But I haven't been in the department as long as my colleague.

Coverdale: Any murders happen in your time here?

Townsend: Sure. The usual domestics and drug disputes. A couple of Philly mob hits we got stuck with because of where they dumped the bodies.

Coverdale: And did you investigate those?

Townsend: No.

Coverdale: You're Black.

Townsend: Gee, I hadn't noticed.

Coverdale: Let me paraphrase something a wise woman once said to me. Who on the force is dumb enough to think I'm going to spill my guts to you just because you're a sister?

TWENTY-TWO

'I swear to God, George, if you pick up that phone, I'm going to . . .'

Sasha stopped.

She would what?

Leave him?

In a million years, she'd never have pictured herself with a White man. For that matter, given her age and how many years had passed since her divorce, with any man. Between her ex-husband's career as a firefighter and hers as a realtor, along with the nonstop juggling required for her son's activities, there'd been little time for each other. When they'd parted after Gerald went off to college, it was with relief as much as sadness.

Things were simpler after that. For years, she'd felt as though her life was nothing but an endless string of negotiations – with house sales at work and every blessed thing under the sun at home. She knew she was lucky. Her husband never ran around, never hit her, didn't drink or do drugs or gamble. He pitched in with the housework and caring for Gerald, and when her friends asked her what the heck she'd been thinking when they split, she had no ready answer. Because the man did icy resentment like no one else, days and days of monosyllabic utterances, and then only in response to whatever question she posed out of desperation.

'I just got tired of the cold,' she told a friend. Once. After seeing the friend's reaction, she began to imply that the decision to split had been her husband's. It wasn't fair to him, but she'd given up on fair.

And then came George. 'You're out of your mind,' she said when Alice first brought up his name.

'How long since you've been with a man?' Alice was never one for tact. 'Look, give him a try. If it doesn't work out, he won't make things awkward. I'm Exhibit A.'

Indeed, there'd been no hint of tension in the Timeless Reads gatherings after Alice quietly extricated herself from whatever arrangement she'd had with George.

Sasha had never answered Alice's question about how long it had been, but the unspoken answer – 'too long' – nudged her so insistently that she finally, in best junior high fashion, told Alice it would be fine to drop a word to George that she wouldn't mind getting to know him better. And she had.

He'd proven brokenhearted but hopeful, appreciative without being needy. And *warm.* At night, he curled himself around her, his light snores puffing gently against her neck, and if she happened to roll away from him, he extended a sleepy arm and pulled her back.

Now he faced her across a motel room, phone receiver in hand. A dial tone buzzed long and loud before breaking into warning beeps.

'Put it down, George. Don't you dare call the police.'

Please, her eyes begged him. Don't make me come up with an ultimatum. She'd always thought their relationship was impossible. They discussed race, sure – God knows, it seemed as though every day brought terrible news about another cop shooting another unarmed Black homeowner/motorist/teenage pedestrian – but never in relation to themselves.

Mia came to the rescue. 'Give her fifteen more minutes. I didn't even know she could drive. She was always pedaling around on that bike. She could have gotten lost. And of course, without the phones, she has no way to call us and we have no way to answer.'

'She could call the motel,' George said, ignoring the hoots of laughter when he suggested that Alice could do so from a pay phone.

'Those don't exist anymore,' Mia reminded him.

But he put the receiver down and checked his watch. 'Fifteen minutes. But the more I think about this, the more I'm worried about the position we're putting ourselves in.'

Sasha's heart sank. She could feel it. Whatever he said next was going to make it impossible for her to stay with him.

'Well?' Mia spread her arms wide. 'Don't keep us in suspense.'

'I have no idea where all this is going to lead. But as I said before, if things go south – and I'd say there's a good possibility they will – we could all be accused of harboring a fugitive. That will be terrible for all of us, but, Sasha, especially for you.'

Mia's eyes went round. 'Why for Sasha?'

But Sasha slumped in gratitude. George was like most nice White people, good on the easy stuff – the man had voted for Obama – but clueless on the countless smaller issues. The salespeople who inevitably stuck close to her in a store, nearly daring her to drop, say, a scarf into her handbag; the 'it's just a joke' two-fer cracks on any job she'd ever held; the looks on clients' faces when they realized their real estate agent was Black, their stuttering excuses as to why they suddenly had no need of her services.

And while her ex-husband and son – Lord, her beautiful boy – were more apt to be pulled over for the most minor traffic offense, more than once she'd been stopped, too, despite the spotless Accura she drove, her pastel suits and the carefully knotted silk scarves designed to put clients at ease. The terror she'd felt each time as a cop approached would be nothing compared to the very real dangers of being associated with a notorious fugitive.

Which George also recognized.

'Fine,' she said. 'Fifteen minutes.' And saw the relief on his face that mirrored her own.

TWENTY-THREE

Alice opened the motel-room door to a frozen tableau: George reaching for the cheap plastic landline phone on the coffee table beside one of the beds, Sasha pointing to the watch on her wrist, and Mia with arms outstretched as though begging.

'What's going on here?'

The receiver clacked into its cradle.

'Alice, where have you been? George was just about to call—' At a warning look from Sasha, Mia stopped.

Alice sank on to one of the beds, resisting an urge to lift the spread, crawl under the covers, curl into a fetal position with a pillow over her head and never, ever emerge.

'Who were you about to call, George?'

He refused to meet her gaze. She looked from Sasha to Mia, each equally reticent.

'The police? That's right, isn't it? You were going to call the police.'

Sasha leapt to George's defense. 'Not immediately, he wasn't. He was going to, but then he decided to wait another fifteen minutes. We were up to fourteen minutes and forty seconds when you walked in. Thank God.' Her nose wrinkled. 'What's that smell?'

Alice climbed out of her refuge, went into the bathroom and washed her hands for a very long time.

When she emerged, George waited with arms folded across his chest.

'Alice, it occurred to us – well, to me – that we could be accused of harboring a fugitive.'

She saw from their faces that they expected a denial.

Instead, she nodded.

'George is right. You could be. And maybe you should call the police. For your own sake.' She picked up a pillow and hugged it to her.

'No way, Alice,' Mia said. 'I'm sure if it came to that, God forbid, we could put together an explanation as to why we didn't give you up that would satisfy the police.' Her tone went from hopeful to commanding. 'Right, Sasha? George?'

Before they could respond, Alice shook her head.

'I'm not worried about the police.'

Mia looked oddly deflated. 'I knew it. This whole fugitive thing, it's all a big misunderstanding, right?'

'No, I've been a fugitive for going on' – she counted decades on her fingers – 'ten, twenty, thirty . . . goodness, fifty years and change now. But that's not the issue anymore.' Alice took a breath and hugged the pillow tighter.

'I told you I'm wanted for murder. Which is true.'

'Oh, God,' Mia moaned.

'And I also told you I didn't kill those people. That's true, too. At least, not directly.'

'What about Babs? Did you kill her?'

'George!' Sasha hissed.

'I had to ask.'

Alice blinked. 'Kill Babs? Over some stupid birds? Don't be ridiculous.'

Mia and Sasha released a collective breath.

'Sorry,' George muttered.

'But you're not wrong to bring Babs into this.'

She hurled the pillow across the room.

'I'm not sure Babs' death was a burglary gone wrong. When I said I might be the prime suspect? I was hoping I was wrong.'

'Why would anyone think you'd want to kill Babs? Apart from the birds, of course. Which' – Sasha hastened to add as Alice glared her way – 'you've already told us wasn't a reason.'

'To shut her up about who I really am. Because I think I might know who killed her. And if I'm right, he was really after me.'

Lavina Township Police Department
Transcript of interview with Mia Sullivan
Present: Detective Travis Meacham, Officer Sherilee Townsend

Townsend: Oooh, a mystery man. I can hardly bear the excitement.
Sullivan: There's no call to be rude.

Meacham: You two being at each other's throats is not going to make this process go any faster. It's already taking way too long.

Townsend: It's just difficult to take all of this seriously. You took us on quite a ride, chasing all over the East Coast, all the way up to Buffalo, trying to find you people. Even now, seems like none of you are done playing games.

Sullivan: Are you calling life and death a game? Because Alice said that's what it was. Life and death.

Townsend: And you believed her.

Sullivan: Turned out to be true, didn't it?

TWENTY-FOUR

If Sasha thought she'd persuaded George to soften his attitude, she'd thought wrong.

He fixed Alice with a hard stare.

'Who is this person?'

Alice met his gaze without flinching. 'He was my college boyfriend.'

'College? But he must be ancient by now.' Sasha clapped her hand over her mouth. 'Oh, Alice, I'm sorry. That came out wrong. But do you mean a man in his seventies might have killed Babs and is trying to kill you? Just hearing myself say that, it sounds crazy. It sounds like something from some cheesy late-night movie.'

She hadn't meant to come to George's defense, but that's how he took it.

'Sasha's right. That's exactly what it sounds like. We're going to need more of an explanation.'

Alice managed a wan smile. 'Apology accepted, Sasha. And you make a good point about his age. He's even older than I am. Before going to college, he bummed around Europe for a while – much to his family's dismay, if I remember correctly. Unfortunately, he's more than capable of it. He knew more about guns than most people. I didn't realize why until later. Still, he's not the kind of person to get blood on his own hands.'

Her mouth twisted. 'He found other people, me included, to do his dirty work for him.'

Sasha made a T of her hands. 'Time-out. This is starting to feel as though it's going to be a very long night. Stressful, too. I think we all could use a little something to help us get through it.'

She rummaged in her suitcase and extracted a flask.

'This was supposed to be for after-dinner drinks around the fireplace at the lake house. Never envisioned circumstances like these. Any objections to Scotch? I can go to the ice machine if anyone wants some.'

Alice went into the bathroom and came out with four plastic cups, peeling off their protective plastic wrapping. 'No need for ice, at least not for me. Please pour generously.'

Sasha obliged, then handed the flask to George.

Mia bent over her own suitcase and, after a lot of rustling, came up with a baggie. She wagged it with a suggestive smile. 'I've got something even better than Scotch. Alice, may I have your lighter?'

George nearly dropped the flask. 'Is that what I think it is?'

'George, please.' Sasha took the flask from him. 'Don't tell me that in your years as a school principal you didn't see a few hundred of these. Not to mention in Vietnam.'

Mia flicked the lighter. An acrid scent filled the room. She inhaled it deeply and passed the joint to Alice, who nearly snatched it from her hand. 'Mia, you're a lifesaver.'

'Take it easy.' Sasha demanded her own turn. 'I suspect you've got a lot to say tonight.'

George's eyes widened as Sasha's cheeks hollowed, drawing the smoke deep. 'Wow,' she said when she finally released it with a light cough. 'It's been too long. Stuff's changed. George? Am I guessing right? You've never smoked weed?'

He drew himself up straight. 'Of course not.'

Her eyelids crinkled. She slipped the joint between his lips.

'Just inhale – wait, not so deep!'

Too late. Hacking coughs wracked his body. Smoke filled the room.

He straightened, face red, voice raspy. 'Tell me why people do this.'

'Try again. You'll see. Take it in – just a little this time – and then hold it as long as you can.'

George tried, with a minimum of coughing and then, before Sasha could stop him, yet again.

'Hey! I did it right.'

She plucked the joint away. 'Ease off, big guy. Or you won't be able to focus on what Alice has to say. I have a feeling we're going to want to remember it.'

Lavina Township Police Department
Transcript of interview with Mia Sullivan
Present: Detective Travis Meacham, Officer Sherilee Townsend

Townsend: Are you telling us you – all of you – were in an altered state when Alice confessed?

Sullivan: She didn't confess. As to your question, no, I wouldn't say that at all.

Townsend: And yet.

Sullivan: Oh, for heaven's sake. Would you be asking that question if we'd all just had a round of drinks?

Townsend: We need to be able to verify the accuracy of the information you're giving us. Because it's not making sense. You're telling me this was all due to a college romance?

Sullivan: Romance. That's such an old-fashioned word. Like out of a fairy tale.

Townsend: Some fairy tale. I don't remember the princess saying it was all the prince's fault. That she had nothing to do with it.

Sullivan: No, Alice was clear that she went along with him.

Townsend: And that didn't give you pause? Just like that, you gave her a pass.

Sullivan: Officer Townsend, you must remember what it was like to be twenty. You're closer to it than I am.

Townsend: Not by much. Anyway, even at that age, I knew right from wrong.

Sullivan: Then let me put it this way. Do you remember the first time you fell in love? Not just teenage hearts and flowers, but the kind that sets you on fire, so that you can hardly breathe?

Townsend: I'm not going to dignify that with an answer.

Sullivan: You're blushing. So you do *remember. Wonderful, wasn't it?*

Townsend: I hardly see what that has to do with anything.

Sullivan: I think it had everything to do with this.

TWENTY-FIVE

Alice had expected scorn. Anger. Implacable judgment.

But pity?

Mia spoke first. 'I've certainly had my share of misbegotten liaisons. And probably if the wrong man – or woman – came along now and said all the right things, I'd tumble all over again. But in your case, if I'm understanding this right, people ended up dead because you were in love? Oh, Alice.'

'You mean, like this?' Alice affected the pose of a starstruck girl, hands clasped before her chest, a tremulous smile on her lips. 'I've always thought that it was because I was stupid. Maybe love is the same thing.'

'What was it about him? The sex?'

'Mia!' Sasha took the joint from Mia. 'No more of this for you.'

Alice tried to remember. She'd hated him for so long, buried those early feelings so deep they were nearly inaccessible.

'He was a rebel – against the war, against the status quo and even against his own family. I didn't know anything about them, only that they were rich and that his sister was the golden child. He said she was the one who was everything his parents had wanted him to be, a perfect "corporate stooge."' She wiggled air quotes around the phrase. 'He said they all stopped speaking to him when he dropped out to backpack around Europe, then switched his major from economics to English when he came back. He read poetry to me!'

Eye-rolls all around.

'I know, I know. But I'd never had the nerve to swerve off the path expected of me. With him, I didn't have to tie myself in knots, trying to be like everyone else. I was so out of place at Holyoke. But by protesting the war, my being different was for a cause.'

George twirled his hand. *Move it along.* He kept twirling, staring mesmerized at the motion.

Sasha reached to halt it. He gave her a goofy grin. 'What are you looking at me like that for?'

'Just enjoying a side of you I never could have imagined. Alice, go on. If George doesn't remember any of this, I'll fill him in later.'

'Right. I'm getting to the hard part.' Alice took a sharp breath, which did nothing to relieve the ache in her chest. On some level, the memories had been with her every day of her life since then. But she'd never talked about them until now, the old emotions erupting in a boiling fury from the mental depths where she'd stored them away.

'You have to remember how urgent it seemed. All that marching and waving signs felt so pointless. Every day, more body bags from Vietnam came into the giant morgue at Dover Air Force Base. Bird – that was his movement name – wanted to do more. The idea was to stage an event that would grab the media's attention the way others were doing with the campus takeovers, things like that.'

George frowned. 'Things like bombings.'

Alice flinched. 'That's quite the fast-forward, George. But yes, eventually, bombings. Bird had a target – an arms company in Connecticut. He said it was safe as could be. The plant had two eight-hour shifts, with the whole place shutting down at ten p.m. And just to be extra-safe, we'd target the executive offices.' She layered her words with sarcasm. 'You know, with our sympathies being with the exploited workers, and all that.'

Mia's eyes narrowed. 'I'm starting to figure this out. This Bird. An English major. What would he know about making bombs?'

'Absolutely nothing.'

'But you—'

'I was a chemistry major. I had the know-how.'

'Oh, Alice.' Sasha shook her head.

'Remember: young, stupid and in love. The trifecta of disaster. And I believed the plan was fail-safe. We even had an insider, one of the assembly-line workers. He'd smuggle the bomb in for us.'

'Any chance he was a Black guy?' Sasha took Alice's silence for the affirmation it was. 'The better to take the fall, right? An obvious suspect.'

'I didn't know it at the time,' Alice protested. 'Bird made the contact. I didn't meet Larry until the night after the bombing. He came to our place.'

'Wait a minute. Back things up. You two were shacking up?'

Alice made a face. 'Bird had a townhouse in Boston not far from Beacon Hill. He positioned sponging off Daddy as a revolutionary act. I'd go down on weekends. You can imagine what that did for my grades. For what it's worth, he's the one who started me smoking.'

George cleared his throat. 'Smoking seems the least of it.'

'I'm getting there. By the time Larry showed up, I'd been crying off and on all day. But that was nothing compared to how upset Larry was.'

She sketched it out for them, putting herself back in that high-ceilinged room with its period furniture, such a genteel setting in the wake of such a violent act. Rain streaked the tall windows of wavy glass and Larry left damp footprints across the Aubusson as he paced, shouting, eyes wild, hands flying.

'You swore, man. You *swore*. Nobody would get hurt. And now somebody's dead. Not just any somebody, but one of the top dogs, along with Mr Jones. It's all over the news. They're looking everywhere for us. We are so screwed. Some level beyond screwed. Man, I've got a wife and a kid. What's going to happen to them?'

Bird trying to calm him: 'We've been over this and over it. We did everything we could to make sure no one would get hurt. Is it our fault somebody was working in the middle of the night? Remember, all over the news is exactly what we wanted. Nobody's screwed. Nobody knows we had anything to do with this.'

Larry's gaze slid sideways.

Bird's voice changed. 'Nobody knows, right? Nobody saw anything. And you didn't say anything to anybody.'

'No, uh-uh. Not a thing.' But he refused to meet Bird's eyes.

Bird clapped him on the back. 'That's great, man. I knew we could count on you. Tell you what. I'll walk you back to the train station. We'll grab a beer on the way. Settle you down, get your head straight. Go home, get some sleep. Everything will look better in the morning.'

He looked at Alice. 'You're all right here alone for a while, right, Babe? I'll pick up some food for us on the way home.'

Larry trailed him through the door, turning to give Alice a half-hearted wave.

Alice's voice trailed off. She looked around the drab motel room and started, as though surprised to find herself there, rather than back in Beacon Hill.

'I never saw Larry again.'

TWENTY-SIX

Alice's voice went so soft the others had to lean in to hear her.

'Bird came back hours later. Way longer than if they'd just gotten a beer. I was frantic. The way Larry had acted, I was paranoid, afraid they'd been arrested or something. But Bird told me everything was fine, that Larry was cool and we had nothing to worry about.'

She drew a long, shaky breath.

'I got lucky, I guess. The next day, I was out on my own. I'd gone to the drugstore to pick up something – toothpaste, I think. Bird said he was worried about me. He wanted us to go away for a few days, someplace beautiful like the Maine coast where we could be alone together while things blew over. His family had a cabin there. I thought it was so sweet, the way he was taking care of me.

'Anyway, I passed a newsstand on the way to the store. Remember those? Every single paper had a photo of Larry on the front page, with a headline, something like "Suspect Found Dead, Second Sought." I snatched one of the papers and ran. I ducked into an alley and read the story to the point where it said that Larry was the main suspect in the bombing and that he'd killed himself. But he'd left a suicide note naming a second suspect.'

She stopped. Let them figure it out for themselves.

'You,' George said.

'Me. I never went back to the house. I've been running ever since. When you see your face on the FBI's Ten Most Wanted List, it's a powerful incentive to keep moving. These last few years at Timeless Pastures are the longest I've stayed anywhere. I thought I'd finally gotten away from him.' She was crying now and couldn't stop.

'From who?'

George turned to Sasha. 'Bird, obviously. She thinks he killed Larry. Right, Alice?'

Alice gulped and nodded. Mia handed her a wad of Kleenex.

She wiped her face and blew her nose. 'I think he set it up to look like a suicide, and the police and the press just accepted it.'

She took a long, quivering breath. 'You want to know where I went tonight?' she said finally. 'To a convenience store to get a newspaper. I had to see what was out there about Babs. Oh God.'

She sobbed anew. 'It was like seeing that photo of Larry all those years ago. But this time, it wasn't a face. It was a name.'

Three voices chorused. 'Who?'

'Hawk Boneham the Third.'

'Who?' It was like an echo.

George rubbed his beard. 'It sounds familiar. Doesn't he have something to do with the company that bought Timeless?'

'A little something.' Alice gulped the last of her tears. 'He gave a statement to the paper about Babs. It said he's a company vice president.'

'That's right.' Sasha snapped her fingers. 'Now I remember. Such a strange name. Who names their kid Hawk?'

'Three times in a row,' Mia added.

'Think about it,' Alice prompted. She held a hand to her ear, the old charades clue. 'Sounds like . . .' She flapped her arms.

George got it first.

'Bird. Sounds like Bird. Hawk Boneham is Bird.'

Lavina Township Police Department
Transcript of interview with George Sterling
Present: Detective Travis Meacham, Officer Sherilee Townsend

Meacham: Even when you had a name, you declined to call the police.

Sterling: Correct.

Meacham: Because . . .?

Sterling: I learned an important lesson in the military that carried over to my career as an educator.

Meacham: Enlighten us.

Sterling: That you should never make important decisions when you're upset or distracted. Alice dumped a lot of information on us at once. It wasn't just the volume. What she was telling us was so far out of the realm of anything that any of us had experienced. It was impossible to process.

Meacham: Given the nature of that information, I don't think that calling the police would seem like a difficult decision. Not even a decision so much as a reflex. You know, if I see a house on fire, I don't hold off because it's an upsetting sight. I just call nine-one-one. Of the four of you – although I guess we could omit Alice from this particular decision-making process – I'd peg you as the one most likely to alert authorities.

Sterling: That's where you'd be wrong. For one thing, Alice actually thought we should call you. I was the one who said we should wait.

TWENTY-SEVEN

George took charge, hoping the others wouldn't see it that way.

He'd spent the year and a half since his wife's death learning to tread far more cautiously around women, a new deference that, as it became ingrained, sharpened his regrets about his marriage. He'd thought himself happy then; heck, he *had* been happy. But had Gayle? He'd just assumed she was. She'd never complained. He pushed the thought away. Time enough to dwell on that later. God knows, he'd already devoted countless hours to that subject since Gayle's agonizingly drawn-out death.

But the present situation seemed dangerously close to spinning out of control and someone needed to rein things in.

'So, assuming Hawk is Bird—' he began.

'No assuming about it,' Alice said. 'Not with a name like that. He is.'

'Fair enough. And now you know who he is. Just out of curiosity, how come you're just realizing that he's been in your orbit ever since that company bought Timeless Pastures?'

Alice hung her head. 'Exactly the same thing I asked myself. All those notes we got from Johnny about the change in ownership; the stuff in the community newsletter. I just didn't pay attention. I only cared about the lot fee increase, not who was behind it. Believe me, if I'd read his name earlier, I'd have been long gone.'

'But you don't need to keep running now. You can just tell the police that he was the brains behind the bombing. They'll probably give you immunity for identifying him.'

Her laughter startled him.

'Oh, George. All those true-crime shows and you don't see the problem with that?'

She waited.

He rewarded her patience with a rueful smile. 'Your word against his.'

'Right. A fugitive for decades against a respected captain of industry. More to the point, a guy with the bottomless pockets to hire the best lawyers out there. Me, I'd get a public defender. And while I think they're among the noblest of people to walk the face of the earth, a public defender wouldn't stand a chance against the kind of firepower he'd aim.'

Badly as George wanted to disagree, he'd seen that scenario too often on his shows.

He took another tack.

'Alice, you need to remember something. Now you know who he is. But he has no idea who or where you are.'

'Unless he does. Babs said something that made me think he might. So I still think the bullet that killed her might have been meant for me. She was on my patio, after all. The newspaper story said one twenty Yorktown Way. That's my house. Babs' is one twenty-one. I can't go back there.'

Mia stifled a yawn. 'Alice, look at it this way. We were all leaving Timeless Pastures anyway. We'll help you find a new place, too. You can even tool around with me in the van if you like.' She caught the look on Alice's face. 'Or not. The point is, we're your friends. We'll help you.'

Minutes ago, George had felt himself out of his depth. Bombs? Murder? Revolutionaries? Fugitives?

He reminded himself that he'd once been able to control a building full of hormone-addled high schoolers, the squirreliest creatures on the planet, with a few calm, well-chosen words over the public address system.

He used that voice now.

'Let's all get a good night's sleep. There's much to discuss – how to deal with this fugitive business for starters. Alice, if you've been on the run for all these years, one more night isn't going to change anything. It's serious, but I'm sure it's not insurmountable. We'll think better when we're rested. And we'll come up with a plan – together.'

TWENTY-EIGHT

Johnny walked up to the front door of Alice's house at nine a.m. sharp on Monday, rang the bell and knocked long and loud before using his manager's passkey to let himself in.

Mindful of his inadvertent discovery of Babs' body, he wanted to be sure Alice and the others were really gone before he called the police chief.

He'd done a cursory stop at Mia's, George's and Sasha's duplexes. Just as he suspected, no one was home and nothing seemed amiss. He'd only been in Alice's home a few times, to help with minor repairs. Residents were responsible for fixing anything that went wrong inside their homes, but Johnny liked Alice, and as long as the job wasn't too big, he was happy to help.

The same held for most of the other residents. Not all – in particular, Babs, who'd been such a consistent pain in his rear that he wouldn't have so much as replaced a beeping smoke-detector battery. He'd said the appropriate things when anyone asked him about Babs' death – 'such a shame' – and hoped his dry tone hadn't betrayed him.

Now, if anything had happened to Alice . . . impossible to imagine, though. Her house was like the others, orderly in the way homes of people with too little to do tended to be. In his experience, single people of a certain age veered toward one of two extremes, either filling the empty hours by cleaning and polishing and straightening everything in sight, or letting junk pile up until it became unmanageable. He'd seen enough of the latter to make the occasional cursory attempt to resist the same tendency in his own life.

He wandered through the three main rooms of Alice's house – eat-in kitchen, living room, bedroom, all of them as bland and opaque as Alice herself. He remembered the furniture from the previous owner, right down to the pictures on the wall, inoffensive landscapes and floral prints. Three framed photos on the nightstand were the only touch of personality.

He switched on the light and studied the images of three people. Two were black-and-white newspaper photos, showing a young

Black man with a short Afro and an older Black man in what looked like a work shirt with a pocket logo, illegible in the small photo. The third, a glossy color image that appeared to be torn from a magazine, showed a White woman posed in hunting gear with a shotgun broken over one arm and a Brittany spaniel with a pheasant in its mouth beside her.

Johnny devoted a minute trying to parse the unusual grouping, then shrugged away the mystery of it. Families came in all sorts of permutations these days.

He glanced at the dresser and considered opening the drawers but knew that, no matter how innocent the impulse, gazing upon Alice's underthings would forever render him the slimiest of creeps.

Instead, he turned to her closet, where her sparse collection of long dark skirts and drab oversized blouses and sweaters barely took up half the space. Bankers' boxes stacked nearly to the ceiling took up the rest. Three sat apart from the rest, one with its lid askew.

He started to straighten it. But this was no dresser drawer, full of intimate things. He lifted the lid and saw a stack of *National Geographics*. He picked up the top one and idly flipped through it. His parents had subscribed, and as a child, he'd loved reading about those exotic, faraway places. He reached for the next magazine and lost himself in sweeping vistas of Saharan dunes.

Just one more, he told himself. Because the cover of the third magazine featured some sort of a monkey holding a snowball. He grinned and reached for it.

Let it fall.

'Holy . . .'

His first thought, God help him, was to wonder why Alice chose to live and dress like a near-pauper when she clearly was not. But – 'Old people,' he reminded himself. They got scared, either like Glenda, seeing bad actors behind every bush, or hoarding all manner of things 'just in case.' He'd seen stacks of foil, smoothed and folded and tied with twine. Canned food by the hundredweight, bought on sale and long out of date. Enough empty plastic containers to stock a take-out joint for years. In the grand scheme of things, cash seemed like an eminently sensible thing to hoard.

But Alice had a *lot* of bankers' boxes. They couldn't all contain cash. Could they?

Lavina Township Police Department
Transcript of interview with J.R. 'Johnny' Natale
Present: Detective Travis Meacham, Officer Sherilee Townsend

Meacham: You waited nearly a day before calling Chief Martinez.

Natale: Was that how long it was?

Meacham: And when you did call him, your report was, shall we say, less than complete.

Natale: I told him four people seemed to be missing. Sounds pretty complete to me.

Meacham: You're familiar with the concept of withholding evidence.

Natale: Evidence?

Meacham: Crucial facts, let's say.

Natale: Crucial facts?

Meacham: I think you know what we're talking about here.

TWENTY-NINE

Johnny sat dazed on the floor of Alice's closet, his phone open to its calculator, an impossible number glowing on the screen.

He'd gone through every box, counted every dollar. More cash than he'd ever seen in his life – and he'd dealt with subcontractors in New Jersey.

The fact that Alice had so much cash on hand made it more likely that something bad had happened to the friends. On the other hand, nothing seemed amiss in the home, and the cash appeared undisturbed. The first box he'd opened had four thousand dollars less than the rest, lending credence to a notion taking imperfect form.

Alice had always paid her loan and lot fees in cash, and he'd thought little of it, beyond considering her an unlikely subscriber to conspiracy theories about banks and corporate control of money. But she'd paid the most recent month's fees just a week ago. He could see needing cash for groceries and other daily necessities, maybe a little more for the long weekend with her friends, but nowhere near four thousand dollars' worth.

Maybe the group had planned some sort of blowout weekend in Atlantic City, staying at one of the fancier casinos, dining on steak and lobster and hanging with the high rollers. That was the most likely scenario, although his mind balked at the thought of Alice – or any of the others, for that matter – leaning over a craps table, arranging a tower of chips and putting pursed lips to the dice before tossing them with a hopeful shout.

Or maybe the long-weekend business was just a ruse, a cover for a more extended jaunt. But it wasn't like Alice to leave Glenda, and especially not the universally adored Sugar Plum, in the lurch. That scenario died a quick death.

More likely, they'd let everyone think they were going to a humble weekend rental and instead took one of those short cruises marketed for senior citizens to someplace warm and wonderful. Johnny frowned, exactly the way he'd imagine a booking agent frowning when presented with that much cash. It was one thing to hand over enough cash to an easy-going community manager to cover a modest, albeit exponentially increasing, lot fee. But didn't airlines and cruises insist upon things like credit cards and passports?

His mind kept coming back to the final, darker scenario, the one he tried not to picture. Someone found out that Alice had that much cash on hand. Maybe one – or all – of the other three. Maybe she'd been murdered, just like Babs, and her body spirited away from the scene of the crime. In fact, maybe Babs had heard something and somehow gotten in the way.

A thought that propelled Johnny up off the floor and outside – the back way this time – to Babs' house, passkey at the ready.

Where he found something that he understood not at all.

Johnny remembered the chief's reaction when he'd called him to report finding Babs' body. Martinez had accused him of unwarranted snooping around the residents' homes. What would he say if Johnny told him about the cash at Alice's and the papers before him on Babs' desk?

Johnny made a snap decision. He took off his shirt, wrapped it around his hand, and wiped off everything he'd touched in Babs' house, finishing with the knob on the back door. He returned to Alice's home and did the same, down to each banker's box and the framed photos on her nightstand.

Only when he was safely outdoors did he take out his phone and tap the chief's number.

'Oscar? Johnny Natale over here at Timeless Pastures. Listen, normally I wouldn't bother you with something like this. I mean, they're all adults, not one of them with any sign of memory stuff, and they can do what they want. But after this business with Babs Stevenson – yeah, sorry, I'm getting to it. Looks like four of our residents have disappeared.'

He didn't tell Martinez about the money. Or about what he'd taken from Babs' house.

Lavina Township Police Department
Transcript of interview with Madison Baker
Present: Detective Travis Meacham, Officer Sherilee Townsend

Townsend: Would you please state your full name and age?
Baker: Madison Marie Baker, thirty-one.

Townsend: Occupation?

Baker: I'm the editor of the Community Caller, *the local newspaper. And just so you're aware, I'm not going to comment on any of our stories or the process we use for gathering news. So you can save yourselves some time.*

Townsend: *Then this will be brief. Are you Bert Miller's supervisor?*

Baker: As much as anyone can supervise Miller, yes.

Townsend: Meaning?

Baker: Bert is the Our Towns columnist. His job is to focus on feature stories in our coverage area. Feel-good stories, you know? But he's always trying to weasel out of them and do news stories instead. Like this.

Townsend: This was pretty big news, though, wasn't it? Like national, right?

Baker: Well . . . yeah.

THIRTY

Bert Miller thanked Police Chief Oscar Martinez, ended the call and forced himself to wipe the wide smile from his face. His Monday was looking up.

The Christmas-season story assignment he'd gotten upon walking into the newsroom had been even worse than usual – a holiday baking project at a local elementary school, with the cookies to be packaged for delivery to a local nursing home.

'Dear God, no,' he'd pleaded with Madison, knowing it was hopeless, but duty-bound to try anyway. 'Think about it – all those germ-laden kids, wiping their noses on their hands before rolling out the cookies, probably licking spoons before sticking them back in the dough, sneezing over everything. Those cookies ought to carry a hazmat warning. And they're going to frail old people? Do we really want to be part of such a tragedy in the making?'

'You never quit, do you, Bert? Even for you, this is shameless. I threw you a bone with that dead-woman story, thinking it might be enough to hold you for a while. Guess I thought wrong.'

Now he stood at her desk, waiting for her to finish a phone call. She swiveled so that her back was to him and spoke for another two minutes before finally hanging up.

'Shouldn't you be headed to the cookie bake?' she asked without turning.

'Depends.' He didn't get many moments like this. He was going to draw this one out as long as he could.

'Depends on what? Come on, Bert. I'm not in the mood for games.'

'On what you'd rather see on the front page tomorrow. A picture of adorable kids, their faces smeared with snot-laced icing? Or . . .'

Madison whipped around in her chair.

'So help me God, if you're not walking out of here in the next five minutes and heading for that school, I'm going to—'

'I said *or.*'

'Or what?'

Really, the grin got harder to hide by the moment. 'The old

woman who was killed over in Timeless Pastures? I just got off the phone with the police chief. Looks like we have a follow-up story.'

'Interview with a family member? Funeral arrangements? As you said, it's a follow-up. Pretty basic stuff. No reason you can't do that and the cookie story, too.'

Bert's lips twitched. He faked a cough to cover his unforgiveable delight.

'Four more people from that development have gone missing.'

Lavina Township Police Department
Interview with J.R. 'Johnny' Natale
Present: Detective Travis Meacham, Officer Sherilee Townsend

Meacham: You told Chief Martinez that you spoke with Hawk Boneham the day the four were reported missing. What was the purpose of that call?

Natale: I'd left him a voicemail about the missing residents. Sort of a CYA move, if you know what I mean.

Meacham: I've been a working stiff for going on twenty-five years. I'm familiar with covering my butt. What was his response to the information?

Natale: He provided a statement to release to the news media, and he asked me if there were any photos of the missing people. I told him the police had asked me the same thing, and I was trying to locate some. He told me to email them to him as soon as I found them, and then to call him so he could verify he'd gotten them. I said I'd cc him when I sent them to the police, but he said to send them separately.

Meacham: Did he say why?

Natale: No. He just said to send them to him first, and when I started to object – I mean, under the circumstances, you guys should take priority, right? – he reminded me who signed my paycheck.

THIRTY-ONE

Bert's initial jubilation at escaping the cookie story faded fast. 'This is the only information we're releasing,' the Timeless Pastures' community manager told him. He struck a computer key. A printer spat a single page, a canned statement from a vice president of the company that owned Timeless Pastures.

Bert took it but lingered in front of Johnny Natale's desk, hoping that the old reporter's trick of simply refusing to leave might spur the man to talk. That, and something else. He'd taken one look at Natale and divined a kindred spirit, the just-shy-of-unkempt appearance of the divorced man pushed back into a bachelor existence that had long ago substituted evenings in front of the television for nights on the prowl.

Natale had the same hangdog appearance, the air of someone who'd given up, that Bert hated in himself. *Buck up*, he reminded himself. His very presence in Natale's office meant he hadn't completely ceded the field.

To buy time, he read the statement aloud.

'We remain shocked and saddened by the news that one of our own was so violently taken from us. As for the other four residents, of course we hope that this will be resolved as a simple misunderstanding about plans that may have changed. That said, Weller Holdings will spare no expense in locating our residents and stands ready to assist law enforcement with whatever they need. Hawk Boneham the Third, vice president for expansion, Weller Holdings.'

He spindled the paper. 'What kind of person has a name like Hawk Boneham the Third?'

Johnny rubbed thumb and forefinger together. 'The kind who has money.'

'Good for him.' But not good for Bert. The terse statement left him with not much of a story at all. He didn't even have photos, although the police assured him they were coming. From the little he'd gleaned about the missing residents, they seemed an unlikely bunch to vanish, especially if traveling together.

A former school principal and Vietnam veteran, a real estate agent, a fitness instructor – all retired – and another woman listed simply as retired, no prior profession given.

He said as much to Johnny Natale. 'Look, I know you can't talk on the record. But these sorts of people don't seem like your typical crime victims, especially not as a group. And even if I let my imagination run wild, they don't seem at all like the kind of people to run off for some sort of nefarious purposes.'

He tried not to let his surprise show when Johnny Natale replied with something other than 'no comment.'

'I'd bet you won't find so much as a parking ticket on their records. None of them was ever late with the lot fees, and that's not something you can say about everyone here, especially these days. That's why I think this is all some big misunderstanding. But better safe than sorry, right?'

Bert, emboldened, pushed a little harder.

'Honest, reliable – how else would you describe them?'

Johnny cracked a knowing smile.

'I wouldn't. As to what I did say, remember that it was off the record.'

Bert shrugged. 'Had to ask. Just like I'm going to ask about that business with the lot fees. What do you mean, that people are late with them, especially these days?'

Johnny's face darkened. 'That's a whole different situation. I'd talk all day about those missing people before I said a single word about it. Now, if we're done here . . .'

Bert took the hint. As he turned to go, he noticed a business card on the floor, halfway behind one of the legs of the desk. It looked as though it had been there awhile, keeping company with some impressive dust bunnies. Under any other circumstances, he'd have said something to Johnny about reconsidering whatever cleaning service was responsible for the office. Instead, he stooped and feigned tying a shoe as a pretext for examining the card. The improbable name of the controlled message-savvy Hawk Boneham III dominated the card, along with both office and cell numbers.

He palmed the card. Who knew? Maybe the company veep would be more forthcoming than his underling.

Lavina Township Police Department
Transcript of interview with Glenda Ferguson
Present: Detective Travis Meacham, Officer Sherilee Townsend

Townsend: It sounds as though you were particularly close with Alice Sanders. Didn't she walk your dog when you got injured? What's his name again?

Ferguson: Sugar Plum. My little sweetheart. Everybody loves Sugar Plum. Alice wasn't the only one who walked him. So, no, we're not particularly close.

Townsend: Yet you wanted to alert the police when she didn't show up.

Ferguson: Just as a good neighbor would. Listen, I see what you're trying to do here. You're trying to link me up with them. But I'm not that kind of person. I'm a decent woman. I would never do the kinds of things they did.

THIRTY-TWO

Bert's attempts to reach Hawk via voicemail, email, text and DM left him with no more story than he'd had before.

He resorted to the time-honored tactic of going door-to-door in Timeless Pastures, hoping to pad his story with what would be predictable quotes from neighbors of the shooting victim and the maybe-missing people.

Only problem was, one door after another remained shut, and not in the closed-door scenario with which every reporter was too familiar – sounds of life within, blaring televisions and whatnot, but no one willing to answer the door to a prying member of the Fourth Estate.

It wasn't just that the homes were silent. They were too quiet, with signs that they'd been that way for too long. Drifts of dead leaves against a long-unopened front door. A stray newspaper moldering under a bush, a birdfeeder dangling empty, landscaping gone unkempt. And more – even in the middle of the day, drapes were drawn tight or, in some homes, missing altogether.

Bert cupped his hands around his face, pressed his nose to the glass and gazed upon one empty living room after another.

After the first few deserted houses, he started jotting down addresses. He did the same on the next street. And the one after that.

In the end, he left Timeless Pastures with only a single interview, from a limping woman walking a Scottie. She gave her name as Glenda Ferguson and told him a convoluted tale about a fight over pigeons.

He pointed to the dog. 'And this cute little guy would be?' You'd never go wrong by praising someone's pet.

'Sugar Plum.'

The name didn't seem to fit the little black dog with the fierce bearded visage and typical Scottie strut. It didn't matter. Glenda Ferguson changed her mind a second later.

'Don't use his name. Or mine either. What if this person is some sort of sicko serial killer? Or maybe he doesn't like interracial couples. Some people don't, you know.'

Bert's head swam, trying to follow it all. 'What person? Interracial couples?'

'George and Sasha. They're the first in the community. Of course, we're all supportive.'

Which meant they weren't, Bert thought.

'Of course, he was involved with Alice first. They thought nobody knew about it. Sneaking around like teenagers.'

'Wait, what?'

But Glenda had already returned to her original theme.

'What if whoever went after Babs – and maybe those others, too – comes after me next? If he's a serial killer, I'd be the obvious target. I'm practically the only one left here.'

Bert grasped at straws.

'What do you mean, you're practically the only one left? Where's everybody going?'

Sugar Plum put an entreating paw against his leg. He picked up the dog as a way to keep the woman from leaving and cooed over it as the woman talk-talk-talked, his recording app running the whole time.

'None of us can afford the lot fee anymore. You wouldn't believe how it's gone up. Pretty much every other month we get a new increase. It's terrible. We're all on fixed incomes, Social Security mostly. I mean, look at this place. It's all prefabs. Does it look like we'd live here if we could afford anywhere else?'

'Uh, it looks nice.' Better a compliment than risk insulting her home, no matter what she thought of it these days.

'Oh, it is!' Her face fell. 'Or it was, until all of this started happening once the new owners came in. We had the nicest group of people here. We were always getting together for holiday parties, barbecues, things like that. Now there's hardly any of us left – and with these four gone, there's even fewer.'

She slumped. 'Take Alice. She was the sweetest person. She used to walk Sugar Plum for me. I don't know what I'm going to do now that she's gone.'

Bert tried his reassuring best. 'She's not *gone*-gone. None of them are. Honestly, this alert just seems like a precaution.'

Glenda reached for Sugar Plum. 'You're still young enough to be optimistic. Wait until you're my age and you've seen enough not to believe in happy endings.'

She limped away, calling over her shoulder, 'And remember, don't you dare use my name or Sugar Plum's in your story.'

He wouldn't. And he'd have to paraphrase most of what she said, given its alarmist and speculative tone. Anyway, her conjecture about the fate of the four was hardly the most interesting part of their conversation.

He went back to the office and filed a bare-bones story. Then he turned his attention to the story he really wanted to do, the one that was going to take some time to unearth.

He was glad he'd been unable to reach Hawk Boneham on the first try. When he finally caught up with the man – and he would, even if it meant going to Weller Holdings' corporate offices in person – he'd have new questions for him. But first, he'd need to do a lot more digging.

Lavina Township Police Department
Transcript of interview with J.R. 'Johnny' Natale
Present: Detective Travis Meacham, Officer Sherilee Townsend

Meacham: At least at first, you gave no indication you took seriously the fact that four people were missing from your development.

Natale: It's not my development. I'm just the manager.

Meacham: Exactly. You're the person who's interacted daily with those people for years. It seems you might have shown more concern.

Natale: I was plenty concerned.

Meacham: Is that why you told every single news outlet that contacted you that you thought they were probably hitting the casinos in Atlantic City?

Natale: Because that's exactly where I hoped they were.

Meacham: I understand you have a close relationship with Chief Martinez.

Natale: We run into each other occasionally at the Dew Drop Inn. Is that a close relationship?

Meacham: We looked at the timing of those comments you made to the media. And we talked to Chief Martinez. He says he told you – because of the close relationship you two have – that our law enforcement partners in Atlantic City put the word out to the casinos, motels and restaurants. Nobody reported seeing them. You had that information, and yet you continued to insist that's where they were.

Natale: Have you ever dealt with the media? Especially during an absolute cluster like this? People's grannies gone missing right before Christmas? Their families frantic? My phone rang nonstop. I just said whatever would get rid of them fastest.

Meacham: Just saying it sounds like you weren't bending over backward to help anyone find them.

Natale: Your interpretation.

Meacham: Yes.

THIRTY-THREE

Johnny knew that Timeless Pastures, with its prefab duplexes and location just a little too far from either Philadelphia or Atlantic City to make for an easy commute, drew a certain type of resident.

Lower-level civil servants. Tradespeople. A few teachers; more teachers' aides. People who'd worked their whole lives at the sort of jobs that paid the bills, just. But they'd never amassed the sort of savings that would allow the hefty down payment demanded by the kinds of well-appointed communities designed as pleasant way stations between retirement and dotage.

The down payments on the Timeless Pastures duplexes were minimal, the homes themselves so affordable that some people even paid cash – something that made people shrug off the fact that they didn't actually own the land beneath those homes. Anyway, the lot fees on the land were negligible.

A few people caught his attention when they arrived. Take Babs. She'd been a forensic accountant in New York. He wasn't sure exactly what that was, only that it didn't sound like the kind of job that saw someone end up in a place like Timeless Pastures. Once he heard the name of the firm, he understood. It had gone belly-up in spectacular fashion during the great greed grabs of the 1980s and 1990s, leaving its employees out of work and their retirement accounts wiped out. He supposed that explained Babs' bitterness, even if he couldn't excuse it.

He knew George's story, too: how cancer had robbed him not only of his wife but nearly all his financial assets as her treatments dragged on for years. George was an easy-going guy, but Johnny learned early on never to get him started on the American healthcare system.

Sasha was another person who seemed out of place in Timeless Pastures, in ways that had nothing to do with race. Everything about her – the suits in tasteful muted hues, the coordinated scarves, the always-perfect hair and makeup – radiated success. But once, when they were talking shop, rental agent to real estate agent, she'd let slip her struggles in a largely White business. She'd shown him the business cards she still kept, sans photo.

'It let people get one step closer to working with me, before actually meeting me in person and backing out of the agreement.' When it came to real estate, she'd chosen to invest her own savings into a college fund for her grandchildren instead of pricier digs for herself.

Under any other circumstances, he'd have asked about the grandkids when Sasha's son called him, virtually spitting nails through the ether.

'What the hell are you people doing to find my mother?'

That's how the call had started. It went downhill from there.

Gerald Coverdale had the same peremptory manner, albeit saltier, that made his mother such an effective organizer. Johnny mouthed the standard platitudes – police alerts broadcast far and wide, tips pouring in, Weller Holdings standing ready with further resources – only to be cut off.

'We're talking about my mother here. You're not telling me anything more than what I've already seen on television. What are *you*, specifically, doing to locate her?'

'I, uh—'

'And that White man they say she's with. What do you know about him? Is my mother being taken for a ride?'

Johnny got a few words farther this time. 'George Sterling is a veteran. He was a high school principal—'

'Which doesn't count for shit. You got priests molesting kids right and left. If that doesn't prove that a person's career is no guarantee of character—'

It was Johnny's turn to cut off the conversation. 'I watched George Sterling nurse his wife through cancer. The man barely slept for months. After she passed, he could've cut a swath through the female population of this community if he'd wanted. But he didn't. He waited a good long time to get involved with anyone.'

Johnny thought it best not to mention that the first 'anyone' had been Alice.

'Your mother, wherever she is, is with a good man. If they're in any sort of danger, and I want very badly to believe they're not, he'd do anything to protect her.'

His forehead dripped sweat by the time the call ended.

The guilty knowledge of the piles of money in Alice's home and the unfathomable spreadsheets in Babs' weighed more heavily on him by the day. He couldn't imagine – wouldn't let himself believe – that anything bad had happened to the four friends.

But something was off. If they hadn't gotten in touch, despite the widespread publicity, they had to have a good reason. At least, that's what he kept telling himself.

His phone rang again. For the fourth time that day, 'CNN' flashed on its face.

For the fourth time, he let it go to voicemail.

THIRTY-FOUR

Alice had to admit that George had been right.

They indeed felt better on Monday morning, so much so that when Sasha suggested they go out for breakfast, she let them persuade her.

'It'll be fine, Alice. It's just like George said. Even if your suspicions about Babs' death are true, that guy Hawk has no idea of the name you go by now or where you are. Anyway, we're fifty miles away from there, in Nowheresville, New Jersey. We'll get a good breakfast under our belts and help you figure out your next steps.'

'As long as it's real food. Eggs and bacon and toast and juice, for sure a piece of pie. And pots and pots of coffee, high-test. Not that fruit cup and decaf business you like to do, Sasha.'

It went against her better judgment. But the sun shone strong, fresh snow glittering beneath it, and besides, her stomach balked at the idea of making do with the motel's version of a buffet breakfast – kid-size boxes of sugary cereals, packets of instant oatmeal, overripe bananas and watery coffee.

Her friends were right about another thing. They'd landed in the middle of New Jersey, such sprawling suburban anonymity that it provoked vocal pushback whenever anyone tried to grant it formal recognition as Central Jersey, denying it the easy acceptance of North and South Jersey.

They found a diner, crowded into a booth at the back and ordered with such enthusiasm that the waitress added, gratis, a cinnamon roll the approximate size of a wagon wheel, to be shared among them.

Alice licked cream cheese icing from her fingers and blew air kisses toward the roll's fast-disappearing remains. 'Normally, you wouldn't catch me dead eating one of these things. All that white flour and sugar. But today, it feels just right. Thanks for being here for me. Now I hate the thought of leaving all of you even more.'

Mia reached across the table and took her hand. 'We were all going our separate ways anyway. And my offer of sharing the van still stands.'

'I wouldn't think of putting you in that kind of danger.' An answer as self-serving as it was true. The van made some of the places she'd stayed over the years look luxurious.

'I'm curious.' Sasha, her continual diet gleefully abandoned, broke a biscuit in half and smeared it with butter and jam. 'How did you manage before you landed at Timeless Pastures?'

'The same way undocumented immigrants have managed for decades.' Alice gave an edited version of her dead-end jobs with under-the-table pay, and sketchy rooming houses in inner-ring suburbs long past their heyday. 'I hate the idea of going back to that. Jobs that kept me on my feet all day, living in dodgy neighborhoods, relying on buses to get me everywhere. It was one thing when I was younger. Now, I just don't know.'

'Which is why you should take me up on my offer,' Mia said.

George wagged a finger. 'We're going to have to come up with a story about how four of us went away for a weekend and only three of us came back.'

Sasha waved her fork at them. 'And whatever she decides, she shouldn't tell us. That'll at least give us some plausible deniability. Satisfied, George?'

Alice could tell he wasn't, but at least he made a show of going along as they kicked around scenarios with varying degrees of seriousness. Mia pushed hard for one involving Alice running off with a younger man or, better yet, woman, while George reeled them back with a focus on three essential criteria: distance, expense and weather. 'You want far, you want cheap, you want warm.'

'Please, God, not Florida.' Alice made a shooing motion. 'Bugs. Snakes. Hurricanes. Humidity. And Florida Man lurking behind every palm tree. Not Texas either. Like Florida, only bigger and crazier.'

'You're narrowing your options. Alabama, Mississippi?'

She rolled some cinnamon bun crumbs into a pellet and threw it at him. 'My second-biggest regret, after this mess I got myself into with Bird, was that I was never a Freedom Rider. More of that, less bombs, and maybe we'd have seen some real progress.'

'There was progress,' Sasha reminded her. 'Just not enough. Good luck finding a place that you can afford and where people are treated right.' She stood. 'I'm going to catch up on the news. I think I saw a TV in the next room. Have to go old-school after you took my phone.'

'I'll reimburse you for the phones. Promise,' Alice called after her.

'Deal.' Sasha peered around the corner as George and Alice continued their Q and A.

'Louisiana?'

'More humid than Florida. Great food, though.'

'Arizona?'

'Tarantulas. And verging on Florida-Texas crazy.'

'California?'

'Too expensive. Earthquakes. Plus, everybody runs away to California. It's too logical.'

'New Mexico?'

Silence: Alice rested her hand on her chin, considering. 'Still relatively affordable, I'll bet. I speak some Spanish – along with learning how to get a fake ID, I picked it up from all that restaurant work. That's a plus. Seriously good food, and because of that, probably plenty of restaurant jobs. I can probably handle a couple more years of those before my knees go entirely.'

Sasha's audible gasp turned heads.

Alice looked up as she rushed back to the table. 'Really, Sasha? C'mon, I'm not the physical specimen our Mia is, but I'm not in a wheelchair yet.'

Sasha spoke low and fast. 'Alice and Mia, get your coats and get out of here. Don't ask; just go. George, you wait a minute, then pay the check. Mia, give him some of that cash.'

Mia started to ask anyway.

'*Go*,' Sasha urged. She led the way.

Mia asked again in the parking lot, but Sasha practically shoved her into the van. 'Start the engine.'

George emerged from the diner a minute later and headed for the van. Sasha held up her hand. 'Drive around to the back,' she ordered Mia, then pointed George that way.

A few minutes later, out of sight of the diner's bank of windows, he climbed in, joining the chorus of questions.

'Just get us out of here,' Sasha said to Mia. Alice stifled a scream as Sasha finally answered Mia's question.

'I guess somebody – my money's on Glenda – got nervous when we didn't come back after our weekend and made a leap in logic I'll never understand. Anyway, the police are listing us – by name – as missing. The TV showed photos of all of us. That includes you, Alice.'

FOUR REPORTED MISSING FROM TIMELESS PASTURES
By Bert Miller
Community Caller Our Towns columnist

The same community that saw one of its residents shot dead last week has reported four people missing.

The four left the community for a weekend together Friday and have not been seen since, according to a release from Lavina Township Police Chief Oscar Martinez.

They were identified as Mia Sullivan, 66; Alice Sanders, 76: George Sterling, 71; and Sasha Coverdale, 70.

All were residents of Timeless Pastures, the 'active adult' community bordering the Pine Barrens where resident Barbara Stevenson, 70, was found slain last week behind the duplex that also housed Sanders, one of the missing residents.

Sterling and Coverdale are romantically involved, according to a Timeless Pastures resident who asked not to be named.

Sanders had been engaged in a long-running dispute with Stevenson, the woman who was shot, according to the resident. 'It was vicious. I was afraid it was going to get physical. But who could blame Alice? Her entire patio was covered with bird droppings.' Each day, Stevenson fed a large flock of pigeons, the resident said.

A news release from Hawk Boneham III, vice president for expansion for Weller Holdings, which owns Timeless Pastures, said he was 'shocked and saddened' by Stevenson's slaying. He said he hoped the matter of the four missing residents would be resolved as a simple misunderstanding.

In the meantime, he added, 'Weller Holdings will spare no expense in locating our residents and stands ready to assist law enforcement with whatever they need.'

Lavina Township Police Chief Oscar Martinez asked anyone with information about the four missing residents to contact the department, either via its anonymous tip line or the online form. He also reiterated his request for the public's assistance in locating any relatives of Barbara Stevenson.

THIRTY-FIVE

Bert knew it was a long shot.

He'd enjoyed his fifteen minutes of Madison's approval when the networks swooped in for their piece of the irresistible appeal of four elderly people gone missing from the same community where a fifth had been murdered.

But beyond breathless speculation on social media – serial killer? – that fast verged into crazy territory – senior sex cult? – the story remained unchanged. Four people still gone, no sign of a crime.

Aside from some outraged quotes from the son of one of the missing people, it made for dull follow-up stories. So Bert braced himself and took his shot, even as he wished for the days of actual shots, when reporters kept flasks in their desks for a courage-boosting slug.

Instead, he made do with the lukewarm dregs of the coffee from the newsroom machine, pale-brown stuff whose only saving grace was that it was free and ostensibly caffeinated. Just the sort of thing given to a condemned man, which is how he felt as he approached Madison, hopeless story idea in hand.

'Hey, Bert. Have they found those missing people yet?'

'Not yet. But—'

'You know, time was when we'd start a newsroom pool on when and where they'd find them. Dead in a ditch or whooping it up at the casinos?'

She'd inadvertently given him an opening.

'Turns out they're not the only ones missing.'

That got her attention. She took her fingers off the keyboard and swiveled to face him. 'What do you mean? Did the police put out another alert? What's going on over there? Did the serial killer thing pan out? Or did I miss an eclipse or something? Have they all been raptured?'

So much for his advantage.

'Look at this.' He thrust a piece of paper at her, a printout of the map of Timeless Pastures, neat oblongs representing the duplexes that lined its cul-de-sacs. He'd drawn red X's over several.

'What is it?'

'It's Timeless Pastures. All those X's? They're vacant houses.'

Her jaw set as she offered the expected pushback. 'So?'

'So, more than half – actually, closer to two-thirds – of these houses are vacant. I talked to a couple of people. As you can imagine by looking at this, it was hard to find anyone, and the ones who are left say the lot fees are going through the roof and they can't afford them anymore.' He'd implied that he'd talked with multiple people. No need for Madison to know at this point that he had only a single source, the chatty Glenda Ferguson.

'Sounds like a good reason for people to leave.'

'But nobody's coming in. I've looked at listings and there's nothing from Timeless Pastures. You'd think someone would want to fill those homes right away to keep the money coming in. It shouldn't be a problem, given the housing shortage. It's weird. You see it, right?'

Dammit. He'd lectured himself not to beg.

'You know what I see?'

Here it came.

'I see a guy who has a column due today, except I don't even know what it's about. In fact, I don't know that he has one at all, because apparently he's been spending all this time wandering around pestering old people on some pie-in-the-sky story that's not even on his beat.'

'But—'

'But nothing.' She laid the map aside, leaned back in her chair, folded her arms across her chest and gave him her patented you're-screwed smile. 'So, Bert. What *is* your column about anyway?'

Bert kept what he called his back-pocket file, a list of story ideas so colossally stupid that they deserved never to see the light of day. Every so often, he'd float one, waiting for the day when Madison bit. Usually, she shooed him away, proving that even she had limits.

'I was going to write about the woman who brings a therapy chicken to schools and nursing homes.'

To her credit, she didn't blink.

'A therapy chicken.'

'Yeah.'

'A real one.'

'The kind that craps all over everything and carries all manner of viruses.'

She looked at the clock. 'You're pushing it, Miller. You'd better hope she's bringing that stupid thing somewhere today.'

Bert reached for the map.

Madison covered it with her hand. 'I'll save this for Don when he gets back. It's right up his alley.'

Bert fumed all the way to his meeting with the chicken lady. Like hell he'd let Don take over his story. What was the isolation period for Covid? The last he'd heard, Don's wife had come down with it, too, meaning Don would have to quarantine that much longer.

At best, he'd have a week to find out what was really going on at Timeless Pastures. Because he'd be damned if he'd hand over his story to anyone else.

Lavina Township Police Department
Transcript of interview with Mia Sullivan
Present: Detective Travis Meacham, Officer Sherilee Townsend

Townsend: Your first reaction when you saw the photos on TV was to run.

Sullivan: Duh.

Townsend: You make it sound as though it was your only choice.

Sullivan: And I repeat: Duh.

Townsend: Do I remember correctly that the story said the police were seeking information on the whereabouts of the four of you?

Sullivan: I believe that's what it said.

Townsend: But it didn't occur to you to contact them.

Sullivan: Duh.

THIRTY-SIX

Car horns blared as the van swerved into the opposite lane.

'Mia!' Sasha and Alice screamed together. Mia gave a weak wave of apology toward the array of raised middle fingers and wrestled the van back under control.

'Sorry, everyone.' Mia fought for breath. She'd just violated the most basic code – do nothing that draws attention. She needed to make up for it, fast. Scenarios, none of them good, flickered through her brain. *First things first*, she told herself.

'We've got to get out of sight. I saw a sign a couple of miles back for a motel just off the road. I'm going to drive right up to the front, and George and I are going to go in and ask for a room.'

'Why you two?' Sasha asked.

'Because a woman getting a motel room alone stands out. And because they're looking for four people and one is a Black woman. Here's the turnoff. Alice and Sasha, get down on the floor. George, climb up front here with me so we look like a normal couple when we pull in.'

'Thanks for defining a normal couple as White.' Sasha managed to kick the back of the driver's seat, hard, as she scrambled to the floor.

Mia congratulated herself minutes later when she opened the room door and – after scanning the motel's eaves and light poles in the parking lot for security cameras – hurried the others into the room. 'We made it!'

Regret chased relief as she pulled the door shut behind her and fastened the chain. Because the easy part was over.

George took one look at Mia's white face, her shaking hands, and correctly diagnosed the panic that sets in once an immediate risk is past.

He'd thankfully never seen it himself but had heard about it during the innumerable training sessions that educators had to undergo to prepare them for mass shootings.

'Sometimes the lucky ones – the ones who get themselves out –

once they're safe, they fall apart. Let them. You don't even want to think about what bottling up that kind of fear can do to someone,' the training coordinator had said.

Mia's experience had fallen far short of dodging bullets sprayed by a teenager with too-easy access to weapons of war. But in the face of a looming emergency, she'd come up with a split-second plan of action and carried it out.

'Well done, Mia,' George reassured her. 'Sasha, can you please bring her a glass of water? In fact, we could probably all use one. I'll help you. Alice, don't let go of Mia.'

Alice sat beside Mia on the bed, arm tight around her, talking in low, soothing tones. 'Sure wish I could have been in that motel lobby with you, watching you and George stroll in just like regular retired vacationers, cool as a couple of aging cucumbers.'

Mia managed a weak laugh. 'Want to know the funny thing? I kept my left hand in my pocket. Didn't want them to know we weren't married. Like anyone has cared about that for the last, oh, I don't know how many decades.'

'Catholic school, right? The guilt, all those rules. It never goes away, does it?'

Mia scrawled something with an imaginary pencil. 'Perfect penmanship, too.'

George and Sasha handed out water. 'There were only two cups for the room. We'll have to share.'

Mia took a sip, then drank the whole cup. 'Better. Thanks. That business about our photos being out there – what a shock.'

'For all of us. My son is going to lose his mind. Probably already has. I have to find a way to call him.' Sasha glared at the empty space on the nightstand that probably once had held a landline.

Alice said what they were all thinking.

'Thanks to that photo, any chance that Hawk wouldn't connect Carol Ann Kaminski with Alice Sanders is gone. What do we do now?'

'Routine,' the facilitators had said during those school-shooting drills. 'Re-establish routine, normalcy, as soon as possible. Even though nothing is normal and won't be again for a long time.'

'Nothing has changed,' George said. 'He still has no idea where you are. New Mexico, or wherever you're not going to tell us you're going, still seems like a viable plan. We need to do two things: get you somewhere else as soon as possible, and come up with a plausible story as to where we've been and why we've returned without you.'

He scanned their faces. He had their attention. Good.

'That's our assignment.' He looked at his watch, glad he'd never given it up when smartphones came along. He'd spent the past day watching the others fumbling for their nonexistent phones whenever they wondered what time it was. 'I'm giving us half an hour to at least come up with a reasonable start.'

It took twenty minutes.

Getting Alice away was the easy part. She'd join Mia in the van after all. But how to explain both their absences when Sasha and George returned?

Mia chewed a fingernail. 'For me, it's pretty straightforward. I just got sick of waiting around for Timeless Pastures to empty out. I already had the van, so why not hit the road the way I'd planned, only a couple of weeks early? Head south, get away from the snow. Let them think I was going to Florida. You can say you all threw a party for me at the lake house – true enough, even though it was for all of us – and then it was bon voyage.'

'What about your furniture?'

'Um, how about this? I'm making a test trip to see how the van goes and work out the kinks of living on the road. I'll be back before my move-out date to deal with it.'

George caught a glint of interest in Sasha's eyes. She took up Mia's narrative.

'George, once Mia and Alice left us, you and I decided to continue the weekend on our own – drive around, see the sights, have a little time to ourselves before we have to move away. If anyone tries to check out that story, you can honestly say that we checked into these two motels. Let's just hope no one remembers you coming in with a White woman.'

George felt his ears redden. 'No one will remember me, anyway,' he said. 'No one remembers anyone who's our age.'

'Exactly,' said Sasha. 'In this situation, it's our superpower.'

'It's not the worst idea. We could play with it. But that still leaves . . .'

'Me,' said Alice. 'I'm still the problem.'

Lavina Township Police Department
Transcript of interview with Sasha Coverdale
Present: Detective Travis Meacham, Officer Sherilee Townsend

Townsend: So you were counting on us being idiots.
Coverdale: That's about the size of it.
Townsend: Gee, thanks.
Coverdale: Worked, didn't it? At least for a while.

THIRTY-SEVEN

One problem solved, at least sort of. Which left . . .

Sasha beat George to the punch. 'This business of harboring a fugitive – I hate to say you were right, George. It's clearly an issue now.'

He surprised her. 'The more I think about it, the less I think it's a problem.'

Alice gave him a wan smile. 'That's sweet of you, George. But I don't get it. I'm pretty sure it's a felony. I've put all of you in a terrible position.'

'Uh-oh.' Sasha knew that look. 'He's got his Cheshire cat smile. What have you cooked up, George?'

'All those crime shows I watch? The ones you like to make fun of? There's a lot of legal stuff in them. For instance, you can't ask about what you don't know.'

'George, what in the world are you talking about?'

'We're the only ones, other than Hawk, who know who Alice really is. So far, nothing has publicly identified her as Carol Ann Kaminski. There's no reason for the police to ask us about that; ergo, there's no reason for us to lie.'

'Ergo? Look at you, turning teacher on us,' Sasha said. But she leaned over and kissed his cheek. 'It's worth a try. And permit me to be your partner in scheming.'

'Gladly. Care to elaborate?'

'We're all sitting here making ourselves crazy, when it's so easy.'

'It is?'

'How's the saying go? We used it all the time in real estate. The simplest explanation is the best. People would fall over themselves, trying to explain away things like, oh, say, water damage. They'd want to convince buyers that the big stain on the ceiling was some sort of modern art project, when all you had to do was say, "It's a leak." And then you'd say either that it was fixed but the cosmetics were never taken care of – and show them the receipts to prove it – or else, "Yes, that's a leak, and here's how much it will cost to fix it, which of course will be deducted from the sale price of the home."'

Alice pulled away from Mia. 'So what's this oh-so-easy explanation? Because I'm not seeing it.'

Sasha beamed. 'One of your house-sitting offers came through earlier than expected. You got the call while we were on our weekend and you headed out straightaway. Much as with Mia, you told us you'd make arrangements to put your furniture in storage later. Heck, we can even do that for you.'

'And where is this supposed house-sitting job?'

Mia raised her hand. 'What about saying it's someplace like upstate New York? Point them in the wrong direction, just in case they decide to look.'

'How did I get there?'

'I dropped you off at Thirtieth Street Station in Philadelphia on my way out of town so that you could catch a train to, say, Buffalo. Thousands of people go through that train station every day.'

Alice put her hands in front of her face. 'Think anyone would notice me doing this in front of each and every security camera? Assuming I didn't miss any.'

'I'm going to add another saying to Sasha's,' Mia said. 'Plan for the worst, hope for the best. What's the worst?'

'That someone will find out I never got on a train to Buffalo. What's the best?'

'That even if our explanation isn't accepted, if for some reason they mount a full-on search for you, it will take forever to scan hours and hours of security tape with thousands and thousands of faces, and to go through all the tickets purchased that day and maybe, just maybe, realize you never bought a ticket or got on a train to Buffalo. At the very least, you'd get a few days' head start. By which point, you'll be in sunny New Mexico – or wherever you're going – scarfing down chili verde or some other place's local specialty and wondering why you hadn't gone there years ago.'

Alice peered between her fingers. 'You know, back when we first heard Babs had been shot, I just wanted to disappear for a couple of days to think things through. I had this silly hope that maybe I was just being paranoid, even though being paranoid is what's saved me all these years. But now I know I wasn't. I've got to disappear for real again, which means I'm going to need the rest of my money.'

Mia stood and bent double, clutching her ankles, stretching her quads and hamstrings. 'Same drill as before? I'll take the van and be back in an hour or so. Maybe longer so that I can legitimately get a run in.'

'That won't work. Not for the amount I need.'

'Just how much do you have?' Sasha blurted.

Mia and Alice exchanged looks. 'More than Mia can carry,' Alice said finally.

'Then I'll go,' said Sasha. 'I'll take the van. It's time to deploy my own superpower.'

George gave her a fond smile. 'Which one?'

'Being Black.'

Sasha looked into their uncomprehending faces. Talk about blissful ignorance.

She tried to keep the resentment from her voice. 'You know how George said a little while ago that nobody registers old people when they see them? Well, that dynamic increases exponentially if you're Black. Nobody sees *me*. Hide these locs under a cap' – she swept them away from her face – 'and I'm Generic Black Woman. Put me in a vehicle nobody recognizes, and I could be just another delivery person.'

Mia started to protest. 'That's crazy, Sasha.'

'No,' Alice said. 'She's right. Unfortunately. Except, under these circumstances, fortunately. Only problem is, you need some delivery person clothes.'

Mia yanked open the nightstand drawer and catalogued the meager contents. 'A Gideon Bible, a Book of Mormon – when did that start? – and, score!'

She tossed an artifact on to the bed.

The others gaped in recognition.

'The Yellow Pages? I didn't even know they printed those anymore.'

Alice picked up the printed listing of area businesses and regarded it with reverence. 'They probably don't. This one must be years old.' She turned the pages. 'I wonder if any of these places still exist.'

'Give me that.' Sasha took it and flipped toward the end. 'Uniforms, uniforms. Here. A few stores sell them. Anyone know what town we're in?'

Lavina Township Police Department
Transcript of interview with Sasha Coverdale
Present: Detective Travis Meacham, Officer Sherilee Townsend

Townsend: Your role up to a certain point seems to have been mostly passive.

Coverdale: I've been called a lot of things in my life, but passive is not one of them.

Townsend: I didn't mean to offend. I'm sure you know as well as I do the benefit of keeping a low profile.

Coverdale: Are you referring again to the fact that we're both Black? If so, then you know as well as I do that – to use your phrasing – a low profile can be anything but passive.

THIRTY-EIGHT

Sasha twisted before the bathroom mirror, studying herself in the uniform Mia had bought for her. She'd gone with a khaki shirt and dark-green pants.

Sasha thought she looked like a forest ranger, minus the Smokey Bear hat, but held her tongue. Mia had done her best on short notice. She'd even bought a khaki ball cap. Sasha wound Mia's stretchy gaiter around her locs and tucked them under the cap.

Finally, she wiped her face free of makeup, hesitating a second before rubbing away the scarlet lipstick she considered a trademark of sorts, emphasizing the megawatt smile she'd flashed in her realtor days.

Mia reminded her of it now. 'Whatever you do, don't smile.'

As if a White person knew the drill. Sasha had spent her entire life code-switching. At least this time excitement overlay the usual resignation and resentment.

Mia gave her a quick tutorial on the van's peculiarities, and it stuttered its way out of the lot, Sasha's spirits soaring as she left the stuffy confines of the motel room behind.

Because now she was the one in charge. George had stepped in with his school-principal best when Mia nearly fell apart, and she was grateful for it, she really was. In fact, his steadiness was one of the things she liked – loved? – most about him.

Safely alone in the van, with an hour before she arrived at Timeless Pastures, she let her thoughts wander. The L-word hovered ever closer with each passing month that she and George were together. She knew he'd have said it long ago had she not stiffened each time a conversation seemed apt to swerve in that direction.

Despite his fling with Alice, he'd still been emotionally at sea, too readily mistaking comfort for love, when she took up with him. But as time sanded the roughest of grief's edges, his neediness lessened. The booming laugh she remembered from their early days in the Timeless Reads book group returned. They became easy with one another, spending evenings stretched out at opposite ends of the sofa, feet entwined as they stared at their respective screens, his with one of his true-crime shows, hers an obsessive stream of home-renovation features.

Because she couldn't kick the realtor habit, looking at every room she entered with an assessing eye. Her own duplex was a marvel of adaptation, given her inability to make significant changes lest she risk the full wrath of Babs.

But she'd covered the regulation-eggshell beige walls with prints and a few precious originals by her favorite artists – Ellen Powell Tiberino, Chéri Samba, Alma Thomas and Amy Sherald – splashes of color echoed in her brightly upholstered Danish modern sofa and chairs. She'd kept the furniture to a minimum to create the illusion of space and banned clutter altogether. Somehow it managed to be both restful and energizing, and it pained her when she walked into clients' homes and saw disasters that could have been remedied with little more than a fresh coat of paint and a thorough tidy-up.

Her home was so different from George's. Claustrophobia gripped her every time she stepped into it. It was clear that when he and his wife had downsized to Timeless Pastures, they'd made the common mistake of bringing as many of the things from their former home as possible. She saw it over and over again, the duplexes' tiny spaces overwhelmed by heavy, dark furniture, commodious sofas and oversize Barcaloungers bumping up against breakfronts full of crystal and china knickknacks. Dining-room suites for eight, king-size beds, huge his-and-her dressers.

She let George think they spent nights at her place to avoid the unseemliness of making love in the bed he'd shared with his wife, but really it was because she feared she'd pass right out from lack of oxygen in such a crowded space. She longed to toss half the furniture, reupholster the rest, tear the heavy drapes from the windows and replace them with sunlight-admitting sheers.

So George slept at her place, and she took no little satisfaction at his repeated refrain: 'Our houses are exactly the same. I just don't understand why yours seems so much bigger.' Her heart swelled the morning he'd clinked his coffee cup with hers over the Sunday crossword and said, 'God, I love this.'

There it was. That word. But . . . *this*.

What if he'd said *you*? Would she have said it back? Or run screaming from her own home?

THIRTY-NINE

Sooner than Sasha expected, the sign for her exit loomed. Another few minutes brought her to Timeless Pastures. She'd only been gone a couple of days, but her heart lurched at the sight of the turnoff. She longed to leave the van in the parking lot outside Johnny's office and walk the few blocks to her own home, lock the door behind her and pretend these last days had never happened.

But for all her disapproval of the way George and Mia had obviously jumped into a real-life version of their favorite forms of entertainment, she had to admit it *was* exciting.

So she trained her gaze away from her own house and steered the van on to Alice's cul-de-sac, parked in front of her duplex and marched up to the front door as though she belonged there, bravado that mattered not a bit since the street was its usual deserted self.

'Just a couple of skirts and tops and some underthings,' Alice had said. 'And all the bankers' boxes in the closet. Oh, and the framed photos by my bed, please. You can wrap them in the clothes. Thanks, Sasha.'

She stuffed the clothing into pillowcases and stared at the photos for long moments before burying them deep within. At the last minute, she pulled the quilt, clearly hand-stitched and soft with age, from the bed and folded it beneath her arm. Wherever Alice ended up, she could wrap herself in it, a hedge against the strangeness of a new life.

She hurried the clothes into the van and went back for the boxes – a dozen in all. She thought to stack and carry two at a time, but they proved surprisingly heavy. She surmised there was cash in one of them, but for whatever reason, Alice was intent upon lugging a bunch of old *National Geographics* to New Mexico with her, too.

She hefted the first box, remembering at the last minute to bend her knees against its weight, and stashed it in the back of the van. Precaution notwithstanding, her back started screaming by the sixth box and her knees joined the chorus a couple of boxes later. Despite the winter chill, she'd sweated through her faux uniform shirt by the time she reached for the final box.

She nearly dropped it as she pulled Alice's door closed behind her, and staggered to the van, shoving it into the open side door with relief. It took all her strength to pull the door shut. Something soft bounced off her ankles.

Sasha jumped back, looking down into the eager eyes and adorable pink tongue of Sugar Plum, tugging hard at the end of his extension leash, gathering himself for another leap at her shins, eager for the treat she usually gave him.

A moment later, Glenda followed the leash around the corner of the van.

'Sasha? What in the world?'

There was only one thing to do.

Sasha dropped her voice an octave, glared hard at Glenda and said, 'Ma'am?'

Glenda stepped back. 'Sasha?'

'Moving company, ma'am. If you'll excuse me.'

She brushed past Glenda and unlocked the driver's side door.

'Moving company? Moving where? Are you sure . . . I mean, you look like . . .'

Sasha's voice dripped venom. 'Because we all look alike?'

'Oh, gosh, no. That's not what I meant at all. I'm not racist. Some of my best friends—'

Sasha held up her hand. 'Do not go there.'

'But you could be Sasha's twin.'

'And there it is. You have yourself a good not-racist day.'

She slammed the door and started the van. If the lumbering thing could have peeled rubber, she'd have laid tracks out of the cul-de-sac.

As it was, she preceded sedately through the gate and on to the main road, wondering just how long it would take Glenda to realize there was nothing whatsoever wrong with her eyes.

Lavina Township Police Department
Transcript of interview with J.R. 'Johnny' Natale
Present: Detective Travis Meacham, Officer Sherilee Townsend

Meacham: Do you consider yourself a reasonable person, Mr Natale?

Natale: I used to. Before all of this happened.

Meacham: Finally, we agree about something. That your actions – rather, your lack of action – were unreasonable.

Natale: Alice taught me a phrase. Situational ethics. I hadn't heard it before, but it makes perfect sense to me. What about you? You heard of it?

Meacham: You're *going to give* me *a lesson on ethics now? Are you freaking—?*

Townsend: I think this is a very good time for my colleague – actually, for all of us – to take a break.

FORTY

Johnny's cellphone pinged with a number he knew all too well.

'Glenda. What is it now? Kids in hoodies sighted out on the main road?'

She spoke over him.

'It's Sasha! It's Sasha!'

'What about her?' He reached for the remote to mute the football game. Decided against it. Over the years, he'd become adept at cutting Glenda off in mid-freak-out.

'I just saw her.'

Johnny hit the mute button.

'What? Where?'

He knew it. This whole missing thing had been blown out of proportion.

'At Alice's house. Just now. She was carrying boxes out of the house and putting them in a van.'

'*What?*'

He grabbed his coat and keys, and was already at the door before Glenda's next words registered.

'She said it wasn't her, but I knew it was. So did Sugar Plum. You know how he is with strangers. But he ran right up to her and asked for a treat. But then she called me a racist! Me!'

Johnny let go of the door. 'Was it Sasha or wasn't it?'

'She said she was from a moving company. But the van didn't have any kind of logo on it. Anyway, it looked more like a camper than a regular van.' Her gasp sounded so loud that Johnny held the phone away from his ear.

'Oh my God. It was one of those burglars you read about. The ones who when they read an obituary, or hear someone was away on vacation – or missing, like Alice and the rest of them – they rob them blind. I can't believe I didn't think of that till now. Johnny, I'm calling the cops.'

Oh, no. Just the other day, Chief Martinez had phoned him. 'Johnny, isn't there any way to keep Glenda Ferguson in check? If we had to run down every tip she phoned in, we wouldn't have time to deal with real crime.'

'Hold on, Glenda. I'm heading over there right now to check it out for myself. If there's a problem, I'll call the police. What did that van look like again?'

'Red. Kind of a dusty red. Either really dirty or needs a new paint job. It headed west out of the community. Oh, and, Johnny, be sure to call me back and tell me what you found out.'

He promised he would. But if he'd learned anything from his dealings with Glenda, she'd call him back first.

West, Glenda had said.

Johnny felt like an idiot, chasing after a maybe-burglar on the word of a certified busybody who saw crime around every corner. The Eagles game had been tied when he left. He'd give this nonsense a few more minutes of his time – the road west, after all, stretched all the way to the Delaware River, ending at one of the bridges into Philadelphia – and then he'd try to get back in time to catch the end of the game.

A sign at the intersection with the main road directed travelers heading for Philadelphia to turn left. A gas station sat just before the exit. An attendant pumped gas into a grimy red van.

'Whoa.' Johnny cut over to the shoulder and hit the brakes. He didn't dare pull into the gas station in his pickup with the Timeless Pastures logo emblazoned on the door. He peered toward the pumps, thinking of the prescription for new glasses that lay largely forgotten on his desk.

He cursed the New Jersey law that forbade motorists from pumping their own gas. How was he supposed to tell if the driver was Sasha? But then a woman emerged from the station's convenience store with a cup of coffee and headed for the van, and even with the ball cap and some sort of uniform, damned if it didn't look like Sasha.

Lavina Township Police Department
Transcript of interview with Glenda Ferguson
Present: Detective Travis Meacham, Officer Sherilee Townsend

Townsend: Am I hearing you right? That you tried to call the police?

Ferguson: Yes, I did. I'm a God-fearing woman. I know wrong when I see it.

Townsend: And what happened?

Ferguson: I was discouraged. No, not just discouraged. I was practically ordered not to. Right then, I should have known something was wrong. But I was raised to be polite, to listen to my elders.

Townsend: Mr Natale isn't exactly your elder.

Ferguson: I just assumed. Because he looks so much older. He really should take better care of himself. I do, and just look at me.

Townsend: I apologize. But you see my point.

Ferguson: He was our community manager. A person in authority. I listen to such people. Even though I now realize I shouldn't have. I don't know if I can ever forgive myself. Oh dear. Do you have a tissue?

FORTY-ONE

Johnny's next move surprised even him.

'Hey, Glenda. You won't believe this. I found the van.'

She screamed into the phone. 'I knew it! I knew it! Thieves, right? I'll call the cops and tell them what I saw.'

'No need. I already called.'

In fact, he had, telling the chief, 'Glenda's on a tear about what she thinks is a burglary at Alice Sanders' home. Yeah, one of the missing people. I checked it out. All good. Just wanted you to know in case she calls.' He chuckled. 'Yeah, you're right. She absolutely will. Feel free to turn your attention elsewhere. Listen, I got a line on Eagles tickets next week. Join me? OK, I'll wait to hear.'

Why didn't he add his own suspicions? He told himself he needed to be sure before he called Chief Martinez, lest the chief slot him into the same category as Glenda. More to the point, Glenda had said she'd seen Sasha/not-Sasha carrying boxes. He knew exactly what was in those boxes. But if he called the chief and told him someone had just removed thousands of dollars in cash from Alice's house, the chief would wonder how he knew that – and he'd have to confess illegally going through Alice's things. Better to postpone that conversation, permanently if possible, at least until he was sure what was going on.

By the time he'd clicked out of the call, the van was on to the four-lane road, still heading west. Following it was easy enough, this time of day and this time of year. Come summer, weekenders from the Philadelphia suburbs would turn it into a parking lot on their way to the Jersey Shore.

The van was so caked with filthy slush that he almost missed the fact that it was signaling a turn on to the Jersey Turnpike entrance ramp, heading north. Were they going to New York? And, if so, were they planning the sort of blowout few days he'd first imagined them spending in Atlantic City, only this time shelling out their cash on Broadway plays and high-end restaurants instead of at the casinos? But why drive such an unwieldy vehicle into Manhattan's gridlock?

One of the turnpike's ubiquitous green signs indicated a New Jersey Transit station ahead. Of course – they were going to take the train into the city. Johnny resolved to follow them until he saw all four depart the van and head into the train station, so that he could assure Chief Martinez – not to mention Hawk Boneham – that he'd seen them alive and well. As to why they were going about their business in such bizarre fashion, he intended to have a good long talk with at least one of them when they returned.

But the van lumbered past the exit for the train station and continued north for another twenty minutes, where it took an exit toward one of the towns whose names Johnny could never remember and turned almost immediately into the driveway of a motel that had seen better days. He barely managed to wrestle the truck into the parking lot of the fast-food restaurant across the street.

The van disappeared around the back of the motel and out of sight.

Now what?

He looked down the street. An insurance office stood next to the hotel. A line of spindly trees divided one parking lot from another. Perfect.

He waited for a break in traffic, shot across the road and parked the truck in front of a slender gap between the trees that gave a clear view of the back of the motel. There sat the van. He waited. And waited. What if she was in for the night? With whom? George? All of them? Or maybe she was all alone? What if he were as confused as he'd accused Glenda of being, and the woman wasn't Sasha at all? He'd known her even longer than Glenda, though. And that business with Sugar Plum – the little dog did his best impression of a snarling Rottweiler at the sight of someone he didn't know.

A motel door opened. Johnny held his breath. The maybe-Sasha woman came out, unlocked the van door, then turned and held out the keys to someone who turned out to be Mia. George and Alice followed.

Johnny pumped his fist. He opened his own door. He couldn't wait to hear how the four had ended up in this unlikely spot.

'Hey! You in the truck! What the hell are you doing?'

Johnny turned. A man stood in the door of the insurance office, cellphone in hand. 'You're not a customer. What are you, some kind of peeping Tom? I'm calling the cops.'

Johnny waved him off. 'No need. The truck was making a funny noise. I just stopped to check it out. Leaving now.' He hopped back in and left the parking lot, just in time to see the van pulling away from the motel. It turned back on to the turnpike, heading south this time.

He fell in behind it. He had no idea what was going on. But at least now, he knew who he was following.

Lavina Township Police Department
Transcript of interview with Mia Sullivan
Present: Detective Travis Meacham, Officer Sherilee Townsend

Townsend: You really had us going with that train station business.

Sullivan: Thank you.

Townsend: Don't know that I meant it as a compliment. We're talking about a scheme specifically designed to avoid detection by police.

Sullivan: You call it a scheme. I see it as a plan.

Townsend: Here we go again with the semantics.

Sullivan: A good plan. One designed to keep someone safe.

Townsend: Which the police could have done, if only they'd been notified.

Sullivan: If only we'd thought you could help. Under the circumstances, it seemed like a long shot.

Townsend: Hence, your scheme. Pretty elaborate, by the way. How'd a yoga teacher come up with something like that?

Sullivan: Personal trainer. I read a lot of spy novels. Maybe you should try it sometime.

Townsend: Maybe you should try following the law sometime.

Meacham: And you say I'm the one who needs a time-out? Listening to you two is like dealing with an old married couple. I think this is a good time for another break.

FORTY-TWO

Mia met Sasha at the motel-room door. 'Don't bother getting settled.' She motioned the others toward the door.

'What's going on?'

'We're getting out of here. I'll drive. Did you get the money?'

'It's in the back. But I ran into Glenda and she . . .'

'Tell us on the way. We have a plan. Hang on to your hat. It's complicated, but I think it's pretty good.'

Of course she did. It was her idea. She outlined it for Sasha once the van was moving.

'It's a massive cover-your-butt. You know, in the whole spirit of planning for the worst. Because what if no one believes you and George when you say Alice went to Buffalo? We're going to prove she did.'

'You're really going?' Sasha turned to Alice, balanced beside her on one of the folding chairs. They grabbed the seats in front of them as the van gathered speed on the highway. 'What if they find you there?'

Mia raised her voice so that Sasha and Alice could hear.

'They won't. Alice is going to buy a train ticket to Buffalo. She's even going to get on the train. The security cameras will show both of those things. Then she's going to duck into the train's restroom, put on a coat and hat, and walk right out again before it leaves the station. She's going to wear one of George's coats – it's about two sizes too big for her – and carry a pillowcase full of stuff. We took one from the motel and filled it with towels. She'll keep her head down and talk to herself, and with luck, if she shows up on the cameras, she'll look like just another homeless person.'

She peeked at Sasha in the rear-view mirror, watching her take it all in, blink and give a slow nod of approval. 'That's pretty good. But won't the van show up in the cameras around the station?'

'We'll park a few blocks away. That whole area has been gentrified, but it's still a little sketchy just north of there. I doubt there's a camera, and if there is, it's been shot out. I'm going to take a roundabout route to get to the station in hopes nothing will pick up the van. It's the best I can do.'

George tapped Sasha on the shoulder. 'Here. A present. Now you can call your son.' He handed her a phone.

'What's this? I thought we weren't supposed to use them.'

'Burners,' Mia said. 'There was a convenience store down the street from the motel.'

'What are we now, drug dealers?' But Sasha took the phone.

'Things are getting complicated. We need them to stay in touch, but mostly to keep up with stuff online. Turns out we're a big story. All the networks are on to it. And you wouldn't believe the things they're saying about us online. They're calling us "The Sexy Seniors." That's your fault, by the way. Well, yours and George's.'

'*What?*' Sasha fumbled with the phone. 'How do I get this thing up and running?'

'George can show you. I walked him through it. Anyway, the good news is that, so far, we're still ahead of the game. Again, this is all precautionary. Once we're done here, I'll take us back to the lot where I stored the van so that you and George can pick up the cars and head back to Timeless Pastures and start spreading BS far and wide as Alice and I make tracks for the place we're not telling you about.'

She cast another look toward Sasha, who was chewing her lipstick-free lip.

'Don't worry,' Mia said. 'My father had a saying when times got tough: "Everything is going according to plan." It was his way of telling us that no matter how bad things seemed in the moment, they usually turned out fine. It drove my mom nuts – she was a worrier. But you know what? He was almost always right.'

She ignored Sasha's response.

'And when he wasn't?'

Lavina Township Police Department
Transcript of interview with Sasha Coverdale
Present: Detective Travis Meacham, Officer Sherilee Townsend

Townsend: I'm just going to start with this question each time we return from a break. Let me get this straight. Even when you had access to a phone again – a burner phone, mind you, so that a call couldn't be traced – you still *declined to call the police?*
Coverdale: I was most concerned with calling my son. Do you have children, Officer Townsend?
Townsend: My personal life is not at issue here.
Coverdale: And yet you seem very concerned with mine.
Townsend: I'm just interested in all the missed opportunities to nip things in the bud, along with the fact that you dragged your own son into this mess by having him make a false report to the police.
Coverdale: He didn't know it was false.
Townsend: Lucky for him. Not so much for you.
Coverdale: Anyway, it wasn't completely false. We told him we were fine. And we were.
Townsend: You have an interesting definition of fine.

FORTY-THREE

Gerald Coverdale's voice rose so loud that the others heard every word, even over the van's rattling progress.

'Mama! Where are you? What number is this? What happened to your phone? They said you were missing. We were afraid you were dead. You wouldn't believe the things they're saying about you online. Your granddaughters are scared to death.'

'Settle down, honey. I'm not dead.' Sasha's laugh was so weak it could have been a sob. 'I'm fine. My phone isn't. I dropped it and had to get a new one. My friends and I decided to extend our vacation by a couple of days. Our neighborhood busybody – you've heard me talk about her – put two and two together and came up with about fourteen.'

'This is a true thing? You're not just saying it because you're tied up in the back of some van with a gun held to your head?'

Sasha looked to the others for help. She was, after all, in the back of a van. George mimed a spirited wave. Sasha forced a broad smile, hoping it would somehow infuse her voice with cheer.

'No, of course not. I'm with my friends. Say hi, everybody.'

'Hi, Sasha's son!' Mia called from the driver's seat. 'We're having such a fun trip.'

Alice raised her voice. 'Gerald, delighted to finally make your acquaintance. Your mother talks about you all the time – you and your beautiful family. She's so proud.'

George opened his mouth. Sasha shook her head, making a zipping motion across her lips. It didn't matter.

A long silence followed. Sasha held up one hand, fingers crossed. Then—

'Mama, is it true what the news said? You're fooling around with a White man? Is he there? I didn't hear him say anything.'

George winced.

Sasha mouthed a silent F-bomb.

'Mama? I don't hear a denial. Did they get that part wrong, too? Or have you completely lost your mind?'

'It's complicated,' Sasha began. But it wasn't. Or, at least until this moment, it hadn't been.

'When are you coming home? Because we need to have a good long talk.'

Sasha had rehearsed this next part in her mind. She was so glad to turn the conversation away from the topic of George that it came out in a rush.

'Listen, baby, we're in an area where the cell service isn't great, so I need you to do me a favor. Will you call the police – the number's listed on all the stories – and tell them we're all fine? That everything just got blown all out of proportion?'

'Yes, but—'

'Oops, I'm starting to lose you. I'll call you as soon as we've got good reception. Probably tomorrow. The important thing is that you don't have to worry about me. Make sure you let the police know. *Don't worry*.'

'Oh, I'm worrying. I'm worrying every minute from now until you tell me you've come to your senses and ditched—'

Sasha grabbed a handful of her coat's nylon outer shell and rubbed the folds together in front of the phone, doing her best to approximate interference in the airwaves.

'. . . losing you. Talk soon. Love you, honey.'

FORTY-FOUR

Johnny followed the van as it crossed the Delaware River and headed into Philadelphia, bypassing the highway in favor of weaving through the city streets.

Maybe he'd missed something back at the motel. His relieved speculation that they were on some sort of innocuous if inexplicable jaunt dissolved. He wondered whether something more sinister was afoot after all.

He'd only seen the four of them get into the van. Maybe a kidnapper, someone who knew about the money, was hiding in the van – had threatened one or all of them with something awful if they didn't go along. But why, if they'd been unguarded in the motel room, hadn't they called for help?

And if what appeared to be a spontaneous trip was truly innocent, who would choose central New Jersey as a getaway? The closest attraction was a huge amusement park, but Johnny couldn't imagine the four shrieking in delight through the stomach-challenging dips and swoops of a roller coaster. Anyway, the park was largely closed through the winter.

The area music venues that had seen Bruce Springsteen's rise reliably drew tourists, but once again Johnny's mind balked at the image of any of them rocking out at the Stone Pony. Besides, the motel was miles from those shore towns.

None of it made sense. He put the crazy-making thoughts aside and concentrated on following the van without getting too close, a task made far more complicated in the maze of streets with unpredictable stoplights. Twice, he thought he'd lost them, only to catch up a few minutes later when he glanced down a side street and saw the van turning a corner.

It finally pulled to a stop somewhere in West Philadelphia, in an area of spacious Queen Anne homes of brick or stone, some of which had been lovingly restored, others whose interiors had obviously been chopped into apartments and were showing the results of decades of habitation by hard-living students.

He'd supervised some contracting jobs in the neighborhood when the area around the University of Pennsylvania and Drexel University saw a burst of new construction, with more campus buildings and corresponding apartment complexes going up all over the place. But he hadn't been back in years.

The van parked a few blocks from the glitzy new development. Here, wooden porches sagged, shutters dangled crooked beside windows, and weeds dominated postage-stamp lawns. He pulled into a space a few cars back, hoping no one in the van would look up the street and see the familiar pickup. A few minutes later, Alice left the van, holding some sort of bulky bag. Johnny slid down in his seat.

She didn't look like someone with anything to hide, walking purposefully away from the truck – thank heavens – without a backward glance. He thought about following her, but that would mean driving past the van, and anyway, wherever she was headed, she'd probably be back soon.

He leaned his seat back a couple of notches and settled in to wait.

FORTY-FIVE

Sasha spoke for all of them. 'I'm hungry.'

'We're near Penn,' Mia reminded her. 'There'll be a Wawa along with a ton of food trucks. Starving students and all.'

'I'm in,' said George. 'How do we want to do this? Because if we head that way, we'll pass cameras for sure.'

He and Mia both turned to look at Sasha.

'Great. So I'm still Anonymous Black Woman?'

''Fraid so.' Mia cut to the chase. 'What does everyone want to eat? There'll be plenty of options.'

George went traditional. 'Cheesesteak for me. But mozzarella, not Cheez Whiz.'

'Pretender,' Mia snorted. 'Falafel for me, please.'

'Me, too. To hell with the diet. What about for Alice?'

They stared at one another, shrugging.

'Whatever,' said Sasha. 'I'll decide when I get there.'

'Could you pick up some bottled water, too, please?' Mia asked. 'We've got a big evening ahead. Gotta hydrate.'

Sasha gave her a thumbs-up and headed out.

Alice, ticket in hand and a newspaper under her arm, made sure to stand in view of the security camera as the train huffed toward the platform. As best she could tell, she'd wandered past every camera in the station. She'd asked the ticket seller far too many questions involving the word *Buffalo*, the idea being that maybe the woman would remember her if the police started asking questions. As soon as the train had disgorged its departing passengers, she pushed her way into the car and went directly into the bathroom.

She shrugged out of the bright-red jacket she'd borrowed from Mia and pulled George's wadded-up down coat, a hat and a newspaper from the pillowcase. The puffy beige parka hung nearly to her knees. She pulled her hair into a ponytail and did her best to stuff it under George's woolen watch cap.

Finally, she took the newspaper and rubbed it hard across her face. It left a faint smudge – nothing like the inky smears of decades earlier – but at least she'd acquired a layer of grime. When she left the bathroom, people were still getting on the train. The crackling canned announcement over the intercom informed her it was leaving the station in two minutes.

She stepped into the line moving through the car, muttering to herself, hunched nearly horizontal, noting with satisfaction the way people shrank away as she passed. She walked through one more car and stepped off the train just as the final 'all aboard' sounded.

She wanted to fling the bag aside, dash up the stairs and bolt for the van. But she forced herself to maintain her halting pace, making sure to stop at a trash can or two and briefly root through them.

She held her breath as she hitched past the officer walking a police dog through the station, resisting the impulse to dodge away from him. Instead, he was the one who gave her a wide berth.

She breathed a little easier once she was back on the street, but there were still a few blocks to negotiate at her maddeningly slow rate. She'd forgotten that she needed to keep talking to herself. She fell back on the old children's story about the little engine who could: 'I think I can, I think I can.'

And if she threw an occasional 'dammit' into the refrain, well, who paid attention to the ravings of a street person?

Johnny squinted.

Sure enough, that was Sasha about a block away, cradling a paper bag, wrapped sandwiches – from the shape he guessed hoagies or cheesesteaks – peeking from the top. His stomach rumbled. When he'd set off for Alice's house to check out Glenda's wild story, he hadn't planned on spending half the day on the road.

Voices caught his attention.

Three young men ambled past, moving with the sort of twitchy energy that Johnny remembered from his days of dealing with subcontractors. Guys like these showed up on the crews sometime, eyes bloodshot, pupils like pinholes. He'd never even bothered with drug tests, just took one look and sent them packing. Dealing with tweakers was just one more thing about his old life that he didn't miss.

They started to pass the dirt-crusted van. Then stopped. One, taller than the other two, with a beard the color of an overripe orange, pulled a Saturday night special from his pocket and everything switched to slow motion.

'Wait,' Johnny croaked from his truck as the man reached for the handle of the driver's side door. It opened.

The man turned to his companions and pumped his fist, then thrust the gun inside.

Johnny fumbled at his own door, fear stiffening his fingers.

The other two men ran around to the van's passenger side and climbed in.

'Oh, no,' Johnny breathed, even as the passenger door opened again and first Mia, then George, was flung on to the street, landing hard.

Sasha dropped her bag and ran toward the van.

'Sasha, no!' Johnny shouted as he leapt from the truck, going in one dizzying breath from slow motion to fast-forward.

The van's engine caught, lurching toward Sasha. She threw herself aside at the last minute, ending up on the street with Mia and George, watching as the van took the turn on two wheels and disappeared around a corner.

'Don't move, don't move.'

Johnny crouched over the trio. Who knew what a fall like that might do to brittle elderly bones? Someone could end up paralyzed.

But the sight of him sent them bolt upright, despite his instructions.

'Johnny? What are you doing here?'

'I could ask you the same thing. Are you OK? Where's Alice?'

Mia looked around. 'There.' She pointed to a homeless woman, a cigarette hanging from her lips, inching her way up the street. 'Alice!' she called.

The woman lifted her head, took in the scene and hurried toward them.

'What happened? Johnny, what are you doing here? Where's the van?'

George struggled to his feet and extended a hand to Sasha, then Mia.

'You shouldn't be moving,' Johnny cautioned again, even as they shook out arms and legs, gingerly at first and then with more vigor.

'All fine,' George pronounced. 'Some bumps and bruises, the worst of them probably to our egos. The question remains – what are you doing here?'

Alice saved Johnny from an immediate answer.

'George. Everybody. *Where's the van?* Did you park it somewhere else?'

Mia looked as though she was about to cry. 'We . . . we . . . oh, Alice, it was awful.'

'They got carjacked. I saw the whole thing,' Johnny said.

Alice whirled to face him. 'And you didn't stop it?'

'Alice.' He took hold of her shoulders. 'There were three of them. One had a gun. They jumped into the van and threw them out. It was over in a matter of seconds.'

Alice sank to the pavement.

'They took the van?'

'The van's gone. But the important thing is that everyone is OK. This could have been much, much worse.'

She looked up at him. 'No, Johnny. Save someone getting killed, this is just about as bad as it could be. All of my money? It was in the van.'

FORTY-SIX

Mia brought them all back to reality.

'We'll deal with that later. We need to get off the street and into someplace safe, ASAP.'

They all looked around, even Johnny, as though expecting some sort of oasis to materialize before them.

Mia waved her hand before Johnny's face. 'What are you doing here? Never mind that. How'd you get here?'

'My truck.'

'Thank God. What's in the back?'

A sizeable cap enclosed the bed of Johnny's pickup. 'Some mulch.'

'Enough room for us?'

'If you squeeze. But there's plenty of room for all of you in the front. It's got an extended cab.'

'No. We can't be seen. Everybody, let's squeeze.' She clapped her hands. 'On the double. Before somebody sees the whole lot of us standing around here.'

They performed the slow-motion scramble mandated by uncooperative knees and hips, made doubly stiff and sore by the slam on to pavement. Johnny shoved the bags of mulch aside and boosted them into the bed.

Mia pulled the door down.

Johnny yanked it back up. 'Isn't anybody going to call nine-one-one?'

Mia grabbed the front of his jacket and jerked him so close their faces nearly touched.

'No. And that includes you. Come on. Let's go.'

'Where?'

'Anywhere but here.' She released his jacket, and he stumbled backward. 'Just get moving. *Now.*'

ELDERLY MISSING PERSONS REPORTED SAFE
By Bert Miller
Community Caller Our Towns Columnist

Four elderly people reported missing from the Timeless Pastures retirement community have checked in with a family member and are safe, said Lavina Township Police Chief Oscar Martinez.

'One of the residents called her son after seeing reports that they'd been considered missing,' he said. 'Apparently, they simply decided to extend a long weekend that they'd taken together.'

Fears for the group's safety arose in light of the recent slaying of Timeless Pastures resident Barbara Stevenson, found shot to death on a patio behind her duplex. An investigation into her killing continues.

Martinez thanked community members for their continued vigilance. 'Law enforcement can't be everywhere. Neighbors helping neighbors – they're our best allies.'

He issued a reminder that authorities continue to seek information that would lead to the apprehension of Stevenson's killer.

'It warms our heart that one story had a happy ending, but we're mindful that a tragedy remains unsolved,' Martinez said.

FORTY-SEVEN

'Happy ending, my rosy rear end,' Bert muttered as he hit 'send' on the story. As far as he was concerned, the tragedy was that his role in the story was over.

He stared into his future, where saccharine stories lurked like pastel demons, teeth and claws dripping syrup.

Not that he wished a bad outcome on the old folks. They sounded like a nice enough bunch. He'd tacked the news release with their photos to the wall of his cubicle. Three of them stared back at him:

A former high school principal with military-buzzed white hair and close-trimmed beard.

A former realtor in a lavender blazer and pretty scarf, scarlet lipstick highlighting her dazzling smile.

A one-time fitness instructor in a technicolor tank top, corded arms akimbo.

The image of the fourth looked as though it had been cropped from a photo at some sort of social event. Indeed, a disembodied hand rested on her shoulder. The woman's face was nearly in profile, a little blurred, as though she'd turned away just as the shutter opened.

The type next to the photo consisted only of her name, devoid of information about who she'd been before she'd landed in Timeless Pastures, where such distinctions were no longer supposed to matter.

'Odd,' Bert said aloud. 'Who are you, Alice Sanders?'

'Whoever she is, I hope she's the subject of your next column.'

Bert jumped, hating himself for it. By now, he should have been familiar with Madison's ability to appear at his cubicle as though she'd silently teleported from her desk to his. She held a piece of paper in her hand.

'What's that?'

'Call me psychic, but I have a feeling you don't have a column in mind. This just came in across the transom.'

Bert forced himself to take it. How bad could it be?

'A collection of Nativity scenes at an old grange hall? You've got to be kidding me. We've done this one before.'

'Oh, don't I know it. But the woman who arranges it every year is a nun . . .'

'Former nun.' Bert knew Sister Alphonse, who insisted upon being called by her former appellation, even though she'd left her order years earlier. He was willing to bet she'd been kicked out. Nuns, at least the ones in his day, had a reputation for employing rulers across knuckles and ping-pong paddles against behinds. Alphonse had probably been a champion knuckle-rapper and butt-paddler.

'. . . and she was most insistent.'

'I'm sure she was.'

'As am I. I assured her you'd be there first thing tomorrow morning. Unless you have something else?'

He didn't.

Or he did, but he wasn't about to tell Madison about it.

'Where are they staging it this year?'

She named a township in the county's northern reaches.

Bert maintained his scowl with an effort.

The card that had yielded the phone number for Hawk Boneham III – resulting in messages Boneham had declined to answer – had also listed a corporate address in the adjoining county to the north.

He'd brave scary Sister Alphonse and the Nativity scenes, then get back in his car and keep on driving. With luck, Tuesday would be the day when he finally scored an interview with Hawk Boneham.

FORTY-EIGHT

Alice folded her knees to her chest and wrapped her arms around them. The truck jounced so hard whenever it hit one of the approximately one million potholes cratering Philadelphia's streets that she'd have toppled sideways had she not been wedged so tightly between Mia and Sasha.

Johnny had pushed the bags of mulch to the sides, blocking the windows. Alice gave thanks for the darkness as a tear slid down her face. Her move into the little Timeless Pastures duplex had felt like a respite from the shabby rented rooms where she'd spent so many years underground. Now it seemed it would prove her downfall. She'd give anything to be back in one of those safely anonymous places, cockroaches and all.

The truck took another hard bounce. Pain vibrated from the steel truck bed up through Alice's spine. Sasha said what they all were thinking.

'There aren't enough painkillers in the world to deal with how I'm going to feel when I get out of here.'

'*If* we get out of here.' Alice fought to control the tremor in her voice. 'Where do you think he's taking us? Can you see?'

George twisted, shoving at a bag of mulch until a stripe of light appeared. He put his face to the opening. 'Hard to tell. I don't know the city.'

The truck sped up, taking a wide turn. 'We're going on to one of the bridges. It's blue.'

'The Ben Franklin,' Alice murmured. 'He's taking us back to New Jersey.'

They sat silent until, once again, Sasha spoke for all of them.

'Do you think he's taking us to the police?'

Alice crawled forward on her hands and knees and tried the door latch. It opened a crack.

She squirmed out of the parka. 'Here, George.'

George took his coat. 'What are you doing?'

'The first stoplight he hits, I'm out of here. It's my only chance.

You all can go with any story you like, but at least this way, you won't be caught up in my problems.'

'That's crazy. What are you going to do? Where are you going to go? You don't have any money.'

You don't have any money.

She closed her eyes and saw again the empty space where the van had been parked. Imagined the hoodlums' delight at discovering the tens of thousands of dollars she'd so painstakingly saved over the decades, the money she'd hoped would shelter her through her final years, when the constant running became impractical or impossible. What would they do with it? How – and how fast – would they blow through it?

'I made it before without any money.'

Because she had. Her legs twitched with muscle memory of the blind dash through Boston's streets after seeing her photo splashed across the newsstand's offerings, until she realized that running would only draw attention.

She'd snatched a baseball cap from an old man's head with a muttered apology as she ducked into an alley and tucked her hair up into it. Shoplifted scissors from one drugstore, hair dye from another, and transformed herself to the best of her ability in the echoey bathrooms of the central library in Copley Square.

Then, her newly shortened and darkened hair still dripping dye on to her ancient navy pea coat, she walked the short distance to the Interstate 90 on-ramp and stuck out her thumb. It was a different time. There was no cable news yet, no wall-to-wall coverage of serial killers prowling the nation's highways. Still, girls and women knew the chances they took. Memories of the Boston Strangler were only a few years old. But he'd killed women in their homes. Alice was young and healthy and strong, and at that particular moment, her fear of Bird trumped any wariness about a would-be assailant.

She got lucky. In a series of rides over the next few days, no one assaulted her, although she sometimes performed some deft verbal maneuvering to fend off the pressure for sex. One particular aging Lothario was so persistent she felt little guilt about the wallet she'd lifted from the glove compartment when he went to the restroom and she went AWOL.

None of that would work now. Even if she'd be willing to sleep with someone for cash, those days were long past.

Sasha took a firm hold of her arm. 'Please, Alice. Whatever you're thinking, stop. What if Johnny does call the cops? Or if Bird – I mean, Hawk Boneham – identifies you from the photo and tells them who you really are. What's the worst that could happen? That stuff was so far in the past. They're not going to put someone your age in prison. All those old radicals, even the ones who killed people, were rehabilitated a long time ago. Last I heard, some of them were even teaching school.'

Alice's eyes were adjusting to the truck's dim interior. She studied her friends' faces: their beautiful, innocent faces. Whatever happened, they'd go to sleep that night having, at worst, faced some uncomfortable conversations with the police and their families.

'I'm not afraid of prison,' she blurted. 'Prison would be safe.'

She inched toward the door. Sasha's grip tightened. 'What kind of nonsense are you talking now?'

'I'm afraid of Bird. He can't risk my ending up in police custody, telling them everything I know. He'll see me dead before that happens.'

Lavina Township Police Department
Transcript of interview with J.R. 'Johnny' Natale
Present: Detective Travis Meacham, Officer Sherilee Townsend

Meacham: Are you Catholic, Mr Natale?

Natale: That's an awfully personal question. Also one that doesn't seem to have any bearing on this interrogation.

Meacham: Interrogation is a pretty strong word. Remember, you consented to this interview. As for your being Catholic and this being the greater Philadelphia area, given your name, it seemed like a safe guess. Here's why I asked. Are you familiar with the concept of sins of omission and commission?

Natale: Of course.

Meacham: Up until now, we've been talking sins of omission.

Natale: How's that?

Meacham: Your repeated and inexplicable failure to notify the police.

Natale: Label it whatever you like.

Meacham: But in my long experience dealing with crime, there's a moment when things cross a line. Whatever a person's involvement has been up until then, that moment requires action. A decision. Intent.

Natale: Just what are you getting at here?

Meacham: I think we both know exactly when you met that moment. When omission turned into commission.

FORTY-NINE

It was nearly dark by the time Johnny pulled up to his house on Monday evening.

He went around to the back of the truck and lifted the gate. Four people cringed away from him.

'Hey, hey.' He stepped back and spread his hands wide. 'Everything's OK.'

'Where are we?' Alice's querulous tone broke his heart.

'We're at my house. I got the distinct impression you guys didn't want to be seen. This was the only place I could think of. Come on inside. I'll put some coffee on, get you warmed up. Oh, and I ordered pizza. Two, actually.'

He offered Alice his arm as they walked toward the house and was relieved when she took it. He hoped they'd trust him enough to explain their actions. From the way they scrambled for cover when the pizza delivery guy knocked at the door, he figured it was bad.

He waited until they'd vanquished a large margherita and a smaller pepperoni to pose his question.

'Anybody want to tell me what's going on?'

They hemmed. They hawed.

'It's complicated,' Mia finally said.

'How about if I tell you what I know – or at least, what I've guessed – and then you can fill in the blanks?'

They sat silent. He launched anyway.

'Partly because of what happened to Babs, the police erred on the side of caution when someone told them you guys weren't back from your weekend when expected.'

'Glenda,' they chorused.

'Actually, it was me. But yes, Glenda's the one who raised the alarm. Then she tells me she sees you, Sasha – or at least someone who looked a lot like you – taking stuff from Alice's house and putting it in a red van.'

'Glenda's got a wild imagination.'

'Exactly what I told myself. Until I went to check it out and saw you pumping gas into a red van at that station near the main road turnoff.'

Sasha sighed. 'Busted.'

'Then I followed the van all the way into Philadelphia, where you parked on a side street near Penn. Alice, you left first and then Sasha.'

'Very thorough. Did you take notes?' Sasha twisted one of her locs, finally free from the cap.

'And then you guys got jacked and, Alice, you came back and started crying about all of your money being gone, and for reasons I fail to understand, you refuse to let me call the police. Just how much money are we talking?'

Glenda had said she'd seen Sasha taking boxes out of Alice's house. If Sasha had taken all the boxes, he knew exactly how much money was missing. But they had no way of knowing that.

'My savings,' Alice said after a beat. She looked to the others as though seeking affirmation and took a deep breath.

'I'm on my way to Buffalo. I got a house-sitting job there and, given that my lease is up at the end of the month, figured I might as well start now.'

Mia jumped in. 'And I was going to take the van on a test drive, maybe head somewhere south, to see what I might still need before living in it full-time.'

'So, it's just like they said on the news,' Johnny said.

'What was that?' Alice's voice sharpened.

'I listened to it when I was driving back. The police said they'd gotten word that the four of you had just decided to extend your vacation. That someone had checked in with their kids—'

'One kid. My son. That was me,' Sasha said.

'—and reported that you were fine.'

Four heads bobbed in agreement. 'Exactly right.'

'Exactly bullshit!' Johnny exploded. 'Mia, you've just lost your van. Alice, you've lost all your savings. Also, three of you were assaulted at gunpoint. That means you're victims of three big-time felonies. But, *nooooo, Johnny, whatever you do, don't call the cops.* And let's not get into this whole business of Sasha dressed up like a delivery person and sneaking stuff out of Alice's house. What's going on here?'

Alice flattened her palms on the table and pushed herself up from her chair, wincing.

Johnny wasn't finished. 'I forgot to add that some of you are probably injured and that it might be a good idea that all of you get checked out at urgent care. But I'm guessing you're not going to do that, either.'

'That's right, Johnny. We're not. We appreciate everything you've done for us today. Deeply, deeply appreciate it.'

George, Sasha and Mia murmured assent.

'But we're not going to tell you what's going on. We can't. As crazy as it sounds, I need you to believe this, Johnny: it's for your own protection.'

FIFTY

The friends asked Johnny to wait in the kitchen while they huddled in his living room.

'Before this happened, we had the perfect plan,' Mia groused.

'It could still be,' Sasha said. 'Mia, you could report the van stolen. That way, you've got a prayer of a chance of getting it back. The fact that you were in Philly when it was stolen is immaterial. Last I heard, it's not illegal to be in Philly.'

'Unless you're a Cowboys fan,' George said. The laughter that followed had a hysterical edge.

Alice cut it off with a sobering reminder. 'Too risky. No matter what, we're – well, I'm – screwed, even if the guys who took it are the worst carjackers in the universe and didn't look in the boxes. If the cops recover a van full of cash, it raises all sorts of questions best not answered. And if they did take it, I've got no way of getting to New Mexico.'

'Yes, you do.' Mia dug into the front of her shirt and handed Alice a warm, slightly sweaty bundle.

Alice's eyes widened.

'It's a thousand dollars. Well, less now. I used some for the burner phones. Count it. I took some extra from your house in case of emergencies. This counts, right?'

Alice fanned the bills. 'Mia, you're a godsend. It's not much, but it'll help me get where I'm going. But it doesn't solve your problem.'

Mia put fingertips to temples and spoke slowly, puzzling it out.

'Worst-case scenario, if the van is gone forever, I've got three more weeks until I have to move out. But I'm going to assume they'll find the van without the cash – and maybe without the tires. I don't think guys like that want to be tooling around in an old beat-up van. If the police do find it, they'll check the registration and notify me – at which point, there'll be a very awkward conversation as to why I didn't report it stolen.'

'She has a point,' George interjected.

'What if I report it, but I wait a day first? That'll buy you some time. And if the police recover it and the money's still in it, well, I'll just say it's mine and thank God the guys didn't find it. Then I'll get it to you.'

Sasha rolled her eyes. 'Dreamer. For all we know, if it's in there when the van is found, the cops will take it. This is Philly, after all.'

'Johnny's still going to want an explanation,' George said.

Alice rose and headed for the kitchen. 'Let's go talk to him. I've got an idea. It's a Hail Mary, but it's all I've got.'

When they returned to the kitchen, Johnny had cleaned the table and thrown away the pizza boxes, along with a stack of old ones he'd moved aside when they arrived. The kitchen counters were free of clutter and bore the streaks of a hasty and overdue wipe-down.

'You're right, Johnny,' Mia said. 'We'll report the van missing. But I'm going to say it was stolen – that I parked it, and when I came back, it was gone. That probably doesn't make sense to you, but it makes things easier for me. For all of us.'

'It's because of Hawk,' Alice blurted. 'The owner.'

'I'm well acquainted with Hawk.'

Alice took heart at his tone.

'You're right not to like him. He's a bad guy, Johnny – as bad as they come. He's done something truly terrible. I'm the only one who could credibly testify against him. I think Babs might have told him about me, but now it doesn't matter how he found out. With my photo in the paper, he knows who I am and that I live at Timeless Pastures.'

Johnny sat still for a long moment. He rose and left the room.

'Alice, how is that going to make any sense to him?' Mia asked.

Alice shushed her. 'He's coming back.'

Johnny carried a stack of paper. He dropped it on to the newly clean table, spreading the papers out to reveal several spreadsheets, lists and a map of Timeless Pastures.

'Maybe this will help.'

FIFTY-ONE

Johnny passed the papers around. His friends studied them, brows wrinkled in the same puzzlement he himself had felt when he'd found them.

George spoke first. 'What is all this?'

'I was hoping one of you would be able to tell me. I found it in Babs' house.'

Alice's head snapped up. 'What were you doing there?'

'The police haven't been able to locate any living relatives. I thought I might find something in her house, maybe a Rolodex, that would help.' It was the best explanation he could come up with on the spot. He wasn't about to say he'd gone to Babs' house after finding the money at Alice's.

'Good heavens, Johnny.' Sasha stifled a laugh. 'Nobody uses Rolodexes anymore. We keep everything in our phones. Which reminds me – as soon as I get home, I'm going to get a new one. I'm so glad I backed mine up, and that I've got insurance on it.'

'What happened to your phone?'

'Never mind.' She waved the paper in her hands. 'These look like lists of company names. A lot look like manufacturing firms. Others are so vague I can't tell what they are.'

Johnny pushed a map of North America to the center of the table. Colored dots were scattered like confetti across it. 'I can't either. But look at this. Check out the legend. These dots correspond to the names on those lists.'

Mia leaned over the map. 'They're mostly in the South and Southwest. Except these.' Her finger landed on one of two dots in New Jersey, then went to the legend. She traced the list. 'Oh!'

'Exactly,' Johnny said.

'Exactly what?' Alice said.

Mia tapped the dot. 'This one. It's Weller Holdings. Our lord and master.'

George moved beside her. 'What about the other one?'

She ran her finger down the legend again. 'Oooh.'

She looked up, eyes wide. 'It's us. Timeless Pastures. Somehow all of these must be connected. Johnny, do you have any idea how?'

'I don't know. But Babs must have had an idea.'

'Do they all make pigeon feed?'

'Good one, Alice. But you'll be glad to know that with Babs', uh, departure, the pigeons seem to have moved on, too.'

Alice looked as though she might cry. 'It's not fair. I could finally enjoy my house, but now I can never go back to it.'

'You want to tell me why?' Johnny cocked his head. Maybe she'd finally say something about the money.

'I do not. But I want you to tell us your theory about these papers. I'm assuming you have one.'

Johnny rolled up the map and tapped the table with it. 'We all know what Babs was like. If she was looking into something with this level of detail, it meant she'd found something bad, or at least something that looked bad. Something that had to do with Timeless Pastures and all these other places. Something she was going to use against someone.'

'Who?'

'At first, I worried that it might be me. After all, I'm the manager. But I'm small potatoes. I don't have any connections anywhere else. I'd be willing to bet that someone is our very own corporate striver, Hawk Boneham.'

'We've got it!' Mia pumped her fist. 'Alice, if we've got something to hold over him, this can only help you.'

Johnny caught the warning glance Alice shot toward Mia, the slight shake of her head.

Sasha brought them all back to reality. 'Yes, we have it, whatever "it" is. But until we figure it out, it's useless.'

Mia's shoulders slumped, then straightened. 'We'd better get to work, then. We can count up the names on these lists, divide them among ourselves, and each of us can look them up, see if we can come up with something they have in common – and with whatever they might have in common with Timeless Pastures or Weller Holdings.'

'How are we supposed to do that? On these?' George held up his burner phone.

'Don't you have a computer? Or a laptop?'

'I have an iPad. But I use it mostly to watch TV.'

'Same,' Sasha admitted. 'Once I realized I could do almost anything on the phone that I could do on a computer, I got rid of my laptop. Tried to pawn it off on my granddaughters, but they laughed at me. George and I should have our new replacement phones in a couple of days. But the kind of research you're talking about is really better done on a computer. We'd go blind staring into our phones, trying to figure this out.'

'I suppose we could use library computers.' Mia immediately contradicted herself. 'Probably not a good idea to use a public system.'

'Computer or no computer, I don't dare do any of it,' Alice reminded them. 'So there's more work for everyone else.'

Johnny rapped the table again, bringing them to order. 'And you seem to have forgotten that I have a full-time job.'

'Maybe we just go with the original plan. I'll get out of here and you all go on with your lives,' Alice said.

Johnny unfurled the map and spread it flat again. 'There's got to be a way to make sense of this.' He snapped his fingers. 'I've got an idea. A crazy one.'

'This entire situation is crazy. Let's hear it.'

George pulled out a chair and offered it to Sasha. 'Let's get comfortable. This promises to be interesting.'

Johnny waited until they'd rearranged themselves around the kitchen table.

'There's this reporter—'

'Hard no,' Alice said before he'd even finished his sentence.

'Hear me out. He's come around a couple of times, first about Babs, then about the four of you missing. But he's picked up on the fact that a lot of our homes are empty, and he won't let go of it.'

He looked at Alice, sitting with arms folded across her chest. She gave him a tiny nod. 'Go on.'

'I say we give him this stuff and tell him it has something to do with the houses.'

'But we don't know that. Anyway, won't he wonder where you got it?'

'I could say it's from – what do they call it? – an anonymous source. Maybe he'll figure out what it means. Maybe he won't. But he's a reporter. Isn't this what they do? Dig into things?'

'Not well enough,' Alice muttered. 'They never even questioned Larry's death.'

Johnny's head snapped up. 'Whose?'

'I vote that we try it,' Mia said hastily. 'Maybe then you wouldn't have to leave, Alice.'

'Oh, I'll have to leave, no matter what. Let's say our wildest dreams come true, and that Babs really was on to something bad about Hawk, and this reporter figures out what it was, and he writes about it and Hawk gets into trouble – which, of course, would be a first in that bastard's long and charmed life. The other matter is still out there.'

'The other matter?' Johnny tried again.

Alice shot him down. 'Nothing you need to know, Johnny.'

'Alice, just give it a couple of days,' Mia begged.

'I don't dare. The longer I'm around, the more I put the lot of you at risk.'

Johnny, puffed up with the success of his idea about the reporter, floated an even crazier one.

'I'm not at risk. I don't know anything about what's going on with you, and that's just fine. Why don't you just stay here for a couple of days? Get some rest – it sounds as though all of you have been through a lot. Nobody knows you're here, and nobody ever comes back here. You probably couldn't tell when we drove in, but I'm nearly a half-mile back into the pines. I've got a spare room that's all yours – well, it will be once I move some junk out of it.'

'That's a great idea; we could get some things together for you, so you're not just heading out with the clothes on your back and the money Mia took,' Sasha urged her.

'Why, Johnny?'

Johnny knew Alice was asking something else entirely. *Can I trust you?*

'Call it a gut thing. I've thought that SOB Hawk was shady from the first time I laid eyes on him.'

Mia jumped up and hugged him. 'Johnny, you're a lifesaver. Alice, he's right. A couple of days after we resurface, people will have forgotten all about us. You can come up with a decent plan about where to go and set out well rested and well equipped. Johnny, can you give the rest of us a ride back to our cars?'

'Sure,' Johnny said. 'Let me just clear some things out of the spare room and find some sheets and blankets and towels for Alice.'

He practically ran up the stairs, so eager was he to escape the room before the others saw the foolish grin and the blush that suffused his face at Mia's hug.

FIFTY-TWO

Bert kicked himself for not having done more research on Hawk Boneham before the man walked into the reception room at Weller Holdings on Tuesday morning.

If he had, he might have been able to contain his surprise at the sight of the elegant elderly gentleman who stood before him, hand outstretched.

'I'm Hawk Boneham. You wanted to see me?'

Bert took the proffered hand and shook. Before he'd been exiled to the column, he'd covered his share of politicians, something that had left him well acquainted with guys who used a handshake as a power move. But Hawk took that a step further. Bert thought the man might actually have crushed a couple of metacarpals.

Hawk grinned in acknowledgment. 'As I've gotten up in years, I've learned that people tend to underestimate me. I like to disabuse them of any such notions.'

Bert flexed his fingers. 'Consider me disabused. Also, possibly permanently disabled.'

Hawk shot his cuff and took a good long look at his watch, ensuring Bert would register the Rolex.

'What's so urgent that you've seen fit to interrupt my workday? A normal person would have made an appointment.'

Just because Bert was happy to be delving into actual news again didn't mean he was inclined to put up with a condescending jerk like Hawk Boneham.

'Probably because you didn't respond to my calls or emails or texts. You know, like a normal person would have. But I'm surprised you deigned to see me today. You could have had your receptionist send me away. You must be curious why I want to talk to you.'

Hawk's lips thinned. The gamesmanship was over. 'Shoot.'

'I'm here about Timeless Pastures.'

Hawk smoothly shifted gears. 'Ah, the missing people. They've been found. Or at least they've checked in. It's only a matter of time until they're located.'

Bert made a mental note to work the word 'unctuous' into his piece. 'I know. I wrote the story.'

'Barbara Stevens, then? The police are handling that.'

'Stevenson. But I'm not here about her, either.'

Boneham flaunted the Rolex again. 'What, then?'

'Your development. Timeless Pastures.'

'I'd hardly call it mine. It's merely one of many properties under the umbrella of Weller Holdings.'

'Are you emptying all of them out? And if so, why?'

The Rolex slid back beneath the monogrammed cuff.

'Whatever are you talking about?'

'The fact that nearly two-thirds of the duplexes at Timeless Pastures are vacant, some for many months by the look of them. What sort of business model kisses all that income goodbye? What's your plan for that property?'

Hawk's expression remained unchanged, but a flush mottled his neck.

'That's the story you're working on? You understand that Weller Holdings' internal operations are none of your business. Not personally, and not legally, either. More to the point, I don't see how anything that happens – short of the unfortunate demise of one of our residents – in a small rural community is of interest to anyone outside that community.'

Any doubt Bert might have felt about the validity of his story vanished. He'd gotten under Boneham's skin. He was starting to enjoy himself.

'Oh, I think people will be very interested in the fact that over the last several months, a lot of old people – working class, mind you – have seen their lot fees raised to the point where they could no longer afford the homes in which they expected to spend their well-deserved retirement. It's a bad look, especially around Christmas time. A news story is one thing, but you know how it is when social media gets hold of something like this. They'll turn you into Scrooge. Or the Grinch. Not the sort of publicity any company loves, especially on top of a murder.'

He'd expected anger. At the very least, the sort of slick doubletalk in which the likes of Hawk Boneham were undoubtedly skilled. But the smile, quick and genuine, surprised him.

'I suppose you're right. That's a story. Not much of one, because I'm not going to comment on it, and neither is anyone else at Weller

Holdings. But I can tell you're the kind of guy who won't leave here without something in hand. So here it is. A real – what do you call it? – a scoop. One that'll make you forget all about those empty houses and those sad old people. Can you handle it?'

Give me a break, Bert thought. But he played along.

'Sure.'

'Have you ever heard of a woman named Carol Ann Kaminski?'

FIFTY-THREE

Bert drove until he could no longer see Weller Holdings' ostentatiously landscaped grounds in the rear-view mirror, then pulled off at a rest stop and went straight to the coffee shop in its food court. Normally, he avoided chains, but this was not a normal day.

He ordered an extra-large – eschewing their fancy Italian terms – with a quad shot, bought a doughy, overpriced scone, found a corner table, set up his laptop and went to work.

Hawk Boneham's tale was so fantastical as to smack of fiction. One of those nice old people on the FBI's Most Wanted List? Landing at Timeless Pastures after being successfully underground for decades?

A few clicks confirmed that at least part of what Hawk told him was true. A young woman named Carol Ann Kaminski was indeed wanted for her alleged involvement in a bombing at a Connecticut arms manufacturer in 1970 that killed two people.

He studied the image in the old news stories, then clicked over to the photos that had run with his own story when the Timeless Pastures residents were reported missing. He could see the resemblance, sort of.

Hawk Boneham said he'd spotted it immediately. 'You see, I have a personal interest in this.'

Bert had waited, itching to pull out his phone, or even a pen and notebook. But Hawk had specified that their conversation was off the record.

'The target? It was my family's company. The bomb killed my sister.' A beat. 'My *little* sister.'

Bert clicked back to the stories. Hawk had taken such pains to emphasize that his sister was younger. Yet the stories described her as the heir apparent to run the company, making much of her youth and her unusual status as a woman in the hyper-masculine world of arms manufacturing.

Photos invariably displayed the cover of a hunting magazine, where she'd posed with a brace of pheasants in one hand, shotgun broken over one arm and a bird dog beside her. Others from her years as a collegiate biathlon champion showed her flat on her stomach in the snow, skis crossed behind her, aiming a rifle at a distant target.

Bert had only spent a little while with Hawk. The man had to be in his eighties. He might have been very different in his youth. But his skin was smoother than Bert's own, lacking the roughened topography that would give testament to a life of outdoor pursuits, and his hands, despite the dominance-establishing handshake, were soft and manicured.

In short, the man looked exactly like the corporate vice president his business card proclaimed him to be.

Which was an interesting detail, but far from the most mystifying one.

Bert had posed the obvious question.

'Why tell me? Why haven't you gone to the FBI?'

Hawk's gaze held a challenge. 'You don't want this scoop? Because if you pass, I'm sure one of the big outfits will take it.'

Oh, Bert wanted it. Not only was it a helluva story, but he was already salivating at the look he'd see on Madison's face when he presented it. Yet his question lingered unanswered, and Hawk's non-response felt final. It also felt insulting. Did Hawk really think he'd jump at the shiny prize dangled before him without determining whether it was mere fool's gold?

'I'll check it out,' he said.

He told himself as he left that the look of annoyance on Hawk's face almost made up for the fact that he was leaving Weller Holdings little more enlightened than before.

FIFTY-FOUR

Bert Miller closed his laptop and looked at the clock. Almost midnight. Paper coffee cups and empty pastry wrappers littered the table around his laptop. Nearby, a lone barista pulled shots for a trucker's venti mocha with a curl of whipped cream.

In too few hours, the alarm on Bert's phone would beep, summoning him to another day in the office and another dreadful assignment. He didn't care. If he played his cards right, the tip Hawk had given him would ensure he'd never write another crapola column for Madison Baker again.

Because the story checked out.

He ordered a plain black coffee for the road, the caffeine kick lasting long enough to get home, although by the time he turned on to the street leading to his apartment complex, he was driving with the windows open to the bitter wind. Once indoors, the bedroom seemed entirely too far away.

He stripped off his clothes and hit the sofa in his underwear, not even bothering to brush his teeth first. Sleep set up a tussle with his buzzing brain, which refused to let him unsee the images that had flashed across his laptop screen during the last few hours.

The devastation wreaked upon an executive office at Gloucester Armaments, the ceiling partially collapsed, a wall torn away. An exterior shot, firefighters training their hoses on the smoking wreckage. Grim-faced paramedics wheeling away two stretchers, each burdened with a body bag. A photo of a young man with a short Afro, under a headline reading 'Suicide Ruled in Death of Arms Company Bomber.'

And photos, so many, of a much younger but still recognizable Alice Sanders – only this time with a different name, Carol Ann Kaminski – invariably with the word 'Wanted' appended.

He read her background – the Vermont dairy farm, the scholarship to Holyoke – with a mix of interest and puzzlement. In his limited experience, girls like Carol Ann Kaminski weren't rabble-rousers. They were too busy working two and three part-time jobs to cover whatever expenses the scholarship wouldn't.

Bert and his friends had worked dining-hall shifts in his years at Penn State, but even the sprawling state school had its share of kids whose parents footed all their bills and provided generous allowances besides, and who therefore had time to raise a ruckus over whatever cause was fashionable at the time. 'Performative,' he believed they called it these days. Although detonating a bomb went well beyond performance.

He'd skimmed story after story, his eyes watering as he peered at bad, blurry scans from old newspapers, their stories recreating a time of massive protests and college shutdowns and a national angst that morphed, among some, into a corrosive self-righteousness that turned deadly.

Better-known groups launched so many attacks on government, academic and corporate buildings that the bombing at Gloucester Armaments would have rated barely a footnote had it not been for the social prominence of its owners, and the fact that one of the suspects remained on the run for so long that many assumed she'd died.

The name of Hawk Boneham – both II and III – frequently featured in the early stories. Hawk II was said to be so shattered by the death of his beloved daughter that he retreated from public life and died within two years. As Gloucester Armaments' new CEO, Hawk III took a different tack, declaring he'd not rest until his sister's killer had been caught. At this point in the interviews, reporters invariably noted his shrug and grim half-smile – 'Well, you can imagine what I'd like to see happen. An eye for an eye, right? I only wish I could be the one to carry out the sentence.'

Which is what Bert kept coming back to.

If Hawk was so bent on revenge, why hadn't he taken his tip straight to the FBI? Who hides information like that?

The answer came as he tossed and turned, so obvious that it destroyed all hopes he'd get any sleep at all.

The person who has something to hide.

FIFTY-FIVE

Johnny set his alarm for five a.m. Wednesday.

He wanted to be up and showered and dressed before Alice came downstairs. They'd gotten through the previous day on sandwiches from Wawa and more pizza, but he'd determined to up his game on this next day, which very well might be Alice's last at his house. She deserved a good send-off. He had plenty of time to make a run to the grocery store for milk and juice and eggs and butter, things that his refrigerator hadn't seen for a very long time.

Not just any staples, either. Everything was organic, as was the loaf of sourdough, although it took him a moment to recover from the sticker shock. After a moment's hesitation – was Alice a vegetarian? – he added bacon, thick-cut peppered slabs that made his mouth water, and headed for the produce section to pick up avocados. He wasn't sure exactly what to do with avocados, but he figured Alice would know.

He'd hoped to surprise her with breakfast when she awoke, but the scent of coffee greeted him when he walked back into the house. Just like him, Alice was showered and dressed, in different clothes than she'd worn the day before.

'Mia got some things together for me yesterday and brought them over this morning,' she said when she saw his raised eyebrows.

'Oh, good. Food.' Mia popped in from the living room. 'Johnny, this place is so cool. It was so dark when we got here that first night I didn't realize it was a log house. I've given myself a tour. I hope you don't mind. How old is it?'

He delivered the grocery bag to Alice's outstretched arms. 'Eighteen-something. It dates to when they mined bog iron here. There was the original cabin, and at some point, they added a second story. The way I heard it, relatives of the family who built it lived in it right up to the time when whatever great-great-great-etcetera-grandchild didn't want to be stuck away in the pines, so decided to rent it out. I'm the lucky guy who got it.'

Mia took the avocados from Alice and rummaged around for a knife. 'Lucky is right. It's like a little woodsy hideaway. It's so peaceful.'

Johnny turned in surprise. He was so used to hearing the house disparaged that he looked hard at her, fearing mockery. 'Some people find it too isolated.' Namely, any woman he'd ever dated after his divorce.

'Are you kidding? I love the way the rest of the world vanishes when you're back in the pines like this. You know, I've probably driven past the turnoff to this place a thousand times and never even noticed it. Alice, I think you've landed in the perfect spot.'

'Not for long, I haven't. The sooner I'm out of here, the better for all of us. Are you sure nobody saw you come here?'

'I ran. And I cut through the woods, just like I did when I went to your house to get the money.'

Alice heaved a sigh, found a frying pan and sliced a chunk of butter into it. When it began to bubble, she cracked a half-dozen eggs into the pan. 'Plates?'

Johnny hustled to set the table, even finding three matching plates and jelly glasses.

Mia sliced the avocados on to the plates and Alice slid scrambled eggs beside them. Johnny cut the bread and toasted it, and filled the juice glasses. Mia clapped her hands. 'It's a feast!'

Johnny sneaked glances at Alice as they ate. Despite the still-damp hair and the clean clothes, dark circles raccooned her eyes. The hand lifting fork to mouth trembled almost imperceptibly. He'd hoped that after a couple of nights of good sleep, she might be more forthcoming about her apparent need to hide out; had even planned to pose a few questions.

Now he decided against it. 'I'll call that reporter as soon as I get to the office.'

'Will you call me and tell me what he says? Except—' Mia glared at her burner. 'I don't even know this thing's number. I guess the first thing I need to do is to get a new phone. Wish I'd been smart like Sasha and gotten insurance.'

'Here.' Alice delved into the pocket of her skirt and came out with a fistful of twenties. 'Buy yourself a new one. I wish I could pay for everyone's, but like you said, Sasha had insurance on hers, and I'll bet George did, too.'

Mia pushed the money back across the table. 'No way. You need that money to – well, to do whatever it is you're doing next. I'll be fine.'

'Speaking of phones.' Johnny patted his buzzing pocket. He held the phone in front of his face. 'J.R. Natale here.'

His eyes widened. 'Yes, I remember you. That would be fine. How about ten o'clock, my office? See you then.'

He put the phone away. 'Well, what do you know?'

'Who was that?'

'You know how we were going to call that reporter and feed him the papers from Babs' house?'

They nodded, twin bobbleheads.

'That was him. He wants to see me. I'd better get to the office. Mia, how about I give you a ride back?'

Her grateful smile flashed dimples he'd not noticed before.

Johnny said something he hadn't been able to say in a very long time. 'I think this is going to be a very interesting day.'

FIFTY-SIX

Mia's day promised to be anything but interesting.

She'd spent the previous one wandering her duplex with a despairing eye. Once she'd decided to join the 'van life' craze, she'd purged most of her things, selling some on eBay to raise money for retrofitting the van and giving others to local charities. In anticipation that she wouldn't live in the van forever, she'd boxed some essentials – kitchenware, seasonal clothing, her favorite books – and rented the smallest storage unit possible, barely more than a locker. The duplex felt as empty as her future.

The van was gone, Alice was about to leave for who knows where, and her own move-out date was fast approaching.

'I'm homeless,' she said aloud, trying it on for size.

She said it again. 'Homeless – ow!' She hopped on one foot to ease the pain of kicking the door in frustration.

She prided herself on her ability to persevere. After her divorce, she'd supported herself by cobbling together jobs with various health clubs and freelance personal training sessions. As retirement age approached, she'd taken a hard look at her life. The health club jobs were drying up. Their penchant for hiring taut-fleshed, shiny-haired young things pissed her off, but she couldn't blame them; despite their name, the clubs were in the image business, after all. For all her own robust health, she knew she was a broken bone away from helplessness.

The Philadelphia trinity she'd rented for years, with its precipitous stairs between its three rooms stacked atop one another, was no place for someone her age. The cheap one-story duplexes at Timeless Pastures fit her bare-bones budget; the instant camaraderie she found in the Timeless Reads group reassured her she'd made the right choice.

Then Hawk Boneham had swooped in and ruined everything. She'd never paid attention to his name when the new ownership had been announced. Now she cursed it.

Except.

It turned out that Hawk Boneham was responsible for the most excitement she'd seen in decades. One minute, she'd been packing away the last of her things and poring over maps, planning her first trip in the van. The next, she was uncovering tens of thousands of dollars, wielding a burner phone and being tossed from the van at gunpoint, all in the name of helping a friend go underground.

Underground!

It had such a thrilling ring to it. She almost wished she could go with Alice. A life on the run sounded so much more interesting than the vague wanderings she had in mind. In fact, the more she thought about it, the more she liked the idea.

Anyone looking for Alice would be looking for one person, not two. They could pose as sisters traveling together. If Alice really needed to stay out of sight, Mia could do the shopping, sign lease agreements, whatever was needed.

She'd showered and changed out of her running gear when she'd returned from Johnny's cabin after breakfast. Now, fired up by her idea to accompany Alice, she found clean tights, socks and a pullover.

Johnny's house was only a couple of miles away. She'd planned a round-trip run when she'd brought Alice her clothes, but breakfast and then Johnny's offer of a ride back had put an end to that. She shook out her arms and legs, bent and touched her toes, then alternated leg stretches.

'Plenty of gas in the tank,' she reassured herself as she set out on her second run of the day, taking it nice and easy.

A large black SUV approached, moving slowly up the main street through Timeless Pastures. Too slowly, barely more than a crawl.

Mia tensed and picked up the pace.

Like any woman runner, she'd dealt with her share of harassment, guys in cars trailing her as she ran, swerving too close and jeering and laughing as she leapt to avoid them, sometimes falling. She'd never worried about it in Timeless Pastures, mainly because she so rarely ran there, but also because what creeper seeks prey in a retirement community?

Still, she was relieved when the SUV turned off the main street into Alice's cul-de-sac.

She slowed to her normal pace and ran a few more yards. She hadn't recognized the flashy car, nor even known its make. People in Timeless Pastures generally drove American-made sedans, usually several years old. Something was off.

She looped back on her route and headed for Alice's street. Sure enough, the SUV was there, lingering in front of her duplex at the end. Mia lowered her head as she jogged past, angling her face away from the driver, but not so much that she hadn't caught the license plate numbers. She repeated them to herself as she maintained her pace, one number per footfall, over and over, playing her old pretend-spy game.

Except, given everything that had happened in the last few days, it no longer felt like pretend.

FIFTY-SEVEN

Johnny was so surprised to see Mia again when he arrived home after work on Wednesday that it took him a moment to realize his house looked . . . different.

He tried to figure it out. Everything seemed to be in its place. It's just that there was less of everything. The old magazines, newspapers and junk mail that littered surfaces had either been tossed – a plastic trash can looked to be newly full of recyclables – or relegated to neat stacks. Surfaces gleamed. Three place settings awaited on the table. Bits of bacon sizzled in a frying pan. A pot bubbled and frothed next to it.

'Water for pasta,' Alice said. 'Thank heavens you had some spaghetti in the cupboard. I'll use the eggs and bacon left from this morning to make a sort of carbonara. You don't have any Parmesan, so it won't be perfect, but it'll have to do.'

She dropped the pasta into the boiling water and turned her attention to a bowl of eggs, whisking them to a froth.

Johnny blinked. 'I hadn't planned beyond breakfast. This is more than OK. And I'm pretty sure I've got some Parmesan.'

He delved into a cupboard and came up with a green cardboard canister of powdered cheese. 'I knew it! Here.'

Alice took it from him and, holding it far from her body, crossed the kitchen to the trash can and dropped it in. 'Johnny Natale, that is not real Parmesan. With a name like yours, I'd expect you to know as much.'

'You sound like my mother,' he said.

'You should listen to her.'

'At least you've got a bottle of wine,' Mia said. 'That's a hint.' The dimples creased her cheeks again.

Johnny played his part. 'Why don't we have wine with dinner? Hope you don't mind the jelly glasses again. Mia, I'm surprised to see you.'

That hadn't come out right. 'I mean, I'm glad.' Sheesh. Was he blushing again? He poured the wine, glad it was a screw top so he wouldn't have to wrestle with a cork in front of them.

'I came back to talk over an idea with Alice. But also because I wanted to hear how it went with that reporter today.'

Alice poured a little milk into the eggs, gave them another swish and turned to listen.

'He didn't show. I got a call just before ten saying he'd gotten a last-minute assignment to cover a holiday pageant and that he had to postpone.'

Alice gave the eggs a vicious turn. 'This sets things back another day. And there's something else. Mia, tell Johnny what you saw.'

Mia started to describe the black SUV. She didn't even get to the license number, which she'd written down as soon as she'd arrived at Johnny's that afternoon.

Johnny was already nodding. 'That's Hawk. Old guy – sorry, Alice – fancy hair?'

'I didn't get a good look at him, mainly because I didn't want him to get a good look at me. I was paying attention to the car.'

'It's got to be him. He swans around in that thing like he's somebody special. Which I guess he is, given that he's a vice president. Strange that someone with that kind of responsibility has enough time to go wandering around down here as much as he does. I don't like the fact that he was snooping around without stopping in at my office.'

'Not just snooping. Mia said he was in front of my place.'

Alice drained the spaghetti in a colander, then dumped it in the frying pan, following it with the eggs, lifting the pan and rotating and shaking it, adding a little reserved pasta water.

'This is terrific,' Johnny said after the first bite. 'I'll get real Parmesan. The next time you make this, maybe you can show me how.'

Alice swirled pasta on to her fork, but only pushed it around on her plate. 'There won't be a next time. If Hawk is skulking around, I've got to get out of here.'

'You forget that he has no idea you're here. Alice, eat that. You need your strength. And this is delicious. Isn't it, Johnny?'

Johnny's mouth was too full to allow him to do anything but nod. He nodded again when Alice took a bite, then looked at her plate in surprise.

'Considering what I had to work with, it's not bad.'

They ate in silence for a few minutes. When their plates were nearly clean, Johnny ventured a suggestion.

'Why not give it one more day? You can make up a grocery list for me. I'll make a run to the store in the morning before I go to work. You can get another twenty-four hours of rest and decent chow. If I don't talk to that reporter tomorrow – well, I don't know what you've got planned next. But whatever it is, you can go ahead.'

Alice cocked her head. 'Do you hear something? Sounds like—'

Headlights raked the kitchen windows before she could finish.

Alice hit the floor.

Johnny jumped up and went to the window.

'I won't have to wait until tomorrow to talk to that reporter. He's here now.'

FIFTY-EIGHT

Bert readied his most apologetic smile.

It vanished at Johnny's greeting.

'What the hell, man? This is my home.'

Bert heard a clatter from what he guessed was the kitchen.

'I know. And I'm so sorry. But you said you had something really important for me, and I got tied up with a BS holiday story.'

Johnny blocked the doorway with his body. 'How'd you get this address? I'm not listed anywhere.'

'Oh, gee, I dunno.' Bert couldn't keep the sarcasm out of his voice. 'Maybe five minutes on Google? Where, by the way, you *are* listed, on several sites. Although I have to say, even with an address, this place isn't easy to find. I must have driven past the turnoff three times before I saw it. Ever think of putting up a street sign out along the main road?'

'Never.'

They stood silent. The sounds from the other room stopped. Finally, Johnny stepped aside and motioned him in. 'If you're that good with the internet, maybe you can make sense of what I have to show you.'

He led the way into the kitchen, where a woman in turquoise tights, a fuchsia pullover and running shoes with some obvious miles on them stood before a sink full of dishes.

'Hi. I'm Mia. Johnny's, uh, friend.' She held up a soapy hand. 'I'd offer to shake, but—' She waved instead. Bubbles danced toward him, iridescent in the bright light.

She looked familiar. The name confirmed it.

'Mia Sullivan, right? I'm Bert Miller. You're one of the people who went missing.'

She gave a throaty laugh. 'Missing. That's a good one. We were having such a good time we just decided to prolong the weekend. Our bad for not letting anyone know. Sorry we caused such a ruckus.'

Bert looked from her to Johnny and back again. She was maybe a few years older than Johnny, but those years had been kind to her in a way Johnny's had not. Although, to be fair, the man looked somehow better than the other times Bert had seen him.

What was it? A closer shave, maybe. Definitely a nicer shirt, and Johnny had taken the time to press a crease into his chinos. But it was something else, the way he held himself. The hangdog expression Bert had noted the first time they'd met, the one he knew he too often shared, was gone.

Given Mia's presence, Bert pegged it to middle-age love – although closer to old age, in this case. He knew he should find it ridiculous even as he resolved, when he finally got home that night, to go back to the dating apps.

'What did you want to talk with me about?'

Johnny gestured to a stack of papers at one end of the table. 'We're hoping you can make heads or tails of these.'

Bert picked one up. 'What are they?'

'They seem to be lists of businesses. I don't know how or if they're related, but Weller Holdings – that's the company that bought us last year – is one of them, and along with Timeless Pastures, it's the only one in this area. The rest are mostly in the South, and some in the Midwest.'

'Where'd you get them?'

'Let's just say it was an anonymous source.'

'That's my line,' Bert said. But he pulled the papers toward him. 'Do you mind if I take these home with me? I can look through them there. But I'm just curious: What makes you think they have any significance?'

Bert saw Johnny's hesitation, caught his glance toward Mia.

She rinsed her hands, dried them and said, 'The source thought it was important. Unfortunately, sh— uh, they didn't say why, and now we can't reach them. But your stories mentioned all the empty houses in Timeless Pastures. Maybe these have something to do with that.'

So the source was a woman, Bert thought. Not that he was tempted to pursue that angle. It didn't seem important. He'd shuffled through the papers as they talked and noted an impressive level of detail. If there was a paper trail, the source wouldn't matter.

Anyway, a more urgent matter had driven him to scour the internet for Natale's address and then to take the fraught step of calling on him there.

'I'll look into it. But in the meantime, I know you contacted me first, but there's something I wanted to ask you about.'

Another long glance between Johnny and Mia. They waited, radiating tension.

'One of the missing people. Well, not-missing.' He tossed Mia a smile. She didn't return it.

'She was on the trip with you, Ms Sullivan. Alice Sanders.'

'What about her?' Mia's voice shook.

'It's been suggested to me, by a *source*' – because two could play that game – 'that Alice Sanders' real name is Carol Ann Kaminski.'

FIFTY-NINE

A grate in the floor of Johnny's second-floor guest bedroom, dating to the days when homes relied on heat from the downstairs rooms to warm those above them, opened directly into the kitchen.

Alice lay flat on the wide pine floorboards, listening hard, barely daring to breathe.

She'd rushed for the stairs as soon as Mia announced the reporter's presence. She peered through the grate, watching in admiration as Mia swept the damning third place setting into the sink along with the other dishes, drowning the evidence in sudsy water just as Bert Miller walked into the kitchen.

The sound of her own name drifted up from the grate.

'No, no, no, no, no,' she moaned silently. She'd have to leave that very night, fleeing with the few clothes Mia had brought her, going – where? She had no idea, just like that first time so many years ago in Boston.

But it had been different then. Easier. Closed-circuit cameras were nonexistent, along with tracker-enabled cellphones and electronic transactions for everything. The cash Mia had returned to her wouldn't last long.

Perhaps most consequential, she was older by decades. *Old.*

She'd disparaged the idea of traveling with Mia in the van. Now she wished it were an option. Hitchhiking would be out of the question, and even though she'd spoken bravely to her friends about working her old waitressing jobs, nobody would hire a seventy-six-year-old waitress, or even a dishwasher. Maybe she could get George and Sasha to give her a ride to a different city, someplace not too far away, like Baltimore, with a network of homeless shelters.

She'd resorted to them sometimes in her younger years. They'd been scary then and she couldn't imagine they'd improved.

But leaning on George and Sasha would make them accessories if she were ever caught. And if the last few moments reviewing her options had revealed anything, it was that she almost surely would be caught.

Raised voices below refocused her attention.

'How can you write a story about this? You don't even know it's her.' For whatever reason, Johnny appeared to be firmly on her side.

'I don't, but the FBI will. I would never write a story just on the say-so of an anonymous source' – Bert waved the papers in his hand – 'but this one will be easy enough to verify.'

'You can't!' Mia's voice was shrill. Mistake. Even with the grille partially obscuring her view, Alice could see the renewed determination in Bert's face.

'According to my research, she's been on the Most Wanted List longer than anyone else. It's a huge story.'

Alice was on her feet and halfway down the stairs before she stopped to think. But just for a second. After all these years, she wasn't about to go down without a fight.

Three faces registered varying degrees of shock as she slammed through the kitchen door.

'Alice, no.'

Alice ignored Mia. She strode up to Bert.

'You want a huge story? If you can wait a bit, you'll have one way bigger – and it'll be on the record.'

SIXTY

It was all Bert could do not to pull out his phone and snap a photo or turn on the recording app.

But the woman before him had made it clear that she wasn't on the record yet, and this was no time for him to abandon principle. He collected himself as best as he could and attempted irony.

'Carol Ann Kaminski, I presume?'

'Who?' said Johnny.

'That woman is long gone. For all practical purposes, Hawk Boneham killed her.'

'That's going to take an explanation.'

Alice, Carol Ann, whoever she was, half smiled. 'You'd better sit down. We probably all should. I think Johnny has another bottle of wine somewhere. You can bet it's been around awhile, although I'm not sure it's the kind that improves with age.'

'Uh, no thanks. Not while I'm working.' Bert had downed the occasional beer while on assignment, but something of this magnitude was different.

By the time Alice finished speaking, he was glad he'd refused the wine. His mind reeled. Across the table, Johnny's mouth hung open, the embodiment of how Bert himself felt.

'Let me get this straight. You're telling me that Hawk Boneham is the person behind the bombing at Gloucester Armaments?'

'Yes.'

'His family's company?'

'At the time, I had no idea he had any connection. All he told me about his family was that they were estranged.'

'Estranged? But all the stories I read said he was distraught over his sister's death.'

'Really?' Alice, so icily calm until that moment, jerked in surprise. 'I never read any of those stories, except for the very first ones. I clipped the photos of the victims from them. Otherwise, I was afraid to go near anything to do with the bombing.'

'From what I read, the sister seemed something of a wunderkind. Trained her own bird dogs, started winning field trials as a teenager.

Went into the family business straight out of Yale. She was developing something – oh, I can't remember all the details – but something like a hand-held submachine gun.'

'Ah. That makes sense. Hawk said he wanted to target this company because it was providing weapons of war.'

'But to kill his own sister . . .'

'Well.' Alice pursed her lips. 'He *said* he had no way of knowing she'd be working that late. Anyway, I'm sure he'd say that, technically, he didn't kill her. He got Larry to actually plant the bomb. Which is pretty smart, now that I think about it, and I've had plenty of time to think in these last decades. Theoretically, Hawk could have gotten into the corporate offices any time he wanted, estrangement or no. But this way, if we got caught, he could say honestly that he didn't plant the bomb.'

'But he made it. With your help.'

She held his gaze. 'I didn't make the thing. I didn't need to. Instructions were floating all over the place in the circles we ran in. But I had access in my college labs to the chemicals he needed. That's as far as it went. So, yes, guilty as charged.'

'Just to be specific, guilty of two deaths.'

'Three. I count Larry as a victim. And, unlike the other two, I think Hawk killed Larry directly. I think he was afraid Larry might crack and implicate us, if he hadn't already. And if he finds me, I'm sure he wouldn't hesitate to do the same. Not just me, but whoever might be with me. I'll give you an exclusive interview. But not until you've gotten the evidence that will rightfully implicate Hawk. You've got twenty-four hours.'

She paused. Gave it time to sink in.

One.

Two.

Three.

'Do you want the story?'

SIXTY-ONE

Sasha asked George to drop her off a couple of blocks from her home on Wednesday evening. They'd spent the two nights since arriving home together, but now, after a dinner out, she wanted some time to herself to think over the events of the last few days.

'I need a walk to clear my head.' As he opened his mouth to object, she pointed to the clear starlit sky and then to the dry sidewalks. 'The sun was out today. It melted all the ice. I'll be fine. See you later tomorrow?'

She blew him a kiss and laughed when he mimed catching it, even as she looked around to make sure no one had caught their moment of silliness. But who was left to see? That somber thought turned her walk into a trudge, one that stopped altogether when she approached her duplex and saw a strange car next to her own in the driveway.

A young man waited on her doorstep, arms folded, either against the cold or to hold in the emotional storm threatening to break.

'Gerald? What in the world?'

'Mama, just open this door so we can get inside and warm up.'

She fumbled with the lock, her hands shaking. Gerald – he'd never been Gerry – marched straight into the kitchen, found the coffee and got a pot going.

'You got something to eat in here? None of that healthy stuff. I mean real food. Something that'll hold us for the conversation we're about to have.'

Sasha didn't want any part of that conversation, and especially not of the role reversal taking place, Gerald barking orders and her scurrying to comply. Yet she was already opening the freezer, pulling out the coffee cake she'd baked a week earlier and frozen in sections for occasions just like this one.

Well, not just like this one. She'd had in mind other occasions – breakfast in the morning with George, who had a sweet tooth, or for their final Timeless Reads gathering. She put the cake in the microwave to defrost and set the table with dessert plates, mugs and cream and sugar for their coffee. Anything to postpone whatever was about to come next.

The microwave beeped. Gerald poured coffee. 'Sit.'

She sat. 'OK. Let me have it.'

She'd expected a torrent of words. But when Gerald opened his mouth, nothing came out. He shook his head, closed his mouth and shook his head again.

'I don't even know where to begin,' he said finally. 'First, you nearly give me a heart attack when you go missing. Mama, I thought you might be dead.' Moisture filmed his eyes.

Sasha reached for his hand. Gerald snatched it away.

'And then I find you've run off with some White man.'

'We didn't run off. We went for a long weekend with our friends.'

Sasha noticed with some satisfaction Gerald's small 'mmm' as he took a bite of the cake. At least her son thought she'd gotten something right.

'You didn't tell me you were going away. You never said a word to me about this White man.'

Sasha studied the cake – maybe a touch more cinnamon in the crumb topping next time, she thought – long enough to let her irritation come to a head.

'That's funny. As an adult, it never occurred to me to ask your permission to take a vacation. Or whom to date.'

'It's not that. Tanya and I, we're worried about you. You're out of this house in a few weeks. You know how I've said you're welcome to stay with us while you figure out your situation? Forget temporary. We want you to stay with us all the time. We can turn the garage into a little apartment – a space all your own. The girls are almost teenagers. In just a few years, they'll be out of the house. How great would it be for them – and for you, too – to have their Mom-mom close during that time?'

The cake went dry in Sasha's mouth. A few months ago, she'd have welcomed such an offer. That was pre-George. Now?

'When you talk about a little apartment, I take it you mean so little that it can only accommodate one person.'

Gerald's fork fell from his hand. 'You wouldn't move that man in with us. Are you crazy? You see why we're so worried about you. When was the last time you saw your doctor?'

'That's the second time you've insinuated I'm crazy. I'm old, but

I'm not crazy. And I'd better not even hear the word Alzheimer's come out of your mouth.'

Gerald drew himself up. 'I flew here by myself, but Tanya is driving up this weekend. We can rent a U-Haul and help you pack up the house and bring you back with us. We'll put your things in storage until the apartment is finished. Until then, the girls can bunk together, and you can have Leesa's room.'

When Gerald was little, he'd once told his mother he knew the signs that told him just how much trouble he was in. If Sasha yelled, Gerald knew he'd get off easy. But when Sasha got quiet, 'Oooh, watch out. I'd be lucky to get away with being grounded.'

So she pitched her voice so low that Gerald had to lean across the table to hear.

'How dare you make decisions for me as though I were a child? I am a grown-ass human, as are you. I'd remind you to give me the same respect you seem to feel you deserve. Which, right now, I'm not sure you do.'

A few minutes after Gerald stormed out of the house, Sasha left, too. Not to go to George. She wasn't ready to discuss Gerald's reaction with him, and she had to sort out for herself her own impulsive insinuation that she might want to live with him. But she needed her friends, badly.

As crazy – ugh, that word – as the last few days had been, she'd felt a sense of purpose she hadn't realized she'd missed. Maybe, by helping Alice with whatever next steps she'd decided upon, she could get it back.

SIXTY-TWO

Headlights, again.

Alice grabbed her coat.

'He's back already?' Johnny went to the window.

'What if it's not him? What if he went to the cops?' Even before the words left her mouth, Alice headed for the back door.

'Wait,' Johnny called after her. 'It's not him and it's not the cops. It's OK.'

He flung open the front door.

Alice, still pale and shaken, returned to the kitchen. Johnny let the curtain fall. Mia sagged in relief. George blew out his breath.

'George? What are you doing here?' Sasha stood in the doorway.

He shrugged. 'I got home and didn't know what to do with myself. So I came over here to see if there was any news. I parked around back, which you might want to do also. What brings you here?'

'Same. I'll go move my car.'

She started for the car, then turned back. 'Have I missed anything?'

'Darned if I know. I just got here a few minutes ago.'

Johnny pulled out some chairs. 'Settle in. It's a bit of a wild ride. I guess you already know most of it, but I'm still trying to digest it.'

Alice went over everything – Bert Miller's surprise appearance, and the even bigger surprise that he knew about her previous identity. The fact that Hawk now knew her as a Timeless Pastures resident. Her offer to give Bert an exclusive interview if he'd help her find details that would also implicate Hawk.

'And you trust him?'

Did she? It was a gamble. But then, hadn't her entire life since 1970 been a gamble? Every single decision – which shabby rooming house to live in, which under-the-table job to take – had been a risk. Then she'd taken the biggest risk of all, settling in Timeless Pastures for longer than she'd ever lived anywhere, slowly spending down her cash reserves.

But it had been so wonderful to sleep without being jolted awake by sirens, to have her own washer and dryer instead of having to use coin-op units in a dank basement, to sit idle on her patio with nothing to do but gaze into the stillness of the pines. She'd fallen victim to that false sense of security, loving it so much that it drove her to confront Babs about the annoyance – and really, that's all it had been – of the pigeons. Those damn birds had led to her imminent downfall.

'I really don't have a choice. But here's the thing.'

She'd rehearsed what she was going to say next, hoping she could get through it without crying. She'd realized, as she'd thought it through, that the hardest thing about going on the run again wouldn't be the omnipresent electronic surveillance, or the labor-intensive jobs, or the lack of cash.

It would be the loss of her friends, these people she'd come to cherish after so many years on her own.

She looked at them in turn, at Sasha and George and Mia and even Johnny, memorizing their faces.

'Alice? Are you all right?' Mia reached across the table and took her hand.

Alice squeezed it, then gently freed herself.

'I've involved all of you way too deeply in troubles of my own making.' She held up her hand as Sasha started to object.

'Hear me out. Given what you now know, you face legal problems. Serious ones. If and when they catch up to me, I'm going to swear, truthfully, that you urged me early and often to go to the police. That might help a little, but the fact that you chose not to turn me in will weigh against you. In fact, if you decide to go to the cops now, I wouldn't blame you.'

Four heads gave decisive shakes.

Alice blinked hard, reminding herself that she'd vowed not to cry.

'Then there's Hawk. I can't say this too many times. The man is dangerous. It's one thing for my actions to put you in legal danger, but if he hurt any of you . . .'

And just like that, the waterworks flowed.

Mia and Sasha came around the table and folded her into a hug. Johnny offered a paper towel in lieu of a tissue.

George frowned, produced a handkerchief and cleared his throat. 'As you might imagine, I've been giving this some thought. Even before you brought up this new business with the reporter, I had some ideas. His involvement will make things easier.'

Alice crumpled the sodden paper towel and blew her nose in the handkerchief.

'What things?'

'How we can work together to get the goods on Hawk Boneham.'

Lavina Township Police Department
Transcript of interview with George Sterling
Present: Detective Travis Meacham, Officer Sherilee Townsend

Meacham: By their very repeat nature, your actions qualify as obstructing an investigation. But did you have any idea how serious it was? Sheltering a fugitive is a felony and not just any felony. In this case, it's a federal crime. The feds don't play. There's no wiggle room in their sentencing guidelines.

Sterling: You call it obstructing an investigation. That's not how I see it.

Meacham: Then please tell me just how you see it. Enlighten me.

Townsend: Detective Meacham . . .

Meacham: These guys have been jerking us around for hours. Excuse me if I'm just a little skeptical of what's about to come out of Mr Sterling's mouth.

Sterling: We were trying to help you.

Meacham: Come again? Because I don't think I heard right. You're looking at me with a straight face.

Sterling: We were trying to get the evidence that would help you convict the real perpetrator.

Meacham: Now I've heard everything.

SIXTY-THREE

George waved an envelope covered with scrawls.

'I've outlined a few things. First, if the reporter figures out what those lists and maps mean, that could be really helpful.'

'How?'

'Because it gives us a two-pronged plan of attack if Hawk is involved in anything illegal, or even just nefarious, on that front. Even if we can't prove he's a murderer, evidence – or at least strong suspicions – of shady business dealings would give us some leverage.'

Sasha had looked so distraught when he'd first arrived at Johnny's that he'd been worried. Now, she patted his arm and beamed at him. 'Good thinking.'

George ran his finger down the envelope. 'To my mind, though, the key to all of this is Larry. That's his name, right? Your partner in the original, uh, incident?'

'You can call it a bombing, George. That's what it was. And yes, that's his name. But Larry's dead.'

'Allegedly by suicide. But you don't believe that.'

Alice winced. 'He had a wife and a baby. I never even met him until after the bombing, but Hawk said he talked about that little girl all the time. She never got to know him. It doesn't seem that someone like that would kill himself.'

George put a pen to the envelope, then shook it and tried again. 'Johnny, do you have a pen that actually writes? This one is dry.'

Johnny pulled open a drawer filled with empty envelopes, rubber bands, paper clips and the like. He found a pen and gave it to George, who resumed his questioning.

'Any idea where they are?'

'None. But they're probably easy enough to find. He had an unusual last name. It was in the stories. Raynolds, with an "a" instead of an "e" the way it's usually spelled.'

'Oh, that's good. That's very good.' George wrote it down. 'Someone needs to find Mrs Raynolds, ASAP.'

'The reporter,' Johnny suggested.

'No.'

George turned to Sasha, eyebrows raised.

'Think about it. That poor woman. Left a widow with a new baby and her husband branded a murderous radical. She probably got hounded to death by the press at the time. Let's hope she had a strong family that could help her through something like that. But no matter what, she had to be traumatized. Probably still is, even after all these years – if she's still alive. What happens if a White reporter shows up on her doorstep and wants her to open up those wounds again?'

'I should have thought of that.' George lay down his pen. 'But she's the only one who could help us.'

'Agreed,' Alice said. 'I doubt she thinks Larry killed himself, either. And maybe he told her something at the time that could help tie Hawk to the bombing. If I didn't have to stay out of sight, I'd go see her myself.'

'I don't believe you people.' Sasha's tone was light, but George felt the sting.

'Here I sit, right in front of you. Just two days ago, you were happy for me to pose as your faux delivery person. Now I'm suddenly useless?'

'She's not wrong,' Alice said.

'I'll go with you,' said George. And, at her look, 'I'll stay in the car. Or you can drop me off somewhere nearby when you go to talk with her.'

Mia raised her hand. 'Isn't there anything I can do?'

'I was getting to that,' George said. 'Even if this place is off the beaten path, I don't think it's a good idea for all of us to be driving back and forth to Johnny's house. If Hawk is cruising the neighborhood, he might be keeping an eye on us. Mia, you know how to sneak through the pines to get here. You can be our conduit to Alice. I know we're all getting new phones, but I think it's safer to keep using these burners, and even better to talk in person whenever possible.'

Sasha beamed approval.

'All the times I teased you about those crime shows of yours? I take it all back. You're turning into a first-rate criminal.'

SIXTY-FOUR

Sasha did some searching online Thursday morning before she gave up and called Bert Miller for help locating Mary Raynolds.

He got back to her five minutes later with an address in New Haven, Connecticut, a four-hour drive from Timeless Pastures. She and George were on the road by noon.

Sasha wasted half the drive with nervous small talk before finally saying, as casually as she could manage, 'By the way, my son stopped by yesterday.'

George, the most careful of drivers, took his eyes off the road for longer than was safe.

'George!'

'Right. Sorry.' He aligned the car. 'You mean, he's here now? Staying in your house? Wish you'd introduced me before we left. Will I be able to meet him when we get back? You know, we could cancel the hotel reservation and come back tonight after you've talked with Mrs Raynolds – if she's even there.'

They'd planned to spend the night in New Haven, exploring the Yale campus and also driving past the arms factory that had been the target of that long-ago bomb.

'No. Keep the reservation. He left.'

A horn blared. 'George, the road!'

George waved an apology to the other driver. 'He came all the way up from Georgia and turned around and left again?'

Sasha, who'd spent hours bracing herself for the conversation, wished she'd kept her mouth shut.

'Not exactly. He's in a motel somewhere nearby. It's complicated.'

'Because I'm White.'

'Well . . . yes.'

'Sounds pretty straightforward.'

'He wants me to move to Atlanta. They want to convert the garage into an apartment for me. He said Tanya – that's his wife – is driving up this weekend so they can rent a U-Haul and move my stuff out of my house and then bring me back with them.'

She grabbed his shoulder. '*George!* Maybe I'd better drive.'

George hit the turn signal and pulled off at a rest area.

'Let's get some bad coffee and worse food and talk this through.'

Over some truly vile coffee and not-half-bad cinnamon-sugar soft pretzels, Sasha offered George as much of an explanation as she could muster.

'He's very protective.' Years of pent-up frustration spilled forth. 'He was so worried about me when his father and I split. He was sure I'd fall apart on my own. Never even gave me credit for leaving the big firm and starting my own realty business in middle age. Maybe my place in Timeless Pastures is nothing fancy – practically a shack compared to that McMansion of theirs in Atlanta – but I've been happy there.'

'He loves you. Count your blessings.'

She knew he had a son. That they were estranged. That drugs and alcohol were issues. And that they'd last seen one another at George's wife's funeral, when the son had shown up drunk. They'd not spoken since.

George's voice had radiated such pain when he'd told her those bare-bones details that she'd never pushed for more. She'd wondered, when headlines declared them missing, if his son might try to get in touch, but that didn't seem to have happened.

'What are you going to do? I thought you were thinking about moving there.'

They'd never spoken in detail about their respective plans after their Timeless Pastures departure, swerving away from the subject whenever it arose.

'I was. It's one thing to think about it. Another to be forced into it. So help me, if they show up on my doorstep with a U-Haul . . .' She looked at the remains of the pretzel in front of her. 'And now I'm stress-eating.'

'Here's an idea,' George said. 'Let them show up with that U-Haul. They'll find me waiting with you.'

Despite herself, a laugh burst free. 'It would be worth it, just to see the looks on their faces.'

'Then it's settled.'

Sasha wolfed down the last of the pretzel. 'No, it's not. Not even close.'

'Of course it isn't. Just this one little piece of it. We'll figure out the rest later. For now, let's go find Mrs Raynolds.'

The woman who answered the door in the two-story brick rowhouse in New Haven was so tiny Sasha had to resist the impulse to stoop when she introduced herself.

'My name is Sasha Coverdale. I'm looking for Mrs Mary Raynolds.'

'You can stop looking because you've found her.' The woman cackled, pleased with her rejoinder. She grew serious. 'And who would you be?'

Oh dear. Sasha looked closer, took in the deep wrinkles, the slight hunch, the trembling hands. Maybe they were too late. If Mary Raynolds couldn't even remember her name from seconds earlier, how could they expect her to recall decades-old details?

'I'm Sasha Coverdale,' she said again.

'No, no.' Mary Raynolds waved her words away. 'I got that part. I suppose I should have said *why* are you? Not who. What do you want with me?'

Deep folds nearly obscured her eyes, but they gleamed curiosity. Sasha had thought to soft-pedal her reason for the visit. Instead, she honored the woman's undimmed intelligence.

'I'm here about your former husband, Larry. Someone who knew him, a friend of mine, doesn't believe he killed himself. She thinks he was murdered.'

The woman gasped and grabbed the doorjamb.

Sasha reached for her, fearing she might fall.

But Mary Raynolds shook her off.

'I suppose you'd better come in.'

SIXTY-FIVE

Bert looked at the map before him, at the red lines he'd drawn from each dot, all of them leading to a single destination, and savored a sensation he'd nearly forgotten.

Triumph.

His phone sounded. 'Madison Baker' flashed on the screen – which also displayed the time.

Ten a.m.

He groaned. Had he really been up all night? At least he sounded genuinely awful when he croaked his hello.

'Are you planning on showing up today? Don's still isolating because now his kids have Covid, too, and I need you to cover the Freeholders meeting for him. You're always pushing for a news story. Now you've got one.'

Bert had covered the Freeholders – New Jersey's equivalent of county commissioners – in his younger days, an experience he likened to root canal, only marginally less painful than the columns he was forced to write.

Bert turned his head away and coughed. 'I'm sorry. I turned off my alarm after I took the test. What day is it?'

'You've got to be kidding me. It's Thursday. And it's after ten. What test?'

'Ten? In the morning?'

'Of course ten in the morning. What test?'

'Geez. I've been out since around seven last night. This thing is brutal. I can't believe I made it all the way through the pandemic without getting it.'

'*What test?*'

'Oh, sorry. Looks like Don isn't the only one.'

He held the phone away from his ear at the string of expletives that followed.

'Gotta go, Madison. Think I'm about to hurl.'

Did people with Covid throw up? It didn't matter. The last thing he heard before he clicked off was Madison, calling across the newsroom to the intern, who apparently was the only person left standing.

'This day just got better,' he chuckled.

By now, he had Johnny Natale's number on speed dial. He punched the button. It was about to get better still.

Bert spread the map across Johnny's desk and tapped the dots in the South and Midwest.

'All of these? They're either old mobile-home parks or developments of manufactured homes, just like Timeless Pastures.'

He moved a finger west, out into Colorado, Wyoming, Montana. Babs had marked dots in red. Bert had added a few blue ones.

'Whoever your source is, they didn't find everything. There are even more. Not as many, just a handful.'

Johnny shivered. 'Man. I'd hate to be living in a trailer in Montana in the winter.'

'They're called mobile homes now,' Bert said. 'But I get what you're saying. I feel the same way about all these in the South. They must heat up like crazy, air conditioning or no.'

'And they all connect somehow? Here?' Johnny put his finger on one of the two dots in New Jersey, north of Timeless Pastures. Bert had drawn a star beside it.

'You got it. Weller Holdings isn't just part of a random grouping. It's the one thing all of them have in common.'

Johnny smoothed his hand over the map. 'What do those SOBs want with a bunch of trailer parks?'

'Mobile-home communities. You think what's been happening at Timeless Pastures is bad? Wait till you hear what's going on in those places.'

Lavina Township Police Department
Transcript of interview with Mary Raynolds
Present: Detective Travis Meacham, Officer Sherilee Townsend

Townsend: Could you please state your full name and age?

Raynolds: Mary Helen Raynolds. I'm eighty-one.

Townsend: Mrs Raynolds, I so appreciate you traveling all the way down here and making yourself available for our questions on what must be a painful topic. I know your interactions with law enforcement have not always been pleasant.

Raynolds: That's an understatement. But you said you're looking into those people who came to my house. They turned my head all around, claiming to be interested in my Larry, trying to clear his name. I want to know: Were they bad people? Just trying to use me for their own ends?

Townsend: I think we can safely surmise they saw you as useful, yes. But were they bad? That's what we're trying to figure out.

Raynolds: And?

Townsend: Still working on it.

SIXTY-SIX

Mary Raynolds collected herself enough to offer Sasha a cup of coffee and some chocolate-dipped lace cookies.

She shook her head when Sasha pushed the plate away. 'Don't tell me you're one of those young women who watches everything you put in your mouth. Nice healthy girl like you. You shake your head at me again and I'm gonna put out a scoop of ice cream to go with those cookies.'

Sasha tamped down the memory of the butter-soaked pretzel at the rest stop. 'In that case, I would love some. But only if you sit down and have some with me.'

Mary Raynolds took a cookie for herself and joined Sasha at the dining-room table, whose cherrywood surface gleamed so brightly Sasha surmised it was only used for holidays and company. Her eyes strayed to the sideboard, to the faded color photo of a young man in Army fatigues and helmet, a rifle slung over his shoulder.

Mary followed her gaze. 'You knew my Larry?'

'No, ma'am. A friend of mine did. These cookies are delicious.' They were, the chocolate complementing their toffee flavor, perfect with the strong coffee.

'What friend?'

'Someone who knew him back in the day.' Sasha needed to steer her away from her tenuous connection to Larry. 'That photo. It's him, then.'

'From Vietnam. I didn't love that photo. Still don't. I think it's undignified. But he wouldn't let me frame the one of him in his dress uniform. Said all that patriotic stuff, wrapped up in a pretty uniform, was a lie. Said the only thing true about the Army was what happened to him in Vietnam. He got drafted. We'd just been married a few months. I was so afraid he was gone forever. And in a sense, he was. When he came back, he was somebody else.'

'How do you mean?'

Sasha dreaded the answer. Even though this was exactly why she'd come, she was inviting a tale, and it wouldn't be a good one.

Heavy drapes hung at the windows, darkening the room and

muffling sounds from the outside world. A mantel clock ticked. A second hand twitched its way around the clockface.

Mary spoke in short, staccato sentences, in metronomic rhythm with the ticking.

'He came back angry. As angry as I'd ever seen a person. He'd seen things there. Terrible things. He said the war was evil. Said it had to be stopped. Took up with those hippies. Those White kids. The ones with college deferments.'

She twisted her hands together.

Sasha had never thought of herself as claustrophobic. Now she longed to fling open the curtains, hit a light switch, stop the clock.

Mary's narrative took on speed. 'I was so scared when he went. So happy when he came back alive. You know what I came to think?' The cookie sat untouched on her plate.

'No, ma'am.'

'That it would've been better if he'd died over there. At least then I'd have had the big military funeral. Gotten a flag. He'd have been a hero. Well, maybe not. So many boys were dying over there every day that they stopped making a big deal over each and every one. But at least it was looked at as some sort of honor. At the time, it made me mad. Like there was anything honorable about getting killed in that useless war. But it would have been better than having everybody see my husband as a murderer. Not just any murderer, but one of those radicals.'

She picked up the cookie and snapped it in two. Crumbs littered the table.

'Turns out getting mixed up with them was worse than anything that could have happened to him in Vietnam.'

Lavina Township Police Department
Transcript of interview with Mia Sullivan
Present: Detective Travis Meacham, Officer Sherilee Townsend

Townsend: Sounds as though you were using the loss of your van as an excuse to continue the, ah, course of action your friends had chosen. That you went along with them because you didn't feel you had much choice.

Sullivan: Officer Townsend, do I look to you like a woman who doesn't know her own mind?

Townsend: That wasn't what I was implying.

Sullivan: Sure sounded like it.

Meacham: It kind of did, Sherilee.

Townsend: I didn't ask your opinion, Detective Meacham. And no, Ms Sullivan, I did not mean to imply that.

Sullivan: Then what are you saying?

Townsend: That the return of your van would have allowed you, as a woman who knows her own mind, to walk away – well, drive away – from an extremely ill-advised path.

Sullivan: I'm confused.

Townsend: About?

Sullivan: The fact that, after the hours we've spent in this room, you think of me as the kind of person who'd walk away from the people she loves. Is that your own MO, Officer Townsend?

Townsend: I'm not the one being questioned here.

Meacham: Kind of sounds like you are, Sherilee.

Townsend: We're starting to spend more time in time-outs than in interviews. That said, I'm ready for another. But for the record, no, that is not my MO.

SIXTY-SEVEN

Two notifications caught Mia's eye when she opened her email Thursday morning.

One from the Philadelphia Police Department reporting her van had been located the same day it had been stolen.

And the second from the Philadelphia Parking Authority.

She clicked on it to find a bill for – 'Five hundred and fifty dollars! What the . . .?'

The single sheet of paper was helpfully itemized.

Three hundred dollars for the abandoned vehicle. 'But it was stolen!' she yelled at her screen.

One hundred and seventy-five dollars for the tow fee.

Twenty-five dollars per day for storage in the impound lot.

That was the bad news. It got worse when she couldn't reach Johnny on his cellphone, hoping for a ride to the Parking Authority lot. She started to try Sasha, but remembered she and George had gone to Connecticut. She took out her new cellphone and added another hundred dollars to her total for an Uber across the river, telling herself the cumulative cost was worth it if it meant getting her van back.

The Uber driver, noting her destination, tried to disabuse her of that notion.

'Those car thieves, they usually take 'em straight to chop shops. You'll be lucky if there's anything left but the chassis' – a gloomy view that figured into the tip she left.

Inside, a woman at a counter protected by a thick, scarred Plexiglass barrier shot her a judgmental glare.

'We don't take kindly to people from New Jersey and Delaware and the suburbs who drive into Philly to abandon their junkers. At least you showed up to retrieve it. That's more than most do.'

'I didn't—'

Mia stopped herself from saying she hadn't abandoned the van. As if she ever would! But she didn't want to invite any questions about the circumstances under which it was stolen – although she very much doubted the Parking Authority cared.

'You're absolutely right,' she said. 'I felt bad about it later. That's why I'm here now.'

'Uh-huh. Not because of how your fine goes up every day it sits here.'

Mia tried a smile and a shrug – 'You got me' – earning only another sneer.

She slid her credit card through a slot in the Plexiglass, cringing as a machine beeped acknowledgment of the amount.

The woman called to someone across the room and gave him a slip with some numbers on it. 'Can you take her to her vehicle?'

The man set off with long strides, not waiting for Mia to catch up. She trotted behind him. 'Where'd you find my van?'

He looked at the paperwork in his hand and named an address not far from the train station. The carjackers had likely abandoned it quickly. Mia let herself hope, taking further encouragement from the fact that most of the cars in the lot, while in various states of disrepair, seemed intact.

She whooped and punched him in the arm when she saw the van at the far end of one of the rows.

'There it is! And it looks OK!'

'It does?' The clerk rubbed his arm and gave her some side-eye. 'Somebody bothered to steal that? No wonder they threw it back.'

She walked all around it, running a hand along its dusty panels, checking the tires.

'I'll wait here to make sure it starts,' the clerk said.

She climbed in the front seat, made a face against the reek of weed, turned the key and gave him a thumbs-up. 'There's even some gas left.'

She willed herself not to speed from the lot. Nor to park on a city street as soon as she'd turned the corner – she'd not make that mistake again.

To wait until she'd crossed the river back into New Jersey, and wait longer still, until she came to a vast anonymous parking lot surrounding a big-box store.

She parked and left the van running. Inadvertently crossed herself and said a little prayer, a throwback to childhood for which she immediately sent an apology heavenward. By her calculations, she and her friends were involved in several potential crimes. The Almighty probably frowned on people who asked for help in such circumstances.

But in this case, she was just checking on what was rightfully Alice's.

Beyond the smell, the van seemed largely unchanged. She crossed her fingers, pushed back the curtains blocking her view of the back, and gasped at the litter of overturned bankers' boxes and *National Geographics*, their yellow borders bright in the van's dim interior.

'Oh, no. Oh, no, no, no.'

She knelt amid the mess, uselessly fitting the magazines back in the boxes and stacking the boxes atop one another, occasionally swiping away tears. What had she expected? She reminded herself that she was lucky to get the van back in working order.

But . . . she bit her lip, thinking. The two stacks she'd made reached only to her waist. They took up the narrow space between the makeshift kitchen and the platform bed that filled the rear of the van.

She'd been so happy with the retrofit that added the bed and its clever storage area beneath, concealed by sliding doors. Now she wondered. Maybe?

Another muttered prayer.

She held her breath and slid open the doors, peering within. Bankers' boxes – unopened – stared back at her. Sasha must have put the first few boxes in the storage space before filling the aisle with the rest.

'TGTBT,' she warned herself. Maybe the carjackers, so sloppy when dealing with the earlier boxes, had a belated attack of neatness when it came to these, removing the cash and replacing the magazines and fitting the lids squarely back on to the boxes.

She said yet another prayer, nearly laughing at the realization that the last time she'd prayed this much had been a years-ago pregnancy scare shortly after her divorce.

She ripped the lid from one of the boxes. Stuck her hand in. Wormed her fingers beneath the magazines. Touched a papery bundle.

And sent a joyous hurrah bouncing off the walls of the van.

She punched dashboard buttons and twisted knobs until she found a radio station. Hearing the word 'oldies,' she started to move past it, but stopped when Bruce Springsteen's 'Born to Run' blared from speakers.

She cringed at the categorization of the song that had defined her college years but cranked up the volume anyway. Was any song more appropriate? She shouted along, at least the words she could remember, all the way back to Timeless Pastures.

Even the sight of Hawk Boneham's macho Range Rover creeping anew along its streets couldn't bring her down.

She flashed a surreptitious bird as she passed and whispered a promise.

'You just keep right on sneaking around. Enjoy it while it lasts. Because we're gonna put you away.'

SIXTY-EIGHT

Mary Raynolds talked for an hour, her voice sometimes going so low Sasha strained to hear.

'The only job he could get when he came back – the only good-paying job – was at the Gloucester Armaments factory. Can you imagine what that did to him, every day working to make the guns that were going straight over to Vietnam to keep the killing going? He hated that job. But enough to do what they say he did? Larry might have come back mad as hell, but he wasn't crazy.'

Her eyes begged Sasha to believe her.

Sasha tried to reassure her. 'My friend thinks that the brother of the woman who was killed in the bombing actually planned the whole thing.'

Mary nodded. 'That's just so. That man, the one with the funny name, he set my husband up to take the fall if anything went wrong. If Larry had told me anything about it before it all went down, I'd never have let him do it. But he kept it from me.'

'How did you find out?'

Mary dug her hands into the sides of her head, mussing hair straightened into soft silver waves. 'Oh, it was awful. One morning he got a call from his foreman, telling him not to come to work. Saying the whole place was shut down because some damn hippies – the foreman's words, not mine – had bombed the place and killed Mrs Carpenter and the custodian. I think that's what set Larry off. The man called Mrs Carpenter by name but didn't give Mr Jones the same courtesy. It's like he was some kind of afterthought.'

'Mr Jones was the custodian?'

Mary patted her hair back into place. 'Yes. I never knew him, of course, but Larry spoke kindly of him.'

Sasha tried not to look at the clock. George had been sitting in the car a long time. Her phone vibrated every few minutes with what she assumed was another text from him. She didn't even dare text him back to let him know she was all right.

'You said it set Larry off. How do you mean?'

'He slammed the phone down – that was back when we still had real telephones – and started cursing and crying. Woke our little girl out of a sound sleep, scared her half to death. Took me a while to get her calmed down. By the time I was able to get her settled again, I was in a state myself. I went back to Larry and begged him to tell me what was going on.

'He wouldn't, at first. Told me to get all our money out of the bank – believe me, it wasn't much – and take the baby and go to my mother's. Said that he was like poison now, and he didn't want us to be tainted. It took me hours to get it out of him, how he'd fallen in with these radicals. How they told him the only way to stop the killing was to scare places like Gloucester Armaments so much they'd quit making the weapons. Have you ever heard anything so stupid in your life?'

Sasha allowed that it ranked high on the stupidity scale.

'He said that man told him he couldn't go into the factory by himself. That there was bad blood between him and his family. He needed someone on the inside to plant the bomb. Guess who?'

Sasha forgot about the ticking clock, George waiting in the car, the stream of despair that had led to this moment. She could barely form the words.

'What else did he tell you?'

'He told me he couldn't live with Mr Jones' blood on his hands and Mrs Carpenter's, too. He was going to give himself up, go to the police and tell them everything. Especially about those White kids who planned it all.'

Mary pointed to another photo, of a smiling young family, husband and wife, boy and girl about middle-school age. 'Our daughter. Her husband. And my two precious grandchildren. Larry would have loved them. Those people who roped him into that thing – they cheated him of so much. If he'd known what he'd miss, maybe he wouldn't have taken himself away from them.'

Sasha jumped in. 'My friend thinks he didn't kill himself.'

Mary Raynolds' mouth quirked in something resembling a smile. 'Your friend *thinks*? I *know*. And I have proof.'

SIXTY-NINE

Mary shook her head when Sasha rose to follow her.

'You stay here. I'll be right back.'

Her halting progress up the stairs was painful to see. Sasha's knees ached just watching her.

She checked her phone as soon as Mary was out of sight. As she expected, a string of texts from George filled the screen, all along the lines of Are you all right? George refused to succumb to the sort of shorthand that would have allowed a quick U ok.

She texted back a thumbs-up and then, realizing George didn't speak emoji – although it should have been clear; that was the whole point of emojis, wasn't it? – went for a complete sentence. She's about to—

But one of Mary's sensibly shod feet appeared on the stairwell, followed by the other, the rest of her appearing by inches as she crept back down the stairs, one hand clinging to the rail, the other clutching a small wooden box.

Sasha had a similar box filled with bracelets and brooches, the latter barely worn now that she'd put away the blazers from her real estate days.

Mary used hers for something else.

'His effects,' she said. 'The things the police gave me after they released his body.'

She caressed it before unfastening the small brass clasp.

Sasha craned her neck. She saw a wallet, keys, some change. A pen, its cap chewed ragged. And an envelope with Mary's name scrawled across it in pencil.

Mary lifted it from the box and held it out to Sasha.

'The note they say he left.'

The paper was soft, the name a bit smudged, as though from repeated fondling.

'Go ahead and open it.'

Sasha hesitated. It felt wrong, far too personal.

'Go on now. Read it.' Mary closed her eyes and recited aloud from memory as Sasha read.

My dearest Mary,

I am sorry to leave you and Belinda this way. I can only imagine the pain it will cause. It is only to save you worse pain and shame that you would suffer as a result of being married to a murderer. I never should have listened to Carol Ann Kaminski. She's the one who planned all of this, feeding me nonsense about how many lives it would save in Vietnam. Tell the families of those people how sorry I am to deprive them of their loved ones. It only seems right that my own family be likewise deprived. Hug and kiss Belinda every night for me.

Your loving husband,
Larry Reynolds

Sasha cleared her throat, folded the paper and slid it back into the envelope. Then she thought again. 'Do you mind if I take a picture? It could be evidence.'

'Oh, it's evidence all right.' Mary's voice dripped acid as Sasha snapped the photo. 'They called it a confession.'

'Well.' Sasha cleared her throat again, raw from choking back emotion. What would it be like to write the last words your wife would ever hear from you? 'He does say he deprived those people. And that you would be known as the wife of a murderer.'

'False!'

Mary pounded the table with surprising strength.

'My husband never wrote that. I mean, he did write it. That is his handwriting. I'd know it anywhere. But it's all a lie.'

'What do you mean?'

Mary looked at her as though she was none too bright.

'It's obvious. It's right there in front of your face.'

Sasha pointed to Mary's name on the envelope. 'This?'

'No, the note. Look at it. What do you notice about it?'

'That your husband had nice handwriting?'

'It's in pencil!' Mary pounded the table again. Sasha feared for the fragile bones in her hand.

'It's in pencil,' Mary said again. 'Larry died with a pen in his pocket. Why would he write a note in pencil?'

'Maybe the pen was dry?'

Another withering look. 'It wasn't. I tried it.'

Mary gently took the paper from Sasha's hand. 'Look. It's right there.'

Sasha tried again. 'I mean, the signature is a little strange. So formal. Why'd he sign his full name?'

The table jumped again, although this time the assault on its surface was one of triumph. 'You're almost there. His full name. Read it again.'

'Larry Reyn— Oh. *Oh.* Oh my.' Sasha rubbed at the gooseflesh pebbling her arms.

'Yes. That's not how my husband spelled his name. R-a-y, not R-e-y.'

'So he didn't write this note? But you said it was his handwriting.'

'It is. He wrote it. But he was sending me a sign that he was forced to write it. Forced by someone who didn't know him well enough to know how he spelled his name.'

SEVENTY

Mia perched beside Alice's bed on one of the boxes of cash. She'd taken the risk of driving to Johnny's to deliver the cash, carrying the boxes up to Johnny's spare room.

'I say we go back to the original plan and head for New Mexico. It's so much safer, now that the police don't know the van was carjacked. And you've still got plenty of money, enough to set you up wherever you decide to land.'

Alice leaned back against the headboard and drummed her fingers on the end table.

'Hawk knows I'm out here somewhere. He'll still go after me. And you'll be with me, and that puts you in danger, too.'

'But you won't have to worry about him much longer. Look what Sasha just sent.'

She showed her the text, the one telling them Mary Raynolds had something that could point to Hawk's involvement. At least, that's how she interpreted the two words: Got proof.

'Sasha and George will bring the information to the police, and he'll be arrested.'

'And he'll be out on bail five minutes later. That's how the system works for people like him – if they charge him at all. Even if that proof is ironclad, people like him tend to skate. Meanwhile, the FBI will know who I am and, until just a few days ago, where I lived. I still think I should just turn myself in. Like I said before, jail might be the safest place for me. And let's face it – I might not have killed those people directly, but I bear responsibility. All this time on the run, it wasn't from jail. It was from Hawk.'

Mia hitched the box closer to the heat wafting upward through the floor vent, an ineffective counter to the chill permeating the old house. Another cold snap had hit, accompanied by a fresh layer of snow. She'd been finding her way through the pines to Johnny's house by following her old tracks through the snow. She'd almost gotten lost this time.

'I saw him again, you know. Hawk. He's been creeping around Timeless Pastures in that Range Rover of his.'

Alice, who'd wrapped herself in the quilt Sasha had retrieved from her house, pulled it tighter around her.

'Did he see you?'

'I don't think so. I mean, he saw the van. And I saw him on my run, but my face was covered. Like this.' She pulled up her gaiter, which hung loose around her neck, so that it covered everything but her eyes. 'Anyway, I'm in the pines during the last mile. Nobody sees me in there. Nobody can see anything in there.'

She didn't add that she might have been almost glad to see someone during her trek through the pines. The trees hung dark overhead, blotting out the sun, deadening sound. The last breeze sent a low moan through them, raising the hairs on her neck and helping her understand how early White settlers had come to believe in a Jersey Devil.

The road was only a few hundred yards away, but it might as well have been miles. Mia had done her best to memorize identifying features along her route, but it was nearly impossible. Each tree, twisted and scaly, looked like every other one. Her jog slowed to a walk once she entered the pines, not only because of the snow, but to avoid tripping over the roots that snaked across the ground, threatening to send her tumbling into the creek that ran beside the trail.

Johnny's cabin, light spilling golden from its windows, stood as a comforting refuge amid the surrounding gloom.

'You're safe here,' she said, as much to encourage herself as well as Alice. 'At least, wait and see what Sasha and George bring back.'

She would never have admitted it, but she wouldn't have minded another day or two of running back and forth between her home and the cabin. Her visits inevitably meant a sit-down over coffee with Johnny, who made her laugh with his tales of the vicissitudes of some of the Timeless Pastures residents.

She was even more reluctant to acknowledge to herself that she liked the way he looked at her, the instant smile, wider and brighter than the professional one she'd seen at community meetings, his eyes lingering an extra beat, but never so long as to be offensive. She probed her own psyche: Was she interested in starting something with Johnny?

As much as she enjoyed the attention, no. She'd had her share of involvement with men – heck, she'd been married to one for years – but lately had leaned toward women. Once this was over, she wouldn't mind meeting someone, although she couldn't imagine how she'd manage that, given her nomadic plans.

Alice's response jolted her back to the present. 'I'm willing to wait for George and Sasha. They're coming back tomorrow, right?'

Mia's phone vibrated.

She glanced at the text and clicked out of it.

'Maybe tonight.'

'Good. I'll try and relax. Thanks for talking me off the ledge.'

'Sure thing.' Mia didn't dare look up. She didn't want Alice to see the fear in her face.

Just to be safe, she put the phone back in her pocket as though to bury the text from Sasha that had flashed across it.

There's a problem.

SEVENTY-ONE

Proof.

Mary Raynolds touched the envelope to her lips, returned it to the box and carried it back upstairs.

Sasha chanced a quick text to Mia. Got proof!

Her fingers were stiff as they tapped the keys. The chill at the realization of the signature's meaning had spread throughout her body as she imagined the steel of a barrel digging into Larry's temple as he wrote, knowing those words on paper would be his last.

Mary Raynolds was barely back in her chair before Sasha's question escaped. 'Did you show this to the police?'

'What kind of fool do you take me for? Of course I did. They insinuated – no, they came right out and said – that maybe Larry was so hopped up on drugs he'd forgotten how to spell his own name. My husband never even smoked a joint.'

Sasha could just see it, the new widow nearly mad with grief, the condescending cop, his hostility toward the authority-defying radicals careening off the charts when race was added to the equation.

Sasha tried to think of the kinds of questions George might ask.

'Didn't they do any tests? Ballistics, what have you.'

'You think you're the first one to ask that? Gun was in his hand when they found him. Made by Gloucester Armaments, by the way. And there was the note. Said they didn't need to do any tests. Had all the proof they needed. You look surprised.'

Sasha shook her head. She wasn't. But she wasn't ready to give up, either.

'That was, what, fifty years ago? Things have changed.'

Mary gave her a look.

Sasha threw up her hands. 'I know, I know. So they've only changed this much.' She held thumb and forefinger a millimeter apart. 'But cases like these get reopened. You show this letter to a good lawyer, put the word out on social media, get people behind the effort, and you might be able to clear your husband's name.'

She tilted her head toward the family photo. 'Wouldn't you like your daughter to know her father wasn't a murderer? At least, not an intentional one? That he'd been assured no one would get hurt?'

Mary Raynolds wasn't that much older, but Sasha felt like a little kid facing the scorn of a respected elder. She shrank in her seat as Mary set her straight.

'My daughter knows her father was a good man, that he was taken advantage of by people who played upon his sympathies to use him for their own evil ends. She's seen this letter. She knows the truth. My grandchildren will see it, too, when it's time. Best to let it lie. This family has been through enough.'

Sasha thought of herself as a strong person, but standing up to Mary took reserves she didn't know she had.

'You can't! He's still out there!'

'Who? Oh, you mean that Hawk person. And that woman, too. They never did find her.'

She tilted her head and pursed her lips. 'What's your interest in this, anyway? Are you from one of those organizations, those Innocence Project-type places?'

'Sort of,' Sasha said, a lie she might have pulled off had George not chosen that moment to knock at the door.

SEVENTY-TWO

Mary Raynolds pushed herself up from the table and went to the door.

Sasha sat frozen, listening to Mary's end of the conversation, George speaking so softly she couldn't make out the words.

'Excuse me? You want what? Who are you?'

Sasha forced herself from her chair.

'He's my . . . he's with me.'

George turned to her, relief written across his face. 'You've been in here so long. And your text worried me. You didn't finish it. I thought something might have happened.'

Sasha found her manners. 'Miss Mary, this is George Sterling. George, this is Mrs Raynolds.'

George held out his hand. Mary took it for a second and snatched it away. She stood aside to let him in but didn't offer coffee or cookies.

Nor did she sit when they returned to the dining room, so Sasha and George also stood as Mary regarded them, arms crossed.

'What do you people want with me? Disturbing an old woman, digging this trash up after all these years, just when I figured I'd finally found peace? Why are you so interested in this?'

George opened his mouth, but Sasha trod on his foot, guessing Mary wouldn't be happy with anything either of them said, but she might be slightly more amenable to something from her.

'As I said a few minutes ago, it's about injustice. A wrong was done. A good man's name was dragged through the mud. His family suffered.'

'True enough.'

Sasha let her breath out. Maybe things would be OK.

'But there's something I don't understand. How do you two know about all this?'

'We read about it,' George said. Sasha pressed his foot again – more of a stomp this time – but he continued undeterred. 'I'm one of those people who's interested in unsolved crimes. This one seems particularly egregious.'

'Oh, it was egregious.'

George nudged Sasha's foot back in an unspoken 'So there.'

'But it wasn't unsolved. According to the police, it was open-and-shut. They say my husband wrote a note admitting to it, and then killed himself from the shame of it all.'

'The note said he planted the bomb?' George was in full true-crime mode. 'That he alone was responsible for the deaths of those two people?'

'George, I saw it. Not in so many words,' Sasha whispered.

'You saw it? May I?'

'You may not,' Mary said, even as Sasha fumbled with her phone, trying to bring up the photo. 'Because there's something I still don't understand. I just remembered something your – your whatever she is – said. Put that phone away.'

Sasha dropped it into her purse. She wanted to do nothing more than drag George bodily from the house. Mary Raynolds was clearly displeased with George's arrival, but she'd also seemed puzzled.

Now, that obvious confusion had vanished. She was figuring something out, and whatever it was, Sasha didn't want to stick around to find out.

Too late. Mary turned to Sasha.

'You said something about a friend of yours. What friend?'

'She's— Ow!' George yelped as Sasha flat-out kicked him.

'She? Who is she? What is it that you don't want this man to tell me?'

'Nothing. George, we should go. Miss Mary, thank you for your hospitality.'

Mary held out an arm that looked incapable of stopping a sparrow. But no way was Sasha going to push past her.

'You haven't answered my question.'

'Which one?'

'Don't be impertinent, young lady. You know very well which one. Who is this friend? Here's another one for you. What are you really doing here?'

Sasha did her best. 'She's like George. She looks into unsolved cases. She has a particular interest in this one.'

'Is she White or Black?'

Sasha looked everywhere but at Mary Raynolds as the woman figured it out, step by step.

'She's White, isn't she? And she's about your age?'

'Yes.'

'What's her name?'

Sasha hesitated. 'Alice. Alice Sanders.'

Mary grabbed the back of one of the chairs and held on for dear life.

'What's her real name?'

Sasha shook her head.

'It's her, isn't it? The woman who was with that man who got my husband mixed up in all of this. The one who's really responsible. She's the murderer – she and that Hawk fellow – not my husband. You don't care one bit about him, do you?'

Sasha searched for an adequate response. She almost told Mary how Alice kept a photo of Larry, along with ones of Roosevelt Jones and Victoria Carpenter, but thought better of it before the words left her mouth. Her reticence didn't matter. Mary was on to her.

She pointed a finger at Sasha, a level of rudeness so severe that Sasha knew the conversation was over.

'Leaving that White man out in the car so you could come in here on your own. Thinking I'd be more likely to talk to you just because you're a sister. You ought to be ashamed of yourself.'

She was. Oh, she very much was.

Still, pride wriggled through her as she and George retreated to the car.

Because no matter what Miss Mary – rightfully – thought of her, she'd at least had the good sense to snap that photo.

Proof.

SEVENTY-THREE

Hawk Boneham had an uncanny ability to appear whenever Johnny least expected him.

He barely had time before the office door closed behind Hawk to slide the papers on his desk – copies of the spreadsheets he'd taken from Babs' house – into a drawer.

'I think I've seen more of you in the last month than I have since Weller Holdings bought the place.' He'd tried for jocularity. It came out like the accusation it was.

It didn't matter. The words were barely out of his mouth before Hawk launched an accusation of his own.

'I'm disappointed in you.'

What had he done now? 'Enough people haven't opted to leave? Not a problem. Another month or two, the whole place should be empty. Is that what you're aiming for?'

'And you'll be out of a job. Is that what you want? Because you're just about there already.'

Was he going to be fired for being a smartass? Other than that, Johnny couldn't figure out whatever sin had provoked Hawk's wrath.

'I've been informed by – well, never mind who – that you've been sheltering a notorious radical. A murderous one.'

Johnny's heart stopped. He wondered how to get a message to Alice that she needed to leave his house immediately. Maybe text Mia? Could she run to the house fast enough to beat Hawk speeding toward it in his Range Rover? Maybe Hawk had already called the police, and at this very moment, Johnny's house was surrounded by cruisers, lights flashing and sirens blaring. Or, even worse, SWAT teams creeping through the woods, bulky in their body armor, rifles raised and ready.

He tried for dumb. It didn't feel like much of a stretch.

'What are you talking about?'

'She apparently lived in Timeless Pastures for years, under your very nose. And now she's escaped, and you haven't lifted a finger to alert the community to this reality.'

Johnny's heart resumed beating with a thud so resounding it left him lightheaded. Luckily for him, Hawk was on a roll.

'Take a look at the FBI's Most Wanted List.' He slapped a printout on to the counter. Johnny stared at a decades-younger version of Alice. 'There will be a story in the local paper soon – but not soon enough. Where are the posts on the message boards and social media? And for our less technologically adept residents, the posters? Maybe someone here had a conversation with this – what is she calling herself now? Alice Sanders? – that might give authorities a clue to her whereabouts.'

'I'll get right on it.' He would do no such thing. 'But—' Johnny trod carefully. 'I haven't seen anything about this from the police.'

Hawk's face darkened. The office door opened again. For the first time in his life, Johnny was glad to see Glenda Ferguson.

'Johnny, that van is here again. The one I thought I saw Sasha driving. Only now Mia was driving. There's something funny going on here.'

Johnny tried to think fast, but Hawk was faster.

'What van? You said Sasha. And Mia. Weren't those two of the people who folks thought were missing for a while? Along with' – he paused – 'Alice Sanders?'

Johnny had always thought the phrase 'perfect storm' a cliché. Now one unfolded before his eyes.

Glenda's head bobbed so hard that Sugar Plum caught the excitement and began yapping.

'Shut up, dog.'

Sugar Plum whimpered and shrank away from Hawk.

'When did you see it?'

Glenda lifted Sugar Plum and covered his bearded face with kisses, eyeing Hawk reproachfully. 'You scared my dog.'

'When did you see it? Where?'

Sugar Plum, now safe in her arms, growled.

'Just now. Over on the main street. Who are you?'

The door slammed behind Hawk.

Glenda set Sugar Plum down. He leaned against her leg, whimpering.

'Oh dear. Did I do a bad thing?'

Johnny, fingers stumbling through an urgent text, didn't look up from his phone. 'I don't think there's anything good when it comes to that guy.'

He put his phone away. He wanted nothing more than to rush past Glenda, jump in his truck and speed to his house to warn Alice. But that might risk leading Hawk straight to her.

'I mean, I told a little lie.'

Johnny looked up. 'You did?'

'He scared Sugar Plum. What kind of person scares a sweet little dog?'

Johnny had a laundry list of answers but kept them to himself.

'So I told him I'd just seen the van over on the main street. But I saw it an hour ago on Alice's street. It's just a fib. It made me feel better, but it was wrong.'

'No. You did exactly the right thing.'

Johnny wasn't sure who was more surprised – himself or Glenda – by the wet, smacking kiss he planted on her cheek on his way out the door.

SEVENTY-FOUR

Alice got the group text from Johnny shortly before five p.m. Code Red. My house. ASAP. Lights off when you make the turn. Park in back.

Those last instructions were, of course, meant for the others. He hadn't included instructions for her. But she knew what to do, thanks to decades of lightning-fast changes in plan, spurred by nothing more than gut feeling.

She took a quick shower – who knew when she'd get another? – and dressed in layers. Wherever she ended up, assuming she arrived in a safe place, she could buy more clothes.

Her winter coat had a zip-in lining. She stuffed bundles of bills between it and the outer shell.

A car pulled up. She pulled the curtain away from the window and saw George and Sasha, barely distinguishable in the fast-falling twilight, heading for the back door.

She grabbed her now-bulkier coat and hurried downstairs to let them in.

Johnny arrived just as she opened the door, hustling past them into the house, flipping light switches off as he went. They gathered as usual in the kitchen, sepulchral in the twilight.

'Call me paranoid – and at this point, that would be an understatement – but it might be best to give the appearance there's no one home.'

A small voice sounded outside.

'Hello? I know you're in there. At least, I hope you are—'

Johnny went to the door and pulled Mia inside, guiding her to the table.

'Whew. What's going on? But give me a minute to catch my breath. I usually walk through the woods, but this time I ran. It's a miracle I only fell a couple of times.' She brushed snow and sandy soil from her legs and took a couple of deep breaths. 'Why are we sitting in the dark?'

'Because as much as I'd like to say that Alice is overly paranoid, she's not. Hawk stopped by my office just now. He wants a full-court press on finding her. He had the FBI photo.'

Mia jumped up. 'Then I'll go home and start loading the van. Alice, we can be on the road in a couple of hours. Even sooner, if you'd like.'

'Mia, that would be great—'

'No, it wouldn't.' Johnny cut her off. 'Hawk knows the van. Glenda came into the office while he was there to say she'd seen a suspicious van again, and mentioned that it was the same one she'd seen the woman she'd thought was Sasha driving it – except that, this time, she saw you driving, Mia. He heard both your names and put two and two together.'

Alice groaned. 'Mia, you'd better leave that van in your carport for the foreseeable future.'

'We can take you.' George and Sasha spoke together. Even in the near-dark, Alice saw the quick smile Sasha flashed at George.

She forced herself to say the right thing. 'I so appreciate that. But you know I can't put you in that position.'

Gloom settled over the kitchen. Alice tried to lighten it. 'What if I just buy another train ticket to Buffalo and get off the train somewhere along the way, just like our original plan? It was a fine idea then and it's still one.'

'I'll drop you at the station,' Johnny said. Then, taking his cue from her tone, 'And I'll keep moving so I won't get carjacked like you guys.'

Nobody laughed.

When his phone dinged a few seconds later, they collectively jumped.

Alice headed for the back door.

'Wait,' he called after her. He motioned to Mia, who ran after Alice and caught her arm.

He tapped at his phone and spoke briefly into it. 'Now, please. Hurry. No lights when you turn off the main road. And park around back.'

He returned the phone to his pocket.

'It's that reporter. He's on his way over.'

SEVENTY-FIVE

Bert killed his headlights seconds before he turned off the road into the narrow track leading through the pines to the house, stifling an impulse to scoff at Johnny's cloak-and-dagger caution.

Then mentally kicked himself as the car inched forward along the sandy track made doubly hazardous by the snow. The steady diet of soft stories had dulled his instincts. He was working on a story that involved a federal fugitive. A possible killer cloaked in corporate mufti. And as another all-nighter of research had shown him, someone without a shred of conscience when it came to exploiting vulnerable people.

But to explain that last one, he needed light.

Bert dumped a stack of documents on the table. 'Is sitting in the dark really necessary? I can tell you what I've found, but it'll make more sense if you can see it for yourself.'

A brief negotiation led to an agreement to use their cellphone flashlights. 'Keep them pointed down,' Mia instructed.

Bert shuffled through the documents, extracting two spreadsheets and the map. 'Your source made a good start in linking all of these places – by the way, I found more still – to Weller Holdings. That person found the what. I think I've figured out the why.'

His forefinger ran down one of the lists. 'Look at these names. Notice anything about them?'

George donned reading glasses and leaned close, reading aloud. 'Pleasant Acres. All Seasons. Willow Estates. Magnolia Gardens. Mountain View. River View. Meadow View.' He looked up. 'There's more, a lot more, but they're all along these lines.'

Mia crowded so close that Bert felt her shrug. 'What am I looking for? As best as I can tell, all they seem to have in common is that they like their views.'

Nervous laughter.

'Try again,' Bert said.

Sasha took a turn. 'These names – they're nearly as bad as Timeless Pastures. Or Out to Pasture as we like to call it.'

'Exactly!' Bert boomed, to a chorus of shushes. He lowered his voice. 'Most of them are retirement communities. And that's not all they have in common. I'd say the vast majority are mobile-home communities, although a few are manufactured homes, like Timeless Pastures.'

'So?'

'I'm getting to that.' He unfolded another spreadsheet.

Once again, George did the honors. 'Central Trading. Parker Plumbing Supply. Main Street Medical Devices. RSC Inc. Evolution Production. McMasters Metals. Sylvester Trucking. Plenty more along those lines.'

Silence reigned.

'I don't get it,' Sasha finally said. 'Some of them – not all – sound like manufacturing companies. Others, you can't tell what they are at all. And none of them seem to have any relation to one another.'

'Yes!' Bert's voice rose again.

'Why don't you just step outside and holler to the whole world that we're here?' Alice hissed.

'Sorry. Just bear with me. You'll see in a minute.'

'I think I see now. Although I'm not entirely sure what I'm seeing.' George lifted the spreadsheet closer to his face. 'There's a name on here that all of us will finally recognize.' He turned to Bert. 'Is this one of the new ones you found?'

'Yes. Gloucester Armaments.'

Alice, despite her earlier warning, yelped. She clapped her hand over her mouth.

Mia spoke for her. 'But what does it mean? What does Gloucester Armaments have in common with any of those?'

Bert pushed the map to the center of the table and planted his thumb on New Jersey.

'It has this.'

He knew he was overplaying the drama. But he wanted them to have the same 'aha' moment he'd experienced when he'd put it all together. He wished he could see their expressions.

But with their phone-flashlights trained away from their faces, he felt only the foreboding hovering over the table.

He moved to dispel it.

'Weller Holdings. Everything comes back to Weller Holdings. They don't just own Timeless Pastures. They own all of these places.'

'So?'

Alice grasped it first, this time confining herself to a gasp. 'Holdings. Isn't that a term for a . . . a . . . I don't know the word. It's been a long time since Econ 101, and I got a C in that course, anyway.'

'Doesn't matter,' said Bert. 'Weller Holdings is about the only thing on these spreadsheets whose name sounds exactly like what it is. It's a holding company.'

'What's that?'

Bert smiled toward the shadow that was Mia. 'It's a company that has a controlling interest in other companies – often many unrelated businesses. Weller doesn't just control Timeless Pastures. It's swept up all of these companies.'

'Hawk Boneham sure falls into robber-baron category,' Johnny said. 'But why would he let his family business be bought up by another company?'

Bert rubbed his fingers together, then realized that those across the table couldn't see the internationally understood gesture. 'Money. He gets money from the sale and, in this case, a vice presidency in Weller Holdings out of the deal.'

'If he gets money, why would he want a job, too?' Alice pointed out the obvious.

'And why would they want to buy a gun company?' Mia pressed. 'Aren't guns already being manufactured like crazy in this country?'

'Exactly right. And that's the reason. Gloucester Armaments was an old-fashioned sort of company, dedicated to high-end guns, none of the plastic parts that the big manufacturers use, and they also refused to manufacture the semi-automatics that have become so popular. Their best models are works of art, and priced accordingly. But people can buy other guns – and bigger ones, too – for way less money. Gloucester's sales were tanking. That fortune Hawk inherited vanished a long time ago. The sale price probably got him out of debt and the job gives him a bit of a cushion.

'And, Mia, you just put your finger on it. The demand for guns is out of sight. Manufacturers can't keep up. Weller got Gloucester for a song, and now they're churning out cheap guns day and night. That dynamic is a whole conversation for another day.'

'I understand Weller might want to buy up manufacturing companies,' Sasha said. 'But why the retirement communities? I could see buying up those fancy ones where people hand over their life savings just to get in, and then pay thousands a month to stay there. But the lower-level ones like ours? It doesn't make sense.'

'Oh, but it makes perfect sense. They're valuable for two reasons. They don't require the high level of skilled staff necessary for assisted-living facilities, and people who live in manufactured homes generally don't own the land under those homes. So, right away it's a property investment. New owners can raise the lot fees as high as they like.'

'We've noticed. When you think about it, that's what got all of us into this mess,' Sasha said, to murmurs of assent.

'I still don't understand,' Mia said. 'Look at Timeless Pastures. They've raised the fees so high that we're all moving out, and nobody new is moving in. Seems like they're cutting their own throats.'

Bert started to speak, but Sasha interrupted him.

'I never handled commercial real estate, but for sure I keep an eye on it. In some of these cases, the property is the valuable asset, not the homes that sit on it. The way I'm reading this, the company gets a bump from squeezing people for the fees, and a second one from redeveloping the property once all the residents are gone.'

'She's right,' said Bert. 'Timeless Pastures is hardly an isolated case. Sometimes they follow the same model you're dealing with – astronomical increases. In others, they flat-out evict people, raze the homes and put up something more profitable. Keep in mind that the people in these places, especially in the mobile-home communities, are there because they can't afford anything better.'

'Evicted? What happens to them?'

'You wouldn't believe the stories I've read,' Bert said. 'Some move in with family members, who are none too well-off themselves. Some end up in homeless shelters. Sometimes the surrounding community puts together some sort of fundraising drive to help them, but that only gets them through a couple of months.'

'But to kick them out?' Mia couldn't let go. 'How can that be legal?'

Once again, Sasha stepped in. 'A new owner can renegotiate the terms and fees, up to and including ending the lot leases. Welcome to capitalism. Alice, all that marching you did to end the war? Maybe you should have stuck around and protested this sort of thing.'

Her comment brought everyone back to the matter at hand.

'If it's legal, then where's the advantage in printing anything about it?'

Bert scooped the papers back into a pile.

'Short term, probably not much. Almost certainly not enough to help anyone in Timeless Pastures. But these are pretty disturbing practices, especially given the affordable housing crisis all over the country. A series of stories about this, and about how widespread it is – and especially with one company at the center of it – could provoke enough outrage to see some laws changed.'

'Which could take years,' George said. 'Look at the age group around this table. Half of us will probably be dead by then.'

'I can't argue with that. But this case is different, thanks to Hawk. Pointing out his involvement in bombing his family's own company will draw a lot of attention to the story. Maybe even national. Companies don't like that sort of thing.'

'You'd better print it fast,' Alice said. 'He knows – at least, he thinks he does – that I'm still in the area.'

Bert hadn't pressed Alice on her offer of an interview, fearing rejection and the resulting disappearance of the biggest story he'd likely handle in his career. Now he didn't have a choice. 'Then I'll need that interview you offered. When can we set it up?'

He held his breath. She'd had enough time to think better of her offer. He reminded himself that even without an interview with a notorious fugitive, he still had a solid story about the exploitive real estate dealings. He braced himself for her inevitable 'no.'

'How about now?' she said. 'I hope you can take notes in the dark.'

SEVENTY-SIX

Bert was so nervous he flooded the engine when he tried to start his car.

He'd acted on every reporter's instinct – get the story, the bigger the better – when he'd first taken Alice up on her offer. And he'd done his due diligence, plunging through decades of background information before sitting down for the actual interview that, truth to tell, he'd never really expected to get.

Everything she'd said in the last hour had checked out. Plus more – so much more. He knew the skepticism that would meet her claim that she'd been unaware of Hawk's family background – that he'd been heir apparent to Gloucester Armaments, only to be passed over in favor of his infinitely more responsible sister. Even before the bombing, Victoria Carpenter's ascendance had garnered a flurry of publicity due to her youth, her gender and her swaggering assumption of a leadership role in that most masculine of industries in a male-dominated corporate world.

These days, anybody with Wi-Fi and a few hours to kill could pull up the same information. He'd need to make a point in his story that the internet was still decades away when Bird had enmeshed Alice in his own peculiar brand of radicalism. What did they call it these days – grooming?

Beyond the bare-bones details he'd already gleaned, Alice had fleshed out her childhood on the dairy farm, her Holyoke scholarship – 'To this day, I can't believe I threw away such a valuable education' – even her participation in some of the bigger anti-war marches.

He twisted the key again. Someday he'd have enough money for a new car with a pushbutton start. And – he blew on his hands – the remote-start function that would allow him to step into a pre-warmed vehicle.

'Come on, come on, come on.'

It was Thursday night. He'd agreed with Alice not to run the story until Sunday. That gave him a couple of days to write up the interview, along with the accompanying story about Weller Holdings.

It also gave him more time to face the fact that the minute the story dropped, the FBI would come calling.

He'd read about reporters who'd gone to prison rather than reveal their sources, and he'd admired them – in principle. But in fact?

'At least,' he said aloud, 'jail would get me out of writing any more stupid columns. Take that, Madison.'

Thus armed with false bravado, he stomped the accelerator, smiled as the engine caught, and maneuvered back through the pines to the main road, flicking on the lights as soon as he felt pavement beneath the tires.

He pointed the car toward the supermarket, intending to stock up on coffee and frozen pizza in anticipation of the long weekend, so focused on the task at hand that the black Range Rover he passed made no impression at all.

Lavina Township Police Department
Transcript of interview with Mia Sullivan
Present: Detective Travis Meacham, Officer Sherilee Townsend

Townsend: I'm trying to figure out how to say this tactfully. It appears you took to your – what should I call them? – your new circumstances with a fair amount of enthusiasm.

Sullivan: Is that a statement or a question?

Townsend: A little bit of both, I guess.

Sullivan: Just what do you mean by circumstances? You mean being priced out of my home? My van being stolen? No, Officer Townsend, I enjoyed nothing about those circumstances.

Townsend: Maybe I went overboard on tact. I meant your involvement in Alice Sanders' issues.

Sullivan: Oh.

Townsend: So I repeat my question.

Sullivan: It wasn't much of a question. What are you trying to say?

Townsend: You seem to have taken a particular pride in your ability to evade law enforcement, despite the legal ramifications.

Sullivan: We were trying to evade Hawk Boneham. Forgive me if we thought life-and-death ramifications were a priority. We needed to keep ourselves, and especially Alice, safe.

Townsend: Which would have been our job. If only we'd been given the chance.

Sullivan: Why do I think law enforcement might not have been inclined to be helpful to someone on the FBI's Most Wanted List?

Townsend: Your usual sarcasm is noted yet again.

Sullivan: You want sincerity? Yes, I'm very proud of the fact that we were able to keep Alice safe for as long as we did.

Townsend: And your skills were crucial to that effort.

Sullivan: Well . . . yes.

Townsend: Until they failed.

SEVENTY-SEVEN

Alice heard Bert's car drive away.

She leaned over the grate, taking in the silence below, anticipation thick within it, everyone waiting for her to come downstairs with a recap of the interview.

Had she done the right thing? It didn't matter. It was done. Maybe, just maybe, Hawk would finally be held accountable. Maybe Mary Raynolds would finally see her husband's name cleared. And maybe she herself finally could stop running, although she wouldn't believe that until Hawk Boneham III was tried and sentenced, had exhausted all of the appeals he'd be sure to file and had finally heard the steel doors of a prison slam shut behind him.

'Alice?'

'Come on in, Mia.'

Mia opened the door and stood just within the room. A rising moon shone through the uncurtained window, revealing Mia's inky silhouette against the hallway's softer darkness.

'Are you all right?'

Was she? Had she ever been, since that moment she found out about the result of the bombing? Or even before, when she'd first met Hawk and succumbed – willingly, so embarrassingly willingly – to his raffish charm?

She shrugged, then realized Mia couldn't see it. 'I guess so.'

'What's the plan? Is he going to publish something?'

'Yes, even though I Mirandized him about the legal danger he faced in talking to me without telling the cops where I was. I asked him to hold off a couple of days. That will give me a head start to . . . somewhere. I don't know where.'

Mia sat beside her, taking her hand between both of her own. 'I wish I could take you. But I have a suggestion.'

Alice leaned her head on Mia's shoulder. Such a gift to take comfort from someone. For years, she'd avoided anything beyond the most casual acquaintances and, yes, the occasional lover. She'd steeled herself against loneliness and even convinced herself she was fine with that. The thought of resuming that solitary life suffused her with dread.

She curled her fingers around Mia's. 'Tell me.'

'I'm going to leave when you do. I'll head for New Mexico anyway. I know you said you might want to go there, but we talked about it so much with the others that someone might let something slip by accident. You go – well, anywhere but New Mexico.'

'But I was looking forward to the chili verde.' *Fake it till you make it*, she reminded herself. If she turned things into a joke, acting like she didn't care, maybe she really wouldn't.

'I'll drop some hints to make people think you're actually traveling with me. Heck, I'll tell Glenda.'

'You might as well put up a billboard.'

'Exactly. I'll lie low for a few days – stop in obscure campgrounds and whatnot – and then I'll try to be really public with my whereabouts. Maybe it'll take the cops a few days to find me and realize they've been led astray. That should give you some extra time.'

Alice snatched her hand away and applauded. 'Mia, you missed your calling. It's a good thing you didn't work for the FBI. You'd have found me years ago. Did you ever think of going into that line of work?'

Mia's deep sigh surprised her. 'Only for half my life. You're not the only one with regrets. But I guess, by this age, we've all got suitcases full of them. Do you feel like coming downstairs now? Also, it's freezing in here.'

'Sorry. I cracked the window a little. I like fresh air when I sleep. I'll be down in a minute. Mind if I take a smoke break first?'

'How well do I know you? Hold out your hand.'

Alice did as commanded. A pack of cigarettes, along with a lighter, dropped into her palm.

'Where did you get these?'

'I stopped by a store yesterday. You've been going through them like mad these last few days. I figured you were almost out.'

'You're a lifesaver.'

'Not usually the word associated with these things.'

They shared a soft laugh and a brief hug before Alice followed Mia down the stairs, donned her coat, its monetary lining rustling as she zipped it high under the chin, and slipped out the back door.

Beyond the clearing, the pines were a wall of utter blackness. She wished she could disappear into them, the way people had done in the old days when the sprawling forest provided shelter to bootleggers, escaped slaves, remnants of Native tribes and people who simply wanted to be left alone.

She shook a cigarette out of the pack, put it between her lips and flicked the lighter, flinching at perceived movement a few yards away.

Her hand trembled as she brought the flame to the cigarette. She was jumpy, her mind playing tricks on her, the wavering light from the flame making her think something was out there. She'd have to get over that, impose the discipline learned over decades. Nervous people made mistakes, and errors were not an option.

She drew the smoke deep into her lungs. She almost wished for one of Mia's joints, despite the imperative to be supremely clear-headed from here on out, even though it all seemed so hopeless – a fact underscored by words spoken from just a few feet away.

'Hello, Carol.'

She blew out the smoke.

'Hey, Bird.'

SEVENTY-EIGHT

Finally, she thought. After all the years of running, the constant vibration of fear, it was almost a relief. Without being asked, she shook out another cigarette, lit it and held it out to him.

He took it, the tip flaring as he inhaled. 'Like old times.' He squinted in the moonlight. 'You look good, Carol.'

She started at the name that, with the exception of that brief encounter with Babs, she was still getting used to hearing again. She took him in, the knee-length black wool coat, the elegant kid driving gloves, the boots that managed to be both stylish and impervious to snow at the same time. The rebellious tangle of curls that had first caught her eye had been tamed into an expertly cut sweep of silver.

'You look . . . different.' He finally looked exactly like what he was and had always been: a scion of wealth. 'How'd you find me?'

His laugh was low, his voice smooth. 'It was easy, once you went missing – again. It's actually funny, after all those years on the Most Wanted List, your photo up in every post office. The FBI couldn't find you. Nor could I, and I had private detectives. A dangerous criminal just vanishes – poof. Nothing, nada, zip. Turns out when an old lady goes missing, it's the easiest thing in the world to find her.'

Alice gave in to the air of surreality: the shared smokes, the casual conversation, just two old friends catching up. Her hand was steady as she waved the cigarette for emphasis. 'Times are different. The internet, security cameras.'

'You led me quite a chase.' Was that admiration in his voice? 'Not like when we first met. You couldn't get enough of me.'

Ah. There it was. The old Bird, arrogance personified. About her, about the bombing. About – she knew this now – his belief that he'd been passed over to head the family company.

'I got smarter.'

'Not smart enough. Because here we are, together again at last.'

If she could just keep him talking . . . but then what? Would the others notice her absence? Assume she'd had her smoke and returned to the room upstairs? Surely they'd check on her. For the moment, he had her alone and at least posed no threat to the others. At best, their appearance likely would force Hawk to turn her over to the police, where she might be safe, at least for a little while. At worst – she didn't want to think about that. The one thing she could not do was to go anywhere alone with him, take him up on the decades-later equivalent of his offer of a beer to Larry.

That possibility, the one that had kept her on the move for so many years, fizzed and sparked through her synapses. Would he stage another suicide? Force her to write a note? What sort of clue would she leave as a signal to her friends? As if it would matter.

She took a savage drag on the cigarette and bent in a coughing fit. She choked out a repeat of her original question.

'I know *why* you found me. But how'd you track me *here*?' Something else occurred to her. 'I didn't hear a car. I thought you drove a Range Rover. Do you have a Tesla, too?'

She peered into the surrounding dark, looking for something that could slink in silence up the road to the house as they sat in blissful ignorance within.

He held up a booted foot.

'It took me a while to put it all together. I was on the lookout for the red van. I found it pretty easily, but it was in a carport. I knew I'd seen it before and had a vague memory of the driver. I didn't make the connection until I saw a woman out for a run and realized she was the same person. Then it was just a matter of following her tracks through the pines. I'll give you guys credit – she didn't make it easy. Take a wrong turn in those pines and you could wander forever without finding your way out.'

Alice resolved that if she somehow escaped alive, she'd never tell Mia how he'd found her. Mia had been so proud of her skills, and until this moment, they'd served her – all of them – well.

He tossed his cigarette into the snow. It hissed, its glow slowly fading. 'I wasn't sure how to handle the lot of you, but now I don't have to. You know what? I wondered if you were still a smoker. Knew that if you hadn't kicked the habit, you'd be out here eventually. And I was right.'

Alice clung to her own cigarette as though that slender cylinder of paper and tobacco were some sort of lifeline.

'Now what?'

SEVENTY-NINE

Sasha said what they'd all been thinking.

'She's been gone way too long for just a smoke.'

Mia pushed her chair back from the table. 'She must have come back inside without us hearing her. I'll go check.'

She stood outside the bedroom door, listening hard. Tapped.

Nothing.

'Alice?'

Still nothing.

She put a finger to the door and pushed it open. The moon had risen further still, throwing furniture into sharp relief. But no Alice.

Mia stood in the middle of the room, turning slowly, half expecting to see Alice magically appearing before her when she completed the rotation. But the room remained stubbornly empty.

She'd turned to leave when she caught a whiff of cigarette smoke. Of course. Maybe Alice was smoking the ones Mia had given her, one right after the other. Good thing she'd donned her big coat.

Mia was at the door when she heard the voice outside.

Make that voices.

Two.

Hawk reached for Alice's arm.

She jerked away. 'I could scream.'

'But you won't.'

She could. She opened her mouth.

'Don't. You know what I'm capable of.'

She put a hand to the side of the house for support. 'You mean Babs.'

'Who?'

'My neighbor. You thought it was me, right?'

He spread his hands wide. 'Guilty.'

'So you had her killed. Who'd you get to do your dirty work this time? Is another Larry lying dead somewhere?'

She'd gone so numb she thought herself incapable of surprise. His next words drew a gasp.

'Give yourself some credit here. I learned something all those years ago. Never involve other people. One of them might go on the run, able to dime you out at any moment. No, I handled this one myself. So much cleaner that way.'

Alice dug her nails into the wall's rough log.

'You shot someone in broad daylight? How is that clean?'

He swung an arm toward the encircling pines. 'Look around you. Your place is so secluded. All I had to do was stay in the trees and wait for you – or at least the person I thought was you – to come outside.' He shrugged. 'Out of sight, with a suppressor.'

'A what?'

'You'd probably call it a silencer. Anyway, piece of cake.'

She hadn't felt the cold before. Now it cut through her coat, through its newly fattened lining, through the thick sweater beneath, seeping into her very bones.

She tried anew to focus. At least he could finally clear something up for her. 'There's something I don't understand. How did you know to look for me at Timeless Pastures?'

'Ah.' He dipped his head. 'I got an email from someone who claimed to have located you at that address. I tried to track the person through the email address, with no luck. Any idea who?'

It had only been a handful of days, but it seemed like years. Babs, standing in her driveway, eyes narrowed in spiteful glee, hissing, 'Don't you think it's time everybody knew? Because soon enough, everyone will.'

'I do, actually. But why would someone go to you instead of the FBI?'

His perfect teeth flashed a grin.

'Maybe a kindred spirit? Someone who didn't want to do the dirty work themselves. Speaking of dirty work, it's time for us to go.'

A door swung open. Light flooded the clearing. Four people jostled to be first through the door.

Mia won.

She walked right up to Hawk, positioning herself between him and Alice.

'Got a minute? We'd like a word.'

EIGHTY

Mia suppressed a tinge of admiration for the man.

He showed neither anger nor annoyance, just strolled ahead of them into the house as though he owned the place.

She followed close behind, flicking on lights.

'Kitchen,' she directed.

He sat – at the head of the table, of course – and scanned with a lifted eyebrow the documents littering its surface.

'What's all this?' He lifted his gaze and took in the faces around him, a survey that ended with a flicker of surprise.

'Et tu, Johnny?'

'Sorry, boss. Except, not.'

'As of this second, I'm not your boss anymore. You're no longer an employee of Weller Holdings.'

Johnny clutched at his chest. 'I'm devastated.'

Hawk pushed at the paper with his gloved finger. 'I repeat my question.'

'Evidence,' Mia said. 'It's part of what's going to put you away.'

He pulled one of the spreadsheets toward him. 'Ah. A list of our assets. Well, I get it now. No wonder you all are so very confident. I imagine you plan to trot this out as proof that . . . what? It's illegal to acquire businesses? Because the last time I checked, it wasn't.'

'It's what you do with them when you acquire them,' Sasha said. 'You run the likes of us right out of their homes. And from what we've learned, we've had it easy compared to some people who were flat-out evicted.'

'Cry me a river.' The first fissure in that smooth, smooth surface.

'You're right,' George said.

Hawk awarded him a regal nod, man to man.

George nodded back. 'Nothing at all illegal about it. It's a bad look, though. The publicity will be brutal.'

'What publicity? What are you going to do, put up some whiney posts on Facebook?'

Mia suppressed an urge to slap him, so strong that she slid her hands beneath her thighs. 'A reporter has written a story detailing all of this. To second what George said, you're right. None of it is illegal. It just looks bad; terrible, in fact, given the housing crisis.'

'And if there's anything a company – even and especially a holding company – doesn't like, it's bad publicity,' Sasha said.

She sat back as George explained the obvious. Hawk would probably take it better from him. 'If I'm not mistaken, the top guy never takes the fall. That's why they have a raft of vice presidents. Most expendable job on earth. Especially when it comes to someone your age.'

Hawk's gloved hand, flattened atop a spreadsheet, twitched.

'I guess we'll just have to see, won't we? Now, if we're done here, Carol – I guess you know her as Alice – and I need to be on our way.'

'Not so fast.' Sasha held up her phone. 'As they say in the commercials, "But wait. There's more."'

'What are you trying to show me now? More of your purported evidence?'

Mia hoped never to see a smile like Sasha's again.

'Larry Raynolds' so-called suicide note. That's right. The reporter will be writing about Larry, too. You see, even though you rich White guys still hold most of the cards, you no longer hold all of them. It's a lot easier to get a case reopened than it used to be. All people need to do is get one look at Miss Mary's face; to hear what that poor woman has been through.'

'That poor woman won't say a word. Gloucester Armaments put her daughter through college and set up trust funds for her grandchildren. You all keep right on living in your little liberal fantasy world. I'm done here.'

Alice had been so quiet throughout that every head swiveled her way when she spoke. 'It used to be your liberal fantasy world, Bird. Or at least that's what you made me think. In the end, it was all just about getting back at your family, wasn't it? You couldn't stand that your sister was going to take over the company, even though you'd done nothing to deserve that responsibility. So you figured out a way to take her out and make it look like some sort of anti-war protest gone wrong.'

Hawk jerked to his feet, sweeping his arm across the table, scattering the papers.

'Shut up, Carol! We're leaving.'

He had her by the arm.

'Stop it!' Mia grabbed her other arm. 'You're not going anywhere with her.'

Alice gave her a sad smile. 'Oh, but he is. I'm just guessing he has a gun. Maybe even the same one he shot Babs with.'

Hawk nodded confirmation, unbuttoned his coat with his spare hand and pulled it aside to show a handgun holstered at his waist, its suppressor-equipped barrel reaching nearly to mid-thigh. 'Now, if you'll be so good as to release your friend.'

'No.' Mia held on with both hands. 'What are you going to do? Shoot us all? That's crazy. You'd never get away with it.'

'Oh, no?' Hawk's smile was nearly as terrifying as Sasha's had been. 'Here's how that would play out. You all lured me here on some flimsy pretext. I'll think of one later. Whatever it is, the police won't question me. Because once I got here, I found myself in the midst of a terrorist cell with the wanted and dangerous radical Carol Ann Kaminski at its core. When I tried to escape, the lot of you rushed me. Self-defense. It'll be messy, sure. But sadly necessary, given the odds I'm facing. *Let go of her!*'

His last words a snarl, accompanied by an expression so icy Mia understood what had sent twenty-year-old Alice running through Boston upon seeing the news of Larry.

'You know we'll call the police,' Mia said.

'The station is five miles away. And, as I've just made clear, I'll be happy to talk with them. *Let go.*'

'Oh, Alice,' Mia blubbered. 'I'm so sorry.'

She threw her arms around her friend, rocking her in a hug so hard Alice stumbled, pulling Hawk off balance.

Mia crouched, propelling herself forward and up on calves toned by decades of running, head-butting Hawk in the solar plexus, yanking the gun from the holster as he staggered back.

'George, Johnny!' she shouted.

They'd already moved to grab Hawk, but he moved faster, wrapping his hand around Mia's wrist, wrenching until she dropped to the floor as something popped in her wrist.

Her fingers fell open, the gun clattering to the floor, Hawk snatching it up and pointing it at her.

George and Johnny fell back.

Mia looked up to see Hawk's finger sliding toward the trigger. She reached high, grabbing and twisting with her good hand, every woman's last-resort self-defense fallback.

Hawk's body torqued.

The gun went off.

George cried out.

Mia squeezed with all her might as Hawk, roaring in pain, wrapped his hands around her neck, his grip vying in intensity with her own.

Somehow, it registered, even as her vision dimmed: he must have dropped the gun.

Someone was screaming. Not Hawk. Sasha.

'You hurt George!'

Hawk's hands fell from Mia's neck. She rolled away, gasping and coughing. When her vision finally focused, she saw Sasha behind Hawk, one hand yanking his silver forelock back, the other pulling tight at her own silk scarf, now circling his neck.

Mia rolled her head to take in George on the floor beside her, hand pressed to his thigh, blood seeping between his fingers.

Johnny had the gun, wobbling in his hands, albeit unequivocally aimed at Hawk, whose face purpled as Sasha gave the scarf a tightening turn when he tried to claw it away.

And Alice, her steady voice a bracing contrast to Johnny's shaking hands.

'Easy. We don't want to kill him.'

'We don't?'

Mia moved behind Hawk and took hold of the scarf.

'Better tend to George,' she told Sasha.

A tearing sound told her George had already tended to himself. She glanced his way to see him ripping the hole in his slacks wider, bending to examine the source of all that blood.

'Just a flesh wound,' he said. 'All that time in 'Nam without a scratch, only to get shot in New Jersey. It's embarrassing.'

'It's not funny. Oh, George.' Sasha crouched beside him, tears streaming.

'Oh, but it is. A little. I've got a handkerchief in my back pocket. Can you please grab it and help me get cleaned up here?'

Johnny waved the gun toward the table. 'Take a seat,' he told Hawk.

'Careful with that thing,' Hawk croaked. 'It's a Glock. There's no safety.'

The scarf still tight around his neck, he shuffled toward the table, Mia close behind.

'Now what?'

'Call the police,' Johnny said.

'Can't.' Mia put a hand on Hawk's shoulder and shoved him down into a chair. 'Because of Alice. She's still wanted. Shut the hell up,' she said in response to Hawk's strangled laugh.

He ignored her command. 'You should have left well enough alone. Now what are you going to do?'

Sasha broke the long silence.

'I know exactly what to do. Johnny, do you have some paper and a pen?'

She looked to Mia as though for confirmation.

Mia held Sasha's gaze for a long minute. They both turned to Alice. She nodded.

'I'm in,' said George.

Alice took the gun from Johnny and tapped it against the top of Hawk's head.

'You must remember how this part goes. You're going to write a note.'

ARMS COMPANY SCION LINKED TO '70s BOMBING FOUND DEAD

By Bert Miller

Community Caller Justice Reporter

Hawk Marcus Boneham III, scion of a Connecticut arms firm bombed in 1970 as an apparent protest against the Vietnam War, was found dead of a gunshot wound in New Jersey's Pine Barrens.

There was no sign of foul play and Lavina Township Police said a note found on Boneham's body points to his death as a suicide, although final determination awaits a medical examiner's review. Police cautioned that any finding would be complicated by the body's exposure to the elements over a period of days before it was discovered.

For many years, Boneham headed Gloucester Armaments, a family arms manufacturing firm founded by his grandfather, Hawk Boneham I. He took over as company head after his younger sister, Victoria Boneham Carpenter, was killed in a bombing attributed to a Boston-based cell of radicals protesting the Vietnam War.

Blame for the bombing initially was placed on a Gloucester Armaments assembly-line worker, Larry Raynolds, an embittered Vietnam veteran who was believed to have died by suicide a few days later. An investigation into that conclusion has been reopened. (See related story.)

A second suspect, Carol Ann Kaminski, Boneham's college girlfriend, was also believed to have been involved, leading to her inclusion on the FBI's Most Wanted List and decades of fruitless searches. (See exclusive interview with Kaminski.)

Boneham's 2024 Range Rover was found parked not far from the entrance to Timeless Pastures, a retirement community acquired a year ago by Weller Holdings. The same firm earlier acquired Gloucester Armaments and, as part of that transaction, Boneham became Weller's vice president for expansion, responsible for acquiring similar communities across the country. (See related story.)

Two area men describing themselves as hikers found Boneham's body partially hidden beneath an undercut along the banks of a creek just off the trail. It is not known how or why Boneham made his way to a location within the Pine Barrens in the middle of winter.

Lavina Township Police Chief Oscar Martinez said that sleet and rain during a recent warm spell washed away any car tracks or footprints in the area, although sandy soil found caked within the lugs on the soles of Boneham's boots indicated he had walked at least some distance.

Martinez would not divulge details of Boneham's note, other than to say it indicated regret over his heretofore unknown role in bombing his family's company. It also appeared to exonerate Kaminski from direct involvement in the bombing, although she remains on the FBI's Most Wanted List pending further investigation. A news release from the FBI said that attempts to locate Kaminski have been unsuccessful.

'I knew there was something shady about that man,' Timeless Pastures resident Glenda Ferguson said of Boneham. 'He's the only person my sweet little dog Sugar

Plum ever growled at, and you know that dogs are a better judge of character than humans.'

In a surprise development, Boneham's note apparently also claimed culpability for the recent shooting death of Timeless Pastures resident Barbara 'Babs' Stevenson.

'It's safe to say we're in shock,' said J.R. Natale, manager of Timeless Pastures. 'People here were already stressed by the fee increases of the last year. Now, you have a murder and a vice president apparently at fault.'

A news release from Weller Holdings attributed those fee increases to rogue management decisions by Boneham and said all those actions are under review.

'Residents should expect immediate readjustments, with reimbursements due to those residents who remain. We are aware of the need Timeless Pastures fills for those with modest incomes and we fully intend to honor that mission going forward.'

Lavina Township Police Department
Transcript of interview with Mia Sullivan
Present: Detective Travis Meacham, Officer Sherilee Townsend

Townsend: I don't know why I'm even bothering to ask these questions, given the answers I've gotten from your compadres. It's also nearly midnight and I'm dead on my feet. Detective Meacham was nice enough to brew a fresh pot of coffee. I brought an extra cup. Want some?

Sulliva: God, yes. I mean, no, thanks.

Townsend: Which is it?

Sullivan: No. I don't want it to keep me up tonight.

Townsend: At this point, I think I could drink a gallon of this stuff and still fall asleep the minute my head hits the pillow, assuming I ever get to see my bed again. Somewhere along the line, I lost hope. So let's get this over with. Under what circumstances did Hawk Boneham leave Johnny Natale's home?

Sullivan: The way most people leave. Through the door.

Townsend: Still with the sarcasm. Alone?

Sullivan: Have you seen the doors on that place? It was built way back when. The 1800s, maybe even the 1700s. Two people couldn't fit through that door if they tried.

Townsend: I am so not in the mood for games.

Meacham: Sherilee . . .

Townsend: Sorry. I'm just very tired. After he squeezed through that very narrow door, did anyone accompany him?

Sullivan: We all left at about the same time. I didn't see where anyone went. I walked back through the woods. He wasn't with me, if that's what you're asking.

Townsend: Was he with Alice Sanders?

Sullivan: You'll have to ask her.

Townsend: Ms Sullivan, I have to give you credit. You're remarkably consistent.

Sullivan: I'll take that as a compliment.

Townsend: Where did Alice Sanders go when she left?

Sullivan: I have no idea.

Townsend: Where is she now?

Sullivan: I have no idea.

Townsend: How would you respond if I said I didn't believe you?

Sullivan: I'd respond that it's your business to be a skeptic. Congratulations, Officer Townsend. You're very good at your job.

Meacham: I've heard about as much from you two as I can stand. As far as I'm concerned, we're done here. Ms Sullivan, thank you for your time. I wish it had been more productive, but as the last many hours have taught me, that was never going to happen. You're free to go.

Townsend: Good night, Detective Meacham.

Sullivan: Goodbye.

EIGHTY-ONE

Mia looked at the closed door and then scanned the room where she'd spent so many hours that she'd ceased to notice her surroundings.

It had defied her expectations of what an interview room was supposed to look like, all concrete and steel. This was more like the waiting room in the public-health dental clinic she used to go to, with mismatched chairs, a worn-out sofa and a coffee table littered with long-out-of-date magazines and, in a nod to the season, a dusty plastic tabletop Christmas tree.

She and Townsend sat at someone's old dining-room set repurposed as a conference table. The officers had interviewed the friends and others in rotating shifts, keeping them apart until it was their turn again. Mia's was the last.

The door opened. Detective Meacham stuck his head in. He'd donned a parka and it glistened wetly beneath the harsh fluorescent light.

'Be careful going home. Some sort of warm front came through and it's raining, but it's going to turn to sleet in another hour or so. The morning commute will be a mess. Better brace yourself for a raft of fender-benders.' The door closed behind him.

Officer Townsend dropped her head into her hands. 'From homicide to slide-offs. Back to normal.'

Mia almost felt sorry for her. 'Speaking of normal, is the interview really over?'

Townsend clicked off the recorder. 'It is now. As is any professional interaction between us.'

Mia attributed the odd twinge of disappointment to exhaustion. She eyed the extra cup of coffee.

'In that case, any chance that's still hot?'

Townsend, who'd started to stand, sat back down. She held the cup out to Mia, their fingertips brushing as Mia took it.

'You're welcome to try.'

Mia took a sip. It wasn't exactly hot, but it wasn't cold, either. Beyond that . . . 'Gahh. You drink this stuff every day?'

Townsend's eyes crinkled. 'I try not to. As for the quality, it's my own fault.'

Mia took another sip, hoping it would grow on her. It didn't. 'How's that?'

'I was the first woman in the department. Between you and me, Travis – Detective Meacham – seemed to think they'd hired me to make coffee. I refused. So he made a new pot, but a little while later, he tried to get me to bring it to him. He snapped his fingers, like a rude customer in a restaurant. "Townsend, coffee!"'

Mia groaned. 'I'm familiar with the dynamic.' How many of the musclebound oafs at the various gyms where she'd worked seemed to think she was there solely to wait on them? And in ways that went beyond fetching coffee?

'I guess we all are. Figured that was why they kept me on night shift as long as they did. But he never asked me to bring him coffee again, and I never made it. Only problem is, I have to drink the swill he makes, which is why I bring a Thermos from home. But today, I drank it dry hours ago.'

Mia took another sip and pushed the cup away. 'I give up. But thanks for offering.'

Townsend knotted her hands so tightly together her knuckles went pale. 'I have a better idea.'

'What's that?'

The officer, so brusque during their interviews, seemed to have developed a stammer.

'T–t–tomorrow—' She looked at the clock. 'Is that really the time? *Today* is my day off.' She took a breath, gulped coffee, made a face and said in a rush, 'Any chance you'd want to meet me later? Say, early afternoon, after I've gotten enough sleep to be coherent? There's a new coffee shop and bakery over on Main that has a sensational kouign-amann, which I've only just learned how to pronounce.'

Mia sounded it out. 'Queen Ah-mahn? I've seen it written but never heard anyone say it. Is the coffee good?'

'Killer.'

Their eyes met.

'Officer Townsend, are you hitting on me?'

'Would you like me to be?'

There it was again, that glimmer of warmth most recently sparked by Johnny's appreciation. This time, instead of shrugging it away, Mia let the flame catch. She grinned.

Townsend's smile in return lit up her face.

'Why don't you call me Sherilee?'

'And I'm Mia. See you in about twelve hours. But do me a favor?'

'Shoot.'

'You've spent an entire day learning everything in the world about me. This time, I'll be the one asking the questions.'

EIGHTY-TWO

Mia had to laugh at her friends' reaction when Sherilee walked into the same vacation rental where they had gathered six months earlier, before Alice had tossed their phones in the lake and launched all of them into national, if brief, notoriety.

Sasha recovered first. 'What are you doing here? Are you coming to question us again? Wasn't twelve hours in those interview rooms enough?' She turned to the others. 'What's she doing here?'

Johnny, lounging in an easy chair with beer in hand, tucked the bottle out of sight, as though they were at a high school keg party and a parent had just walked in. 'I have no idea.'

'Don't look at me,' George said. 'But if you're here to question us, I'm calling a lawyer.'

Sherilee looked toward Mia. So did everyone else.

'I, uh, invited her.'

She registered their baffled expressions, crossed the room to Sherilee and took her hand. 'Now do you have an idea?'

Mia half expected to hear a thud as jaws collectively dropped. She especially avoided looking at Johnny, who reliably found ways to run into her every couple of weeks, always with a suggestion of something so casual – sharing the pizza he'd just ordered, offering to give her a ride when he saw her running miles from Timeless Pastures – that it let him save face when she inevitably refused.

She led Sherilee to a loveseat and settled next to her, draping an arm over her shoulders. 'George, you're closest to the kitchen.'

George took the hint. 'May I offer you something, Officer Townsend? We have wine, beer, sparkling water.'

'First of all, you can call me Sherilee.' She looked at the glass of Pinot Grigio on the coffee table in front of Mia. 'Some of whatever that is, please.'

Mia was grateful that Sasha at least waited until Sherilee had sampled the wine before asking what they all wanted to know.

'How long has this been going on?'

'I can tell you exactly.' Mia picked up her phone and scrolled through her photos. 'At about seven past midnight at the end of the day when we were all interviewed. I know because I took a screenshot of the time as soon as I left the room. Somehow I knew I'd want to remember the moment.'

George looked at Sasha. 'And here we thought we were the romantic ones. Making goo-goo eyes during a police interrogation? Wish I'd known that before I wasted all that money on flowers and nice meals.'

Sasha swatted him. 'Be serious. Isn't that unprofessional? Some sort of conflict of interest?'

'Believe me, it wasn't deliberate. The opposite, if anything.' Mia nodded vigorous agreement as Sherilee spoke.

'She was such a pain in the butt. You all were.'

'Hey.' Johnny raised his hand. 'I tried to be helpful.'

'And yet you were stunningly unhelpful. But at least you didn't have Sullivan's attitude. Every time it was our turn to talk with her, I'd tense up.'

Mia looked pleased with herself. 'I didn't know that. Good. Your buddy, Detective Meacham, was the one who noticed it first. He told us we squabbled like an old married couple. At some point, I started deliberately thinking of things to say that would get under your skin.'

'And I started looking forward to ways to smack you down.'

They gazed so fondly at one another that a collective, middle-school-worthy 'Ewwwww' arose.

'I wish Alice were here to see this,' Sasha said. 'She's the one who told me George would be right for me. I wonder what she'd make of you two.'

The room fell silent. Sherilee shifted in her seat. 'Any idea where she is?'

Mia jerked away from her.

'You promised.'

'Geez, Mia,' Johnny muttered. 'What were you thinking?'

She made a good guess as to what he was thinking. She could have had him – easy-going, problem-free Johnny. Instead, she'd chosen to complicate her life with a cop.

She looked to the others. 'She promised. I want you all to get to know her better, but the one rule is that she can't ask about Alice.'

Sherilee threw up her hands. 'You're right. I'm sorry. It slipped out. I'd blame it on being a cop, but, more than anything, on being human. It's an obvious question, but I withdraw it, with apologies. Mind if I ask another?'

Mia began to regret having unpacked her bag. She'd hoped this would go differently; had visions of including Sherilee as part of their group, the way they'd brought Johnny into the fold. Beyond the unquestioning help he'd offered during their adventure, as they'd come to refer to that time, he'd worked with Weller Holdings to reinstate the leases they'd canceled, allowing them to stay on in Timeless Pastures.

So far, Mia had used the van mostly for weekend trips, neglecting to mention – until now – that she'd timed them to Sherilee's days off.

'You might as well,' she told Sherilee. 'Everybody's already mad at you.'

Sherilee smiled, undaunted. 'Just like old times, then. I hope this one doesn't cross a boundary, but it's something I've been wondering about ever since this happened. If you really don't know where she is, I'll bet you've been wondering, too.'

'Just spit it out.' Johnny again, glowering.

'Why'd she disappear again? There was no need. The note made clear she wasn't a murderer. The FBI still wanted to talk with her, sure, but mostly to clear things up. Her underground days would have been over.'

Mia let the others answer, their responses a word salad that added up to the fact that they all found it equally inexplicable.

Afterward, helped by a few more glasses of wine, along with the fact that Sherilee dropped the subject, and even more by the lemon cake she'd brought for dessert, the evening turned into exactly the sort of gathering they'd planned.

Because they finally could all move forward. The publicity had died down. Sasha's son had mostly forgiven her and even unbent enough to watch a Phillies game with George during a visit a few weeks earlier, though Sasha feared they'd come to blows over George's comments about the Braves. George and Sasha had shifted from their separate duplexes and moved into Babs' and Alice's side-by-side units, an almost-living-together arrangement that worked for two people admittedly set in certain ways but happy that a shared bed was only steps away.

Johnny had thrown himself into supervising the rehabbing of Timeless Pastures' vacant units and advertising their new status as housing for people on fixed incomes, turning the community into a poster child as a solution to the housing crisis, something Weller Holdings trumpeted at every opportunity.

And they all followed Bert Miller's stories in the *Newark Star-*

Ledger, the biggest newspaper in New Jersey, where he'd landed a job about a minute after his stories on Alice and Weller Holdings went online.

That night, Mia lay awake as Sherilee slumbered beside her. They'd all dodged her second question, and she was grateful to Sherilee for not pressing the issue.

Because who really knew why Alice had disappeared again?

Mia knew.

That's who.

They all did.

She slipped from the bed and stood beside the window, pulling the curtain away so that she could see the lake. She wondered about their phones, whether they were sunk deep in silt, or lay glittering on the lake bottom, their secrets no longer significant.

Still, their abandonment was the first step that had bound them in a pact of silence that remained to this day, one that Alice, by her continuing absence, helped them keep. Because any lingering attention remained focused on Alice.

Not on those she'd left behind.

The ones who waited until Hawk had finished writing the note Alice had dictated, with insertions insisted upon by Sasha and Mia absolving Alice from responsibility for the bombing.

'They'll never believe that,' Alice said.

'She's right,' said Hawk, wincing as Alice rapped him again with the gun.

'Shut up.'

He finished writing, waited as they inspected the completed product for the same sort of clue Larry had left – 'Looks like he's not that smart,' Sasha snorted – and then folded it and put it in his jacket pocket, as per their instructions.

Alice scanned their faces, their dear, frightened faces as the full realization hit them. Because the note to which they'd all agreed so quickly could have only one outcome.

'I'm going to walk Mr Boneham back to his car.'

Alice, gun in hand, walked toward the door with Boneham right in front of her. George balanced on his good leg and took Sasha in his arms. Johnny sagged in relief.

But Mia stepped forward.

'It's pretty dark through those pines. I know the way. Besides, you'll need help with him.'

Again, their eyes met. Again, Mia nodded. *Yes, I'm sure.*

And Alice had done her best to shield her. Because it was Alice who took Sasha's scarf and tied Hawk's hands tight behind his back, peeled the leather gloves from his hands, and donned them herself before wiping the gun with a kitchen towel.

Alice who held tight to the scarf with one hand and clutched the gun in the other as they set off through the pines.

Alice who stopped by the gurgling creek. Mia, a little ahead on the narrow trail, heard a scuffling noise and a thud.

'Oops. He fell,' Alice called softly. 'You go on back, Mia. We'll find our way to his car from here. Thanks for your help.'

She tried not to look and later thought maybe she hadn't; that she'd only imagined she'd seen Hawk on his knees beside the creek, Alice beside him. Because it was so dark under the pines. Impossible to be sure of anything that happened after she left.

And for that, Mia pressed her nose to the glass and whispered into the night.

'Thank you, Alice.'

Acknowledgements

Huge thanks to agents Sarah Yake and Richard Curtis, along with the editors at Severn House, who encouraged me to step off a familiar path and try something new. Specifically, at Severn House, senior commissioning editor Victoria Britton, assistant editor Tina Pietron, editorial assistant Sianna King, cover designer Panagiotis Lampridis, managing editor Lianne Slavin, and senior brand manager Martin Brown. A shout-out to Montana journalist David Erickson, whose reporting on practices affecting housing in low-income communities proved both sobering and educational. And forever and ever to Scott, who has always believed.